SURRENTEP

"Do you operate ...... smuggling ring?" Sir Owen suddenly demanded. He smiled at Antonia's reaction. "You look shocked, I see. But are you really so taken aback?"

"I would only tell that even if I were what you say, I would never harm my country," Antonia replied carefully. "And I want your promise as a gentleman you will say nothing about this."

"You have it," Sir Owen said, smiling even more broadly. "Shall we seal that bargain with a kiss?"

Antonia well knew that Sir Owen was no more a gentleman than she was a lady in the game they were playing . . . and that there was no end to what he wanted of her . . .

MARGARET WESTHAVEN is a native of Oregon. She is married and has a young son.

THE LADY
IN QUESTION

Margaret Westhaven

A SIGNET BOOK

Signet
Published by the Penguin Group
Penguin Books USA Inc., 375 Hudson Street,
New York, New York, 10014, U.S.A.
Penguin Books Ltd, 27 Wrights Lane, London W8 5TZ, England
Penguin Books Australia Ltd, Ringwood, Victoria, Australia
Penguin Books Canada Ltd, 10 Alcorn Avenue, Toronto, Ontario, Canada M4V 3B2
Penguin Books (N.Z.) Ltd, 182-190 Wairau Road,
Auckland 10, New Zealand

Penguin Books Ltd, Registered Offices:
Harmondsworth, Middlesex, England

First published by Signet, an imprint of New American Library,
a division of Penguin Books USA Inc.

First Printing, December, 1991

10 9 8 7 6 5 4 3 2 1

Prologue

He paused at a thicket of gorse bushes, crouched down behind, and waited in the darkness. The whipping rain had already soaked him to the skin, but such was his concentration that he hardly noticed.

He was clad all in black, hair hidden under a knitted cap. A mask fashioned from a black silk cravat covered his face, for he knew that to be seen would mean the end of his mission this night. Perhaps even the end of himself. He had no idea how cutthroat this particular gang of smugglers was, and he did not desire to meet with them and find out. His purpose tonight was merely to observe.

His lips curved upward under the concealing mask. Did he really wish to avoid all smugglers? No. In fact, there was one in particular he would not mind encountering. The Lady.

She might only be legend. If she were no fairy tale, but real, she was a dastardly lawbreaker. Still he admired her as he admired no other woman. The stories related by the country folk, tales he had listened to ever since he was a boy, told of a valiant Lady, a leader who served her people well, a contraband-landing philanthropist who never feathered her own nest but saw her share of the smuggling profits into the hands of the poor.

And this reputed altruism was the most fanciful point of the story. The Lady of the Kentish coast, the most notorious, the cleverest smuggler of them all, could not really exist.

No smuggler, surely, had ever failed to profit by the trade.

The Lady was not a new legend. She would have to be a couple of hundred years old by now. Unless—and some, including the man in black, considered this a real possibility —her position were handed down, perhaps within the same village or the same family.

It could be that she was not a woman at all, never had been. Smugglers were a knowing lot. When the original gang had formed, long ago, they could well have given their leader a woman's identity to throw the excise man off the track.

The watcher's wishes were fanciful, and he knew it. He would like to see her, though, that Lady of legend, dressed in garments of floating black—for she was said to disdain the easy practicality of men's clothes—the giant emerald, her signature ornament, flashing on her breast. He cocked his head, the little smile still playing about his lips, and wondered if he could listen a little harder and hear a feminine voice calling men to the night's work.

But smugglers never shouted, never made the slightest noise, of course. The roar of the sea, the din of the wind and rain were the only sounds he heard. From his position he could see down to a shingle banked by chalk cliffs. Soon the boats would land. Either that or they would not land, which would leave him to think himself a fine fool. Carefully he had culled rumors and whispers, and had made out his own version of what was to happen this night.

But in this part of Kent, everyone was hand in glove with the free traders, everyone knew who was who, and though he was a native of the county, he was a foreigner thirty miles from home. He might think he had been subtle, he might have taken care that no one should suspect his purpose in asking questions, but all the same he could have been led a dance.

He stiffened. Was that movement on the beach below? He raised his head slightly to get a better view and met a homely but effective wooden cudgel.

1

Antonia Worthingham came down the cellar steps in her sister's shadow, holding a bed candle safely away from her nightdress and the woolen shawl she had draped about her shoulders. She was still blinking with the effort of returning to consciousness. Even at dark of the moon, she had never been routed out of her bed in the middle of the night.

When she reached the bottom step, she caught her breath and stared at the ancient floor. "Really, Laura, this time you've gone too far."

The black-clad figure of a man was stretched out at Antonia's feet upon the stone flags of the cellar. He wore the breeches and guernsey of a fisherman and was large, with strong shoulders and powerful thighs.

Laura spun around to face Antonia, her dark skirts brushing the unconscious man's outstretched arm. "Sister, I'm doing all I can for the creature."

Her smile almost shocked Antonia with its brilliance. Laura's raven curls, her white skin flushed with excitement, her purple-blue eyes, all seemed even more vivid and lovely than they usually did, and Laura was the acknowledged beauty of the neighborhood. The exhilaration of the night's work was what caused this extra glow, Antonia supposed. "He was spying on our operations, or about to, and he had to be put out of the way," Laura continued. "But he's breathing normally, and all I need from you—"

"You know I've no desire to take part in any of this,"
Antonia said. "How do you know this person was about to
spy on you? He's dressed like a fisherman. Perhaps he's new
in the area and was simply in the wrong place at the wrong
time."

"On this particular night, with a mask on?" Laura said
with a certain superior look that Antonia secretly found
infuriating, especially when, as now, Laura was right.

"Very well, then, he is an officer about to catch you out.
I like my tale of the fisherman more," Antonia said with
a sigh. "Oh, Laura, what am I to do with you?"

Her sister's silvery laugh rang out. "Why, there's nothing
to be done with me, my love, so you must help me. You
and Barrows must contrive to identify this person and see
him safely to wherever he belongs. Blindfold him in case
he awakens. I don't have to tell you that all must be done
in the utmost secrecy."

"Indeed you don't." Antonia put her candle down on a
step and knelt beside the man. His pulse was steady, and
his chest rose and fell with a regularity that relieved her
mightily. "What happened to him?"

"I merely gave him a tap on the head, ma'am, and
managed to carry him here on my shoulders. No one else
in the gang knows," came a masculine voice from the
shadows.

Antonia looked up, not surprised to see Thomas Vale,
Laura's right-hand man. A groom at their neighbor Lord
Hambrey's by day, Vale was clever and coolheaded in the
most outrageous situations. Laura had come to rely upon him
in nearly all things since he had joined her band a few months
before.

Antonia nodded curtly. Something about Vale made her
uneasy, and she hadn't learned to treat him as she would any
other servants. She couldn't say why his presence called up
such discomfort. She was not attracted to him, though she
supposed his thick red-brown hair and aquiline features would
appeal to many women. Nor did she suspect Laura of a
preference there.

Antonia could only put her feelings down to her suspicious

nature, a defect she was often sorry for but couldn't seem to correct. She didn't trust any smuggler, not even her sister.

"We must get back to the load, Antonia." Laura glanced at the watch that hung on a chain around her neck. She tucked the timepiece back into her bosom, and straightened the emerald brooch that ornamented her black dress of linsey-woolsey. She and Vale disappeared into the shadows of the cellar behind the wine racks. They would take the secret way out of the house and back to the shore. That passage had been useful to the Worthingham family more than once over the years, but it had been invaluable, Antonia suspected, to the free traders.

"Ah, yes," Antonia said to their backs, "the Gentlemen won't wait, and neither will the night." She looked down at the unconscious man. "Whereas you, sir, should have waited before you tried to outfox Laura. An excise man? I wonder. Well, we must get you out of here."

And for that task she would need help. Of all the servants in the house, Barrows, the butler, was the only one officially in the know about Miss Laura Worthingham's more colorful activities. His had been a trust handed down from his father, also a Worthingham butler, much as Laura's present position as the scourge of the Kentish coast had been handed down to her by her serious-minded Great-Aunt Harriet. Picking up her candle, Antonia hurried away to rouse Barrows.

He always kept to his pantry on run nights in case he should be needed, and there she found him, snoring gently in his big chair. The chair had to be big to contain the butler's bulk; he was a veritable giant who would have looked more at ease in rough farmers' clothing than he did in the sober garb of an upper servant. He was middle-aged now, but in his youth he had been known to perform undignified feats involving the lifting of farm animals, a talent that had won him many a wager. Antonia knew he could handle one sizable man with no trouble at all.

"Eh?" He woke with a snort when Antonia shook his shoulder. "What's toward? Riding officers?"

"Heavens," Antonia said in a soft voice, "you really

ought to curb your dreams, Barrows. Do remember that you'd have no reason to fear the riding officers.''

"Miss Antonia?" Barrows's red-rimmed eyes looked up in astonishment, and he was on his feet as quickly as his somnolent state would allow. "Why you? That is, ma'am—is something gone wrong?"

"Yes, I would say so. There is an unconscious man in the cellar, and you must help me with him." Quickly Antonia explained the little she knew of the situation. The butler couldn't hide his relief that the injured man, whoever he might be, hadn't been allowed to do whatever damage he had in his sneaking mind to do to the elder Miss Worthingham's operation.

Antonia hid her irritation. Barrows, no less than Laura and Vale, seemed to think nothing of the fact that a man had been knocked senseless and might be seriously injured. Calmly she explained the task ahead of them. Barrows's job must be to carry the stranger upstairs where he might rest in more comfort, she told the butler. Antonia would search the man's pockets for identification, though she had scant hope of finding anything.

"Perhaps I'd better do that, ma'am," said Barrows stiffly.

"Yes, I suppose you had." Antonia had a little half smile for the butler's strict notions of propriety. "But the chief thing is to get him off those cold stone flags. I know nothing about head injuries, but common sense tells me that lying unconscious on stone can't be good for anyone."

Antonia hastened back to the cellar, Barrows at her heels. The man still lay motionless in the position she had left him. Somehow she would not have been surprised had he been gone. Nothing would surprise her on a night the Gentlemen were out.

The butler matter-of-factly hoisted the black-clad man onto his back, and lumbered his way upstairs with Antonia close behind. "You'd better put him in the small saloon," she said, marveling at how Barrows's strength had not decreased with age. He seemed not to feel what must be a considerable weight. The unconscious man must be over six feet high.

Barrows dumped the man onto the sofa in the small saloon,

a room that was never used for receiving visitors and had thus been allowed to sink into a genteel shabbiness. The striped damask the stranger was laid upon was worn in places, and the pillow Antonia tucked carefully beneath his black-swathed head was fraying badly.

"His pockets, Barrows," she whispered.

The butler grunted and made a quick and complete search, coming up with a wallet, a purse, and a letter as well as a small pistol. "Loaded," he said of this last. "Take care, ma'am."

Antonia nodded. She had not expected such clear confirmation that Laura was right. This man was evidently no simple fisherman. "You may go now and ready the horses. I'll come and fetch you when I've discovered who he is. And if I can't do so—well, I suppose you may take him to the inn. From the weight of this purse, he'd have enough to pay the shot."

When Barrows had gone, Antonia sat down close beside the candle, which was now guttering low, and took a deep breath. The man's possessions were spread out before her, and her duty was clear. But never had she searched through another's belongings.

The man moaned once, sharply, and relapsed into silence.

Antonia jumped at the noise and turned to the stranger. "Are you waking, then?" she murmured, but there was no answering sound. She crossed the room and knelt beside the sofa, looking closer at the man. The closed eyes, dark-lashed, could be seen through the slits of that black mask. What color would they be? What color was his hair, for that matter? And what sort of a face did he have? Most importantly, why should she not find out?

A few moments' reflection convinced her that unmasking him was a practical idea. She had forgotten to tell Barrows about the blindfold Laura had suggested, and there was no likely handkerchief or scarf in the room where she sat. If she removed the black cloth that covered the man's face, she would be able to roll it up and mask his eyes with it.

With a deep breath, she set to work. The stranger kept still; once a sort of sigh escaped his lips. It was with some trepidation and guilt that Antonia drew off the knit cap. A

wealth of short, thick light hair was revealed, and Antonia
ran her fingers through it in surprise. She had imagined,
somehow, that a person who would skulk about a smuggling
operation would be dark-haired. Feeling for the stiffness that
would mean blood, she was glad to find no such thing; only
soft hair the color of a wheat field in the sun. She must have
touched a tender place, for the man moaned again. Antonia
waited until he was quiet, then gingerly began to unknot the
mask.

She lifted it away as gently as she knew how, and drew
in her breath at what was revealed. What a handsome fellow!
The strong planes of the face, the endearing cleft chin, were
most striking.

As Antonia gazed, the man's dark lashes stirred, and his
eyes suddenly opened. She found herself staring into their
clear gray depths for one of those moments outside of time.

"You!" he said in a hoarse voice, breaking the spell. Then
the eyes closed again.

Her fingers shaking, Antonia folded up the black scarf and
bound it around his eyes. She had taken a foolish chance to
unmask him. Would he remember her? At least he was not
an acquaintance. She would never have forgotten meeting
such a man. He was probably not even a gentleman; he had
certainly been found in no gentlemanly situation.

She shrugged. More likely than not, he would not recall
having seen her. She hadn't a memorable sort of face.
Nothing like Laura's. Resolutely, she reminded herself how
lucky she was that this was so in this instance. Then she rose
from her place beside the stranger, and fetched a lap robe
from a nearby cupboard. She covered him, tucking in the
robe around his shoulders, as she might have for her younger
brother. Then she turned to the next order of business.

The purse contained coins in the amount of a couple of
pounds, which Antonia counted out of curiosity, then quickly
replaced. She opened the wallet. This was mysterious in its
barren state. There was only a lottery ticket and a receipted
bill with the direction torn off. Antonia reached for the letter.
How much easier it would have been if this person had only
not torn the identifying marks off that bill.

The cream-colored sheets of the letter were folded with precision and sealed with a pink wafer that somehow made Antonia feel she was about to pry unforgivably. Written in an untutored hand on the cover was "O.L." That was no identification at all. There, she soothed her conscience, she would have to open it to discover a name.

She scanned the first page of round hand and blushed. The letter was from a woman. She got to the second page and gasped once, then skipped over the rest until she got to the end, looking, as she told herself, for other identifying clues. She truly meant to skip. Here and there a particular tidbit caught her eye in spite of her best intentions.

Someone cleared his throat, and Antonia jumped.

If Barrows thought it odd for his young mistress to be discovered with flaming cheeks and wide eyes, looking at him as though he were a ghost, he gave no sign. "Madam, all is ready," he said. "Do you know who he is?"

"Yes and no. His Christian name is Owen. I could discover no more," Antonia said, busily refolding the letter. "Do you think he could be an excise man? And have you heard that anyone of that name is in the neighborhood?"

Barrows furrowed his massive brow. "Ah! I believe it's familiar, ma'am. I heard say only today that a Sir Owen Longfort has arrived to Lord Hambrey's house party. Longfort's the name of an old family over North Downs way."

"A gentleman!"

"Gentle is as gentle does," Barrows said with a snort. "Mayhap working for the government somehow, ma'am, for why else would he be crawling about after Miss Laura's folk?"

"A knight," Antonia said thoughtfully, looking at the man on the sofa. "Or a baronet, I shouldn't wonder, if he's intimate with Lord Hambrey."

"Don't know, ma'am, but we'll find out soon enough," said the butler.

Antonia didn't doubt that they would.

"Odd," she said. "With the season about to begin in town, I mean, it's odd that Lord Hambrey should be having a house party. We can assume, then, that this man is visiting his lordship under false pretenses, or that Lord Hambrey knows of this Sir Owen's skulking and is less of a friend to the Gentlemen than he pretends. He's known not to refuse the occasional gift.''

The butler nodded in serious agreement to this.

Antonia went on voicing her suppositions after a reassuring glance at the recumbent gentleman. His eyes were still closed. ''Perhaps this Sir Owen is only curious about the free trade. Many people find it fascinating. At least this makes our task easy. You may quite safely take him to the gates of Ham Hall and ring the bell. Make sure no one sees you.''

Barrows gave her a look, and Antonia nearly apologized for instructing him in a caution so basic. She restrained herself, though, and watched as the butler lifted Sir Owen up on his strong shoulders and maneuvered him out of the room. She hurried ahead then, opening doors and trying as best she could to ease Barrows's passage to the kitchens, where a boy slept and must not be wakened, and thence to the place near the stables where the butler had tethered a stolid farm horse—the one horse in the Worthinghams' possession that was up to Barrows's weight—and another, slighter animal onto which he hoisted the unconscious gentleman.

The wind and rain, or perhaps the rough handling of Barrows, seemed to rouse the injured Sir Owen; he was stirring quite frequently now. Antonia hoped he would not slip off the horse, but Barrows tied something around him and assured her, in a rough whisper, that there was no such danger.

Shivering as the rain quickly drenched her nightclothes, she watched the two horses disappear down the avenue and around a bend.

Sir Owen Longfort! A personable young man and a ''sir'' into the bargain. He must have just arrived, otherwise the local gossips would never have neglected to tally up his assets of person and fortune in every drawing room in the neighborhood. Antonia smiled. She had gotten a march on the Simpkins sisters for once, and without even trying.

She wondered how those scandal-loving spinsters would

like to read that letter. *My darling Owen,* it had begun, and
that had been the only line fit for family reading. Antonia's
cheeks grew warm as she thought over some of the topics
the letter writer had introduced and not hesitated to develop
with a lusty disregard for propriety.

Antonia blushed the more because she knew she ought not
to have given in to the temptation to read the letter. She was
despicable; she need not have looked past the salutation.
Nobody with any right notions of honor would have done
so, but she had been so curious, so eager to know more about
a handsome man that her sense of fitness had meant nothing
to her. And she had been served right. She now knew that,
though handsome, he was a rake. Antonia had no desire to
become attached to a man who carried such letters about in
his pocket for the unwary to read.

The woman had signed herself as his devoted and given
no name. Anyone, Antonia reasoned, would hesitate to own
authorship to such heated prose.

Antonia made her silent way into the house and up the dark
staircase to her room. What a shocking libertine Sir Owen
Longfort must be to receive such a letter from a female . . .
then it occurred to her that there was a perfectly simple
explanation that reflected no ill on Sir Owen's personality
or habits. The missive could be from his wife.

But this comforting thought gave Antonia no pleasure.

2

"A lovely face. A pale, perfect oval surrounded by masses of light brown hair that waved about her neck like a cloud. A pair of the bluest eyes I've ever seen." Sir Owen Longfort, baronet, smiled at his companion. "A sight well worth this nasty bump, I'd say," he added as his hand went to his head.

Lord Hambrey, a bluff man in late middle age, glared across his library table. "No rhapsodies, now, Longfort. This is serious business."

"You don't think it a serious stride forward that I've seen the Lady?"

Hambrey laughed. "I don't believe in the Lady, young man. What you saw, you dreamed. When we found you, you were blindfolded, remember. I think you might have seen a village girl who passed by as you lay at my gate and peeked under your scarf. Out trysting, I don't doubt, even in this weather, for the freedom of the farm girls hereabouts is— but that's neither here nor there." His ruddy complexion deepened in hue. "You didn't see the Lady, for the Lady is a myth." Lord Hambrey paused and glanced about the paneled walls of his sanctum. "At the very least, I know you didn't see any of the ladies hereabouts. No one answers to that romantic description."

"So if the Lady exists, she must be out of our social sphere," Owen completed the thought. "Makes no difference to me. I'll look about me. Perhaps I'll see her again."

"What's more important than imaginary lady smugglers, man, is the case of the real traders. They're on to you. You needn't waste anymore of your time down here, I say, and others say the same. We'll bring in someone else to rout out the evidence we need."

Sir Owen bristled. "I could have been hit by anyone. I don't see that it's worth taking me out of the picture."

"I do," Lord Hambrey said, "and my word's law in these matters. Longfort, it's enough that you've pieced together the rumors as we hoped. We're next to certain now that the spies are being landed by our local traders. We'll catch them at it, never fear." He shook his head. "Devil take it. I've never been a friend to the free trade, but dash it all, I never thought they were traitors. My family's taken its share of brandy for turning a blind eye like many another, but landing French spies! I never dreamed—not our own Gentlemen."

"Not the Lady's," Sir Owen said with a sigh. "Well, the word on the coast here, if you call 'word' the hints that can be gotten, is that it's the truth. And if we catch them landing one of the Frogs, we can slow Boney down by that much at least. A shame, but we'll take out a goodly portion of the brandy supply while we're about it."

"Unfortunate but necessary," Lord Hambrey said with a rueful laugh. He poured his guest and himself another draught of a rare cognac that had never passed by any customs officer.

"Upon reflection, you may be right," said Sir Owen. "About taking me off the case, I mean to say. They evidently unmasked me last night. Someone knows who I am, and I'm useless as an agent. But I mean to keep my eyes open. I trust I'm still welcome at your house party?"

"Would look suspicious if you left," Lord Hambrey assured his guest.

When Antonia entered the morning room at a little past her usual hour—thanks to the sleep she had missed by the night's adventure—she found her sister, Laura, seated at the window and busy about her work, a footstool cover she was embroidering in an intricate pattern of medieval-looking foxes and grapes. Antonia never ceased to be amazed at how little sleep Laura required. It was all of a piece, perhaps, with an adventurous temperament.

Laura looked up. Her large eyes, such a dark blue as to be almost violet, were clear and untroubled, as Antonia had known they would be. Not for the first time, Antonia surveyed Laura's glossy black curls, heart-shaped face, and glorious figure with a touch of envy mixed with the usual pride. Attired as she was in a demure morning dress of white cambric, Miss Laura Worthingham was the picture of serene and frivolous beauty. She could never be connected with the dangerous Lady she sometimes turned into when night fell.

"Did you get rid of that spy with no trouble?" Laura asked eagerly.

"Barrows must have told you he did." Antonia sat down at the table opposite Laura and pulled out her own work from the drawer. She was making a shirt for their brother Montgomery, who was growing faster than any weed and had written a desperate appeal from Eton expressive of his urgent requirements. She had set several tiny stitches in the linen before she realized that her sister was still watching her.

"You goose," Laura said, "I thought you would know what Barrows can't. What did the man look like? And what was his name again?"

"Sir Owen Longfort," said Antonia. "At least so we concluded on the basis of his Christian name." She didn't mention how she had found out the name. "He was quite handsome. Tell me, since he's of our class, are we likely to meet him?"

Laura shrugged. "It depends. Lord Hambrey might entertain the neighborhood while he has guests; he might not. It might be a masculine party formed solely for cards, or billiards, or wenching, in which case we'd have to meet by accident. Though I think Lady Hambrey's down. I simply don't know."

Antonia thought of the letter in Sir Owen's possession, and a smile played about her lips. Wenching was not out of the question for that gentleman.

"What's so amusing?" demanded her sister.

"Why—nothing. I was only thinking that it's a shame he's a spy of some kind. He was quite handsome, and perhaps you and he could meet," Antonia said, inventing quickly.

Laura shook her head. "Give up matchmaking in my direction, Sister. Those days are over."

Antonia bristled at the implication that she spent her time in trying to arrange a match for her older sister. She had never done anything of the kind. In fact, she well understood Laura's need for independence. She hastened to excuse her words. "Well, just because you didn't meet anyone during your season, and because you find all the local beaux to be lubberheads, doesn't mean that it would be impossible—"

"Antonia," Laura interrupted with a soft smile. "Those days are over precisely because I *have* met someone. Haven't you noticed how different I've been for these past weeks?"

Antonia stared. She had noticed nothing of the kind, and of all the things she might have expected to hear Laura tell her, this news was nowhere on the list. "You've . . . met someone? You?"

"Do you think that because I've turned five-and-twenty, I'm past my last prayers?" Laura teased in evident amusement at her sister's expression.

"Laura, you know you're the loveliest creature in the county, and you'd never reach your last prayers if you crawled on your knees for twenty years. I'm merely surprised you've found someone you could like—and behind my back, it seems."

"Well, that's hardly anything new," Laura said. "You prefer that I conduct most of my life behind your back. Why not my romance, too?"

Antonia frowned. This was an old grievance. "I don't approve of smuggling. I've never liked being privy to all you do. Is that wrong of me?"

"Not wrong, surely, but quite unusual in our family," said Laura with a touch of severity. "You know a Lady of our house has led—"

Antonia had all the family lore by heart despite her lack of a wish to add to it. "Yes, yes, a Lady of our house led the local Owlers back when they were smuggling wool out of England, not brandy in, and a Lady of our house it was who piloted her own lugger to Calais that time when half her crew was laid low by fever, and it was old Aunt Harriet herself in her young days who denounced the Hawkhurst gang at the peril of her life, and—need I go on? I do understand,'' Antonia finished with a pleading expression, ''I simply don't approve.''

''You have no sense of adventure,'' Laura said.

''You made off with all of that quality, I admit it. Now aren't you going to tell me about this man you've met?'' Antonia held her breath. For one moment she was certain that Laura had somehow encountered Sir Owen and been captivated by him. He would certainly intrigue any woman if his personality were at all to be compared with his looks.

Laura's smile was now so dazzling as to be almost blinding. ''I was hoping to take you to see my friend later today. We can go out for a ride and visit him. But I'd like to say no more until the two of you meet.''

''Mysterious as ever,'' said Antonia. ''Do you mean to tell me that you and this unknown gentleman have an understanding?''

''I understand that he's going to marry me,'' Laura said.

Antonia swallowed hard. ''Laura, I must know. Is it Sir Owen Longfort?''

A peal of laughter from her sister set Antonia's mind at rest on that score. ''Good Lord! I've never seen the man. Oh, how delightful. You've developed a fancy for him yourself, and on a moment's sight. He must be handsome, indeed.''

Antonia, much to her annoyance, found herself blushing like a rose.

''He's connected with the excise men in some way, though, I'd swear it, or why would he have been skulking about to watch our boats come in?'' Laura gave her sister a warning glance. ''Be careful if you should meet him again.''

''To be sure. But as you say, it's most unlikely,'' Antonia responded. ''Do tell me more about this gentleman of yours.''

Laura waved off her queries with a laugh. "My dear, you know how I love surprises. You must wait."

Antonia waited, but it was with a bad grace. Extraordinary that Laura should come out with such a tale as having met a man she could love! Laura had never yet known a man she could feel her equal, that much Antonia understood, and she didn't wonder at it. How many men could measure up to the legendary Lady?

On Great Aunt Harriet's death, Laura had assumed the mantle of the Lady with eagerness. She was talented, clever, mad for adventure: under her leadership, the local free trade had prospered. Theirs was one village where no one starved.

The trade might have prospered, but the Worthinghams had not. One reason suspicion had never rested at their door was that all the Worthingham Ladies, following the lead of the first smuggler of their name, thought of themselves as female Robin Hoods and donated their services to the traders of their little coastal village without taking anything for themselves, save the occasional cask of brandy or card or lace—for it might have raised suspicions, indeed, had the Worthingham family abstained from the duty-free merchandise that circulated so freely about the coast.

Antonia was of a practical turn, and it was she who kept the household accounts. She sometimes had the ungenteel thought that, if Laura must smuggle, she might as well take her share of the profits. From young Monty's wardrobe to Antonia's threadbare bed curtains, a thousand domestic needs plagued the Worthinghams. But Antonia knew that her thoughts of profit were unworthy of her heritage, and she never voiced them.

More practical, certainly, would be to convince their trustees to allow them more of an allowance, but these worthies remained unbending. Antonia's father had held stringent ideas on economy and women's duties, and the Worthingham estate was tied up in strange and convoluted ways. There was the entail, of course, which held the house and land for Monty, and enough was allowed to keep the farm in good order and the house from falling down. But

Antonia's and Laura's portions were under the power of a particularly glum firm of solicitors whose partners, obstinately following the instructions of the late Mr. Worthingham's last will and testament, allowed them only the meagerest of household monies. Each young lady, though, was to be franked for a lavish London season.

Laura and Antonia both called it criminal that their money existed only to enrich a future husband, and could be used by them solely as a means to catch that husband. They weren't great heiresses, but the interest on their dowries, if paid to them quarterly rather than hoarded for the future, might have solved a multitude of little problems for Easton Grange, the ancient family seat of the Worthinghams. The farm was indeed in good order thanks to an excellent bailiff, they had beasts enough to do the work and carry them about, but they had to practice a host of miserly tricks in the housekeeping, which they would as soon not have thought about.

Since Laura had been bound by the will to make her debut, so she had done a scant year and a half after her father's death. Her experience had followed the usual pattern of a well-dowered beauty's appearance on the London scene. Her godmother had brought Laura out. Her looks had duly taken the town by storm, and she had met and received offers from crowds of handsome young men and lecherous old ones. And she had told Antonia, an impressionable schoolgirl, harrowing stories about the falsities of the London set. Laura had returned home to Easton Grange heart-free, and the trustees, though disgruntled, had been unable to find a clause in Mr. Worthingham's will that would compel his daughters to marry against their inclination.

Laura had proceeded to remain single for seven years. How, Antonia wondered, could her sister have found, in this out of the way corner of Kent, what she had failed to find in the greatest metropolis in the world?

When the sisters set out later that day for the ride and meeting with Laura's mysterious paragon, Antonia voiced this thought.

Laura shrugged and set her black mare off at a canter,

throwing back over her shoulder, "The heart can never choose where it goes. Trite words, sister, but true."

Antonia gave up her queries and admired the picture Laura made. Her violet blue riding habit flattered her so, no one would have guessed how venerable the garment was, a relic of her season that had been refurbished many a time. Beside such brilliance, Antonia felt like a mouse in her soft gray habit, though it was much newer than Laura's. She clucked to her own mare and took off after her sister.

Easton Grange lay on a section of the coast that boasted a few chalk cliffs, and it was to these cliffs that Laura now led the way through the thin March sunshine. A brisk wind was blowing, and the day was perfect for a ride. The sisters soon reached the cliffs, then headed south toward a wood that the locals claimed was haunted. Antonia knew, as every unsuperstitious native of the place must realize, that if the wood were thought to be haunted, it must really be a depot for smuggled goods, and she had never gone near the Haunted Wood alone.

A narrow track led under ancient oaks and waving beeches. Antonia had been trailing, but now she came up close to her sister. In spite of herself, she was a little uneasy, though none of the trees were yet in leaf, and the place was much less gloomy than it would be in summer. The sea breeze lifted the veil tied around Antonia's hat and ruffled the bare branches of the trees. She shivered.

Laura glanced at her. "You look as though you believe in spirits like all the villagers. Well, so much the better. He won't be found easily."

"Why shouldn't he be found?"

"Ask me no questions," Laura said with her tinkling laugh. "We're almost there, and you may ask him."

When they rounded a bend in the narrow path, Laura leading the way, a male rider met them. A gentleman by his clothes, and mounted on an Arabian, which even Antonia, who was not much interested in the finer points of horse-flesh, recognized as the best. The rider politely moved aside to let the ladies pass, and as they did, each giving him a courteous nod, a shock of recognition shot through Antonia.

She found herself looking, for the briefest moment, into the same gray eyes she had seen the night before. Yes, it was he. The blond hair, the cleft chin, left no doubt. There was no sign that the man knew her, though, and she gradually felt her breathing return to normal as his horse's hoofbeats receded into the distance.

"That was the man!" she said to Laura, speaking in an excited whisper, though he was surely out of earshot. "That was Sir Owen."

"Was it?" Laura's voice was puzzled. "I had thought—didn't you tell me he was very handsome?"

"He is!" Antonia was indignant.

"Well, if you say so. He seemed nothing out of the ordinary to me. Good seat. Magnificent horse. Perhaps I was too busy looking at the Arabian to take full note of its owner's many charms."

Antonia had the feeling her sister was laughing at her, but she let it pass.

The track wound deeper into the woods, and then Laura directed her mount away from the path altogether. Antonia forgot about Sir Owen in her curiosity. Who was this man of Laura's who hid himself so deep in the wood?

"We're nearly there," Laura said.

"Thank heaven. The suspense would surely do me an injury," Antonia replied, only half in jest.

Sir Owen Longfort was thoughtful as he emerged from the wood. He had been drawing some conclusions of his own. If it hadn't been for those beautiful blue eyes, so unmistakably the eyes he had seen the night before, he might not have recognized her.

A clever woman and very young, much younger than he would have judged her to be. She might bind up her wonderful hair, dress in quiet colors, subdue her face into a bland expression, but she could not hide those eyes.

He wondered about the flamboyant beauty with her. It would be easy to find out who they were, for even if the Lady's qualities had gone unrecognized by the neighborhood—as he must assume from Lord Hambrey's denial that anyone of her description lived hereabouts—her companion's too obvious charms could not.

They were ladies of quality, that much was evident by their mounts and their well-cut habits. So the local smugglers were led by a daughter of the gentry.

Sir Owen laughed aloud and spurred his Arabian back to Ham Hall.

3

Antonia had never ventured so deep into these trees, though she knew Laura had made the Haunted Wood her second home ever since she was old enough to climb the trees and rob the birds' nest—which dismal occupation she had been good enough to stop on her tenderhearted little sister's pleas.

Finally the riders emerged into a minuscule clearing, and Antonia instantly knew where they were.

"Old Hannah's cottage," she exclaimed. She had never seen the old woman's tumbledown little house of ancient stone. "How very odd that the roof should be in such good repair. Nobody ever comes this way, and she is so very old."

"Oh, we take care of our own," Laura said with a twinkle in her eye, and Antonia realized that Old Hannah, who had been scaring village children for over two generations and doctoring most of the neighborhood for all that time, must be connected to the free trade. A smuggler's widow, perhaps.

The girls dismounted and tethered their horses to a tree growing in front of the house.

Laura knocked at the cottage door, and it was opened, after an interval, by a tiny, black-clad figure. The hooked nose emerging from under an outsized mobcap tied with widows' ribbons, the beady dark eyes, the gnarled hand resting on a walking stick: these Antonia recognized from many a trip to the village, where Old Hannah was a feared but typical sight. In her own habitat, though, the power, which was only

a subtle aura when she strayed out of the wood, surrounded
her like a cloak.

"Aye, so ye've come again," the old woman said with
a flashing glance at Laura. Antonia found it impossible to
tell whether Old Hannah was angry or pleased at the sight.

"Yes, and brought my sister," Laura answered briskly.
"May we come in? How is he?"

"Mendin', mendin'," said the ancient, standing aside to
let the young ladies pass into the dark interior of her abode.

Antonia blinked to accustom her eyes to the gloom. In the
fireplace hung a black pot, much as one would have expected
to find in a rumored witch's den, but the smells emanating
from it proved to be nothing more sinister than a hearty
pottage. The few furnishings were simple, but strong and
unbroken, and though the place was cluttered with many
sinister-looking bunches of herbs, and a black cat sat on the
mantelshelf, the feeling in the room was not of evil, but of
good cheer.

Laura had instantly run to one side of the room, and
Antonia turned in that direction. She saw a narrow white bed,
and on that bed a man with a bare chest. Laura was embracing
this person with energy.

"Now, then, Miss Laura, not so hard, you'll burst the
stitches," cautioned Old Hannah in a creaking voice. "And
don't sit down on the poor soul's leg. So you're here indeed,
Miss Antonia," with a look up at the younger girl. "They
finally told you. Sit you down. There's naught more worritin'
than lovers' talk for them as ain't doin' it."

"No, no, Antonia, do come right over and meet Jean-
Baptiste" was Laura's plea. She had sat down on the bed,
and the man's arm was around her.

Antonia advanced in fascination. Laura was leaning her
head on the man's shoulder. He was a black-haired individual
with a decided nose and dark eyes. Antonia supposed he
might be considered good-looking in some circles. Certainly
the proper clothing would help. Antonia's eyes passed over
the hairy chest and, embarrassed at the liberty she had not
meant to take, she raised her eyes to his face again.

"Jean-Baptiste de Fontanges, my little sister Antonia

Worthingham," Laura said with a dazzling smile. "Jean-Baptiste has been staying here with Hannah during his illness."

"You are French, sir?" Antonia offered her hand, which the man shook with his free one. "An émigré?"

Fontanges' eyes twinkled as he released her hand. He looked at her sister. "You haven't told her?" he asked in affectionate tones. He spoke English well, with an accent Antonia thought quite pleasing.

Laura blushed and looked confused. Antonia watched in amazement, never having seen her sister exhibit any of the coy behavior associated with femininity. "I thought it best that we tell her together," Laura said.

"Please do tell me." Antonia sat down on a little stool beside the bed and looked at the pair earnestly. Old Hannah, Antonia noticed out of the corner of her eye, had retired to the hearth near the bed, where she was stirring the pot.

"Well," Laura said, "Jean-Baptiste is indeed French. He is here quite by accident, you see. He is—he is a spy."

Antonia's jaw dropped. "A spy?"

Fontanges burst out laughing and kissed Laura on the forehead. "Ah, *ma petite,* you know how to break a piece of news. Is she always like this, mademoiselle?" The last words were addressed to Antonia.

She nodded. "Sir, I begin to think you understand my sister quite well. Do you care to tell me what this is about?"

"Heavens, I can do that," Laura said with a toss of her head. "It's quite simple. A couple of months ago, when I was out with the lugger—"

"You were out with the lugger?" Antonia burst out, dismayed at the thought of Laura actually taking part in the transfer of smuggled goods from one boat to another. "You know you've promised never to put out to sea again, since that time you fell over the side and nearly scared Mama to death coming home drenched and feverish."

"Well, so I did promise, but it was just this once," Laura said. "You know I need excitement, Sister. I can't merely stay on shore when I know the most intriguing things are happening at sea without my being there.''

Antonia shook her head.

''Here is what happened,'' Laura went on, undaunted by her sister's evident disapproval. ''We were putting in to shore, when we saw a man struggling about in the waves. It was one of those nights a month ago, you know, when it was blowing a gale. The men's favorite time for landing goods, but that's neither here nor there. And Vale, who had just lately joined the Gentlemen, was the one who threw Jean-Baptiste a rope and saved his life. Except that Jean-Baptiste had been seriously wounded, on the rocks or perhaps on a piece of broken lumber from his small boat, and so we brought him here.''

''And what were you doing out in the waves, sir?'' Antonia asked.

''I see no harm in telling you, mademoiselle, for those days are over,'' said the Frenchman. ''My identity had been carefully established. I was to be an émigré of good fortune, and I was to mix with the society of London and find out what I could.''

''A spy indeed. And you don't plan to carry on with that work?'' asked Antonia. She was astonished at her own calm. Here she sat, in a witch's cottage in the woods, listening to a seemingly naked man tell her of his plans to spy against her country in time of war. ''You are a Bonapartist, are you not?''

He moved his shoulders, and for the first time Antonia understood the true look of the fabled Gallic shrug. ''Mademoiselle, I have always made it a rule to owe allegiance first to myself. I have had that idea even more since my friends forgot about me, assuming me dead, and did not even try to help me. Now I am not here to spy, no. Would you risk your life if you were not to be paid for the honor or even acknowledged as a living creature?''

''It was rather cruel of your comrades to forsake you,'' Antonia said. ''How did you find out what they did? Do they know you're still alive?''

"In answer to your first question, Antonia, we simply listened," Laura said. "I have ways of finding out many things."

"And no, mademoiselle—Antonia, if I may?—my compatriots do not know I live. They might find it most expedient to put me out of the way if they did. You see, I can no longer serve my purpose. Your sister's Gentlemen have seen my face. They know who I am."

"Meanwhile," Laura said, "while Jean-Baptiste has been laid up here, I've been visiting him to see to his comfort, and one thing led to another, and I've accepted his offer."

"Oh." Antonia could think of nothing else to say in response to this lightning-quick description of the courtship.

"You would ask what I can offer your sister," Fontanges informed her, causing her lips to curve upward as she realized that the thought had not yet crossed her mind. "Well, dear sister-to-be, I can offer her a new life in America. We take ship soon for La Nouvelle Orleans, where I have a brother in a good way of business. He will help us."

"I can definitely picture Laura fighting wild beasts in America, but how—" Antonia turned from the Frenchman to her sister. "How can you leave your country? Your family?"

Laura looked momentarily dismayed, but she soon recovered her bright smile. "I'm not talking of dying, Sister, merely of moving on to bigger and better things. True, the Gentlemen will be lost without me, but perhaps I can train Vale to take my place until another Worthingham Lady is ready to take up the emerald. I know there's no use expecting you to do it."

Antonia shivered at the mere thought. "You're right, the line ends with you. So the Lady's Gentlemen won't work this section of the coast anymore. It's rather sad."

"Heaven knows I'd never meant to abandon my men," Laura said. "But there's nothing else to be done. Jean-Baptiste must go out of the country as soon as can be, and I must be with him. I have connections in the maritime trade. We're to take ship to Bermuda, where we'll change to another vessel to go to the mainland. Even with the unrest on the waters these days, there ought to be no problem. Nothing to signify,'' she amended her last words.

Antonia thought that Laura's idea of no problem likely meant that the ship would only be boarded once by privateers, or that there would only be one or two shocking gales and epidemics of fever. The situation with the former colonies was growing tense; there was talk of war. It would indeed be best for the travelers to be off soon if they were to arrive at their destination safely.

"And when do you leave?'' she asked.

"Though we would wish for time for my leg to mend, we are resolved to take the first vessel that my Laura can arrange. It may be a matter of days or months,'' Fontanges said.

"Do you plan to see Monty again?'' Antonia asked Laura curiously.

"If time and circumstances permit,'' Laura said. "As Jean-Baptiste has told you, we'll be off as soon as a proper transport can be arranged.''

Antonia had long known that her sister had very little family feeling; or, more likely, that what little she had, had been channeled into the bond she had forged with her smuggling crew.

Antonia realized further that it would be up to her to hold what was left of the family together; to keep the estate up until her brother should come of age seven long years down the road. She sighed.

"Oh!'' A dismaying thought struck her. "I can't possibly stay on at Easton Grange alone.''

Laura laughed. "You can't. That's true. Tell me, my love, do you care to come with us? It's the custom for a bridal party to take along the bridesmaid on the wedding trip, and you would surely love America. An untamed country, Antonia. Think of it!''

Antonia shook her head. "I'm flattered, but no, I belong here. I'm English through and through. A chaperon, though. I'll have to come up with a chaperon.''

"I suppose you will at that,'' Laura said, wrinkling her

nose. "We've barely squeaked by as it is; only my advanced age is holding the slender threads of our respectability together."

Antonia considered their situation. Since they had pensioned off their governess when Laura attained her majority four years before, and Antonia, at sixteen, came out of the schoolroom, the sisters had had a succession of elderly matrons residing with them. The latest had been Miss Phipps from Margate, an elderly and eminently respectable relic of the last century, who had surprised everyone, last summer, by running off with an actor in a provincial touring company.

Since that surprising incident, the sisters had lived alone. They had exhausted the neighborhood's supply of genteel companions and really preferred their privacy. Laura had turned twenty-five and let it be known that she was quite capable of playing propriety for her younger sister. The neighborhood behaved as did the rest of the world, and found it extremely difficult to say no to Laura. But now—Antonia, at twenty, could not possibly inhabit Easton Grange by herself.

"I'll have to write letters at once and come up with another old spinster," Antonia said. "Vexing, but perhaps it won't be so bad."

"Naturally I'm sorry to leave you in such a predicament," began Laura, having exchanged a look with her Jean-Baptiste, "but—"

"Yes, love must conquer all. I do agree with you." And Antonia patted the entwined hands of the couple, giving them her sincerest smile.

"If you marry, mademoiselle, the problem ceases to exist, and so does the need for a *suivante*," the Frenchman pointed out.

Antonia shrugged. "Well, it isn't likely that I'll marry. I'm not like Laura. I'm not the type to attract offers."

"That, my dear sister, remains to be seen," Laura said. "You haven't even tried yet."

A rare dimple appeared at the corner of Antonia's mouth.

"How do you know that I haven't been trying, as you call it, for years now without succeeding?"

"Because you're a Worthingham," Laura said. "We remain single only for a cause. And you, Antonia, have no cause."

Antonia could only laugh and dismiss the question of her marrying with a wave of her hand. She turned the conversation back to Laura's own concerns, and Laura, it must be said, was more than willing to go along with the change.

4

Antonia was frowning when she sealed the letter. Leaning her chin upon her hand, she stared out the south window at the rose canes and bare shrubberies of the garden. She very much feared that her godmother, Lady Pomfret, would respond promptly to her plea. There was no lady who loved more to be of use, and her ladyship would likely call it a pleasant task to put Antonia in the way of a suitable companion. Antonia shuddered. She would be lucky if Lady Pomfret didn't send a severe duenna down by the next mail.

But there was no choice. Lacking female relations to advise her, Antonia had cast about her narrow circle of acquaintances and found nobody so suitable as Lady Pomfret for the task at hand. London, which her ladyship made her home, was likely full to bursting with females in quest of a position, whereas the neighborhood of Easton Grange was not and, in any case, had been mined already.

Antonia tucked the letter in her reticule, meaning to go into the village later to post it herself. Looking around her, she saw not a drawing room fast growing shabby, but a haven of peace and solitude soon to disappear.

Elderly companions, Antonia had reason to know, were likely to be great talkers and to exercise that weakness incessantly. She wasn't looking forward to sharing her home with a stranger. It would be odd enough to have Laura gone.

Laura came into the room that moment, laughing to herself.

Antonia looked at her sister with more fondness than she usually displayed.

"I'll miss you," she said wistfully.

Laura looked up from the card she was perusing. "Oh. Antonia. Good morning. I'll miss you, too, my dear, to be sure I will. But only think how amusing this is. We were wondering if the Hambreys would entertain and throw us— you—into contact with Sir Something Longfort, and here's the invitation already."

"You don't say." Antonia took the card from Laura's hand and perused it. "Why, this is for tomorrow night. We scarce have time to rifle your cupboards."

The sisters made a practice of refurbishing those gowns of Laura's that she had collected during her long-ago season. The trustees had denied her nothing she might use for the husband hunt and she had been wise enough to come home with a carriage loaded down with baggage. The superfluity of gowns for that one season served still to eke out their present meager dress allowances.

"Well," Laura said briskly, "let's get to work by all means. I should be organizing my wardrobe for America in any case. But I intend to wear my jade green gauze tomorrow night. I'm not trying to capture any hearts, and I've only appeared in it a few times."

"I've been seen in my depressing white muslin more times than I can count," Antonia said, "and with your kind permission, I'm going to make a good turnout tomorrow."

"For any special reason, my dear?" asked Laura with merry eyes.

"Heavens, no." Antonia knew, as her sister must know, that this was not strictly true, but she didn't intend to admit out loud that she wouldn't mind if that intriguing stranger, Sir Owen Longfort, found her attractive. As attractive as a young lady could be, that is, who must appear at the side of Laura Worthingham, the acknowledged beauty of the neighborhood.

By the next evening, Antonia's nimble fingers had retrimmed and practically recut a pretty dinner gown that had first made its bows, along with eighteen-year-old Laura, in the year Four. Antonia was satisfied that she could look no better given the raw materials nature had left her to work with, those being, besides the gown, hair that was only soft brown, not raven, and a figure that, though adequate, came nowhere near Laura's dazzling proportions. Men's heads simply did not turn when Antonia Worthingham entered a room.

Bearing this unfortunate truth in mind, Antonia dressed her hair a little more frivolously than usual, decided against the gauze scarf, which she had planned to drape about her neck, and put on a pearl pendant, which actually drew attention to an unusual display of bosom. A critical glance into the glass told her that the rose color of the silk seemed to add a glow to her pale skin, and that no one would ever guess that the costume wasn't of recent date. What a shame that the sewing she had had to do to update the ensemble had taken away from it the unmistakable stamp of the London modiste.

Ham Hall was at a distance of about three miles from Easton Grange, and thither the sisters were driven, at precisely the proper hour on the night in question, in the boxy Worthingham post chaise, relic of their parents' wedding journey. (The Worthingham vehicles, like the Worthingham females, in the trustees' opinion, needed no refurbishment beyond the absolute minimum.) They were announced to a drawing room filled with their friends and neighbors, as well as a goodly number of strangers who must be the house party. Antonia stood aside, as was her habit, to allow the first enthralled reaction to Laura's beauty to subside.

The neighbors were quite used to Laura; she had come out at the age of seventeen and lived among them ever since. Considering all this, Antonia thought that it really was too much for the Underwood brothers to stare in such fascination, and for old Sir Laverton MacKay to wipe his forehead with quite the air of agitation. The strange ladies and gentlemen, on the other hand, reacted as Antonia expected them to and exhibited either envy or worship, according to their sex. At least no one fainted or burst into poetic flights.

Laura, as always, didn't care for the reactions she was provoking and moved across the room to their hostess with easy grace. Lady Hambrey, a middle-aged woman in purple net, offered her usual warm welcome to the Worthingham girls, who were next to her in importance in the neighborhood.

"And my lord is somewhere about with Sir Owen, one of our guests. You will doubtless see him soon. Now, my dears, let me take you around and present you to these people." Lady Hambrey, who was somewhat stout, surged from her chair and began a stately progress down the room, stopping here and there to introduce the Worthinghams to a Lord This, a Mr. That, a Miss Somebody. The house party appeared to be composed of about a dozen people Antonia had never seen before.

One or two gentlemen claimed acquaintance with the magnificent Laura. Lady Hambrey's brother went so far as to comment on the stir Miss Worthingham had made in her season. Lady Hambrey stared him down and reminded him, in a furiously whispered aside, which Antonia could just hear, how indelicate it was to refer to a time so distant in a young woman's life.

Laura nudged Antonia in amusement during this exchange. She was not at all vain and would admit to her age without being asked. The Worthingham women, besides being lengendary smugglers, tended to bloom late, and Laura felt no shame at having attained her venerable time of life.

An impulse of either mischief or kindness prompted Laura to stay by Lady Hambrey's unfortunate brother and treat him to a dose of her famous charm, saying that she did indeed remember him. Hadn't they stood up together at a private ball? Or had it been Almack's? Antonia's eyes opened wide at her sister's drawling tone and the easy way she spoke of high society. There was no mask Laura could not wear.

The gentleman basked, and Lady Hambrey and Antonia moved on. Antonia knew her duty as guest and detached herself from her hostess to do the polite to the Simpkins sisters, elderly spinsters who had known her since she was in leading strings. The little ladies hailed Antonia. She had earned their favor long ago by being quiet, domestic, and the exact opposite of her sister. They began to regale her, in whispered tones, with the biographies of many of the house-party guests.

Antonia murmured the proper things and kept her eye on the door, watching—she might as well admit it—for the entrance of Sir Owen Longfort.

Startled, she realized she had heard his name. The elder Miss Simpkins was starting in on the information she had gleaned on the man by those mysterious methods in which she excelled.

"A single man and a baronet, my dear, and wealthy, they say. Lady Hambrey is acquainted with his mama, a dear lady who was unable to come down from London for some reason or other which I forget, and who is related to the Duke of—which duke, Cecilia?" She turned to her sister.

"She is only the distant cousin of the Duke of Arlebury, and I must say this for the Longforts, they do not puff up the connection," said Miss Cecilia. "You know Sir Owen's seat is only thirty miles from here." She looked significantly at Antonia. "Not a great title, perhaps, as your sweet sister could certainly have laid claim to in her younger days, but time does march on, does it not? A baronet would be a most eligible connection for Miss Worthingham now. And do but think, dear Antonia, then it would be your turn."

Antonia wondered if she was, indeed, considered to be figuratively in the schoolroom because Laura had not chosen to marry up to now. Could the same, then, be said of Miss Cecilia Simpkins?

"Oh! Here is Lord Hambrey with Sir Owen now," Miss Simpkins whispered excitedly into Antonia's ear.

Antonia hadn't needed the lady's information; her eyes were already fixed on the gentleman who had just entered the room in company with his host and a couple of other, lesser males. Lord Hambrey she barely glanced at, she had known his grizzled and hearty form from her childhood. The other men she passed over as quickly to focus on the real object of her interest.

Sir Owen, whose cool gray eyes were sweeping the room

with such seeming boredom, was handsomer than Antonia remembered him. Some credit must be given to the tasteful evening attire, but she truly wondered how he could improve so vastly with each viewing. She had thought him extra-ordinary when he had been unconscious, dressed in rumpled and dingy garments. She had been even more intrigued by the brief sight of him in his riding clothes. Now, in all the glory of a perfectly fitting dark blue coat and biscuit-colored pantaloons, he was simply enthralling.

Laura, by now the center of a court of admirers, flashed a look at Antonia and winked at her. Antonia straightened her back and resolutely turned her eyes from Sir Owen.

The elder Miss Simpkins began to discuss the intricacies of her latest tatting pattern.

"Miss Antonia Worthingham?"

The deep voice startled her, and she glanced up, her eyes, which had been beginning to glaze over at the recital of needlework, now alert. Sir Owen was smiling at her.

"We are to be seated together at dinner, ma'am, and I hope you'll allow me the liberty of making myself known to you now. Longfort is my name."

Miss Simpkins, who had already been introduced to him, took over and presented Sir Owen to Antonia.

"Delighted, sir," Antonia said demurely.

Sir Owen looked at a vacant seat between the two Miss Simpkinses, hesitated, and said, "Miss Antonia, would you care to take a turn about the room? Dinner won't be announced for some time yet, and you might like to see Lord Hambrey's collection of snuffboxes."

Antonia had seen the snuffboxes on every visit to Ham Hall since she could remember, but she didn't mention this. She was by no means reluctant to accept Sir Owen's arm. The Simpkins sisters began to twitter as soon as she turned away from them.

"This part of Kent is very retired, despite its relative proximity to Margate. Wouldn't you say so, ma'am?" said Sir Owen with an amused look in the direction of the two spinsters.

"Yes, I'd say so. Why do you ask? Is it the fashion in

which any visitor out of the common way seems to set local
tongues a-wagging?'' Antonia responded in a defensive
manner, feeling an odd mixture of mortification and pro-
tectiveness on the Simpkins spinsters' account. She squirmed
at the sharpness of her own tone.

"I was merely wondering if my singling you out will have
the unfortunate effect of making you the subject of gossip,
Miss Antonia.''

Antonia couldn't think of a quip clever enough to suit her,
and remained silent as a result. At that moment they passed
by Laura and the group of adoring males that now surrounded
her, and she hailed Antonia with a wave.

"This gentleman and I haven't met,'' Laura said with a
smile that had struck many a male into sheeplike worship.

"This is Sir Owen Longfort. My sister, Miss Worthingham,'' Antonia said, and the gentleman expressed his honor
at the acquaintance. Laura received his compliments with
the dignity of a queen.

"Sir Owen, I merely wished to warn you to be circumspect. I act as my sister's duenna, you know, and a stern
and strict one I am.'' Laura's dazzling dimples caused her
surrounding flock to heave a collective sigh, but Sir Owen
seemed unaffected.

"Your point is well taken, ma'am. You've no doubt heard
that no young lady can be trusted with me.''

Laura's dark blue eyes widened. "Heavens, you don't
mean it. No, I had no idea. Well, Antonia, do be careful,
but at least this encounter will give you a certain cachet
among the country belles.''

Antonia laughed and threw Sir Owen an embarrassed
glance.

"Shall we go and look at those snuffboxes, Miss Antonia?''
he said smoothly. There was a twinkle in his eye that made
Antonia wonder if he really did have a dangerous reputation
or had merely been roasting her sister.

They promenaded in silence for a while, stopped in front
of the japanned cabinet that held the snuffboxes, and
examined them studiously, from the jeweled gold box once

owned by a French monarch, the prize of the collection, to the tiny opal stopper bottle, carved with a rose, which was Antonia's favorite.

"I don't even take snuff," Sir Owen remarked, looking through his quizzing glass at a chinoiserie specimen. "Shall we go on, ma'am, now that we've done with the nominal object of our walk?"

He led the way to a corner that was fairly secluded, between the cabinet and the pianoforte. Lady Hambrey never opened the instrument until after dinner, and so the area was untenanted.

Antonia followed him, curious. In the few moments they had been together, she had been vaguely dissatisfied and wishful that something else might happen. She couldn't really say whether she had embarked upon a flirtation or not. Sir Owen wasn't particularly attentive, though she could feel his eyes on her whenever she looked away from him. Did he have something particular to say to her now, or did he simply mean to be a little outrageous by taking her into semiprivacy? He would set the Simpkinses and their ilk to talking, that was sure.

Sir Owen gave her an intimate smile and spoke in a low voice. "I didn't wish to let the evening pass by without telling you how delightfully direct I find your methods." His hand came up to touch his light hair at the back of his head.

Antonia jumped. She knew that spot, for she had touched it herself. She wondered if the lump had yet gone down. So he did remember her face from his brief moment of consciousness on the night of the smuggling. He thought she had been the one to hit him! And she couldn't set him right.

"I must also mention, ma'am, just this once and for your ears alone, that I have always wished to meet the Lady—a lady of your well-known capabilities," Sir Owen continued. He was looking right into her eyes.

Antonia cast hers down, thinking quickly. What odd development was this? It couldn't be more clear. He thought she was the Lady! Why, then, did his expression hold no sternness, no disapproval? He seemed absolutely delighted.

On reflection she imagined he would be thrilled on uncovering her supposed identity, a secret closely guarded for two centuries.

And now what was she to do?

"I don't know what you mean, sir." She looked up again and tried for an innocent stare. "We've just become acquainted, and I'm not at all well-known. Did you perchance hear me giving advice to Miss Cecilia Simpkins on her lacework? I am said to be a needlewoman of no mean skill."

He smiled, seized her hand, and kissed it so quickly that she couldn't be sure, five seconds later, that he had really done so. "I understand, ma'am. Discretion is everything. But take one piece of advice from me and watch what you do. The business that's gone on for so long on this coast is one thing. Treachery, betrayal of one's country, is quite another."

"What?" Antonia couldn't imagine what he meant by the last remark and spoke quite loudly. Several nearby people glanced over, and their position now noticed, Antonia and Sir Owen moved away from the confidential corner in mutual accord.

Sir Owen was looking at her sharply. Antonia thought he must realize that she honestly didn't know what he was talking about, but they had no more chance for private conversation, and she soon decided that more discourse with this man was the last thing she wanted.

Dinner was announced, and Sir Owen and Antonia went in together. Antonia developed an unprecedented interest in the gentleman on her other side, one of the Underwood brothers, and talked to him as much as she could. All the while the meal went on, her mind was working busily.

Sir Owen Longfort thought he had indentified the Lady. But what could he mean by treachery? Antonia knew that he couldn't be referring to simple evasion of the king's customs; he had seemed to tolerate that. Betrayal of one's country! What could that signify?

There was only one thing to do: discuss her strange experience with Laura as soon as possible. Meanwhile Antonia agreed, in her abstracted state, to have the first dance at the upcoming assembly with the unprepossessing Bertrand Underwood, who was leering at her unusually deep décolletage. She didn't remember the promise five minutes later.

Her thoughtful mood continued when the ladies withdrew, and Laura came up to her, put an arm around her waist, and whispered, "My dear, what is it? You look as though you're sleepwalking. Didn't the great Sir Owen's company have its expected exhilarating effect?"

"Yes and no," Antonia said, dismayed that she had been caught out in a less than sociable mood. "I'll tell you about it in the coach going home."

"Do you still think him handsome?" asked Laura, head to one side.

"I must admit I do," Antonia said. "Much good may it do me." Since he thinks I'm a smuggler, she added to herself.

"Not at all in the style of my Jean-Baptiste," Laura said. "When I think how *he* would outshine all these useless fribbles, it makes me quite wild. I hope there are some parties in America. I would love to see him in society."

Antonia murmured something appropriate and wished for the gentlemen to come in. Sir Owen disturbed her. She didn't like to think of speaking to him before she consulted privately with Laura, but she did so wish to see him again. What a tangle of contradictions her mind was this evening.

She and Laura settled down in a companionable silence. The sisters were happiest when sticking close to each other in their little country society, a preference which was just as well, as Laura's looks were not the sort to inspire willing companionship from members of her own sex.

The gentlemen soon joined the ladies, and, as though he knew what Antonia had been thinking and sought to tempt her, Sir Owen gravitated to her side immediately. "Do you care to walk in the conservatory, Miss Antonia?" he asked courteously. "If your sister would permit?"

Laura gave him a look of mock severity and adjured Antonia to be careful to cause no tongues to wag.

"I never do," said Antonia. She could think of no way out of this invitation without being missish, and, hoping that the conservatory would be too crowded to allow for more probing questions from the baronet, she accepted Sir Owen's arm.

In the conservatory, Lord Hambrey was holding forth on the parentage of his latest rare plant to a group of matrons. Not, at first glance, the place for a romantic rendezvous. But Sir Owen steered Antonia behind a potted orange tree before she could think about whether a romantic rendezvous was what he had in mind.

"I can't help it, and I know a lady of your adventuresome nature won't be insulted," he said in a rush. He bent down to Antonia and kissed her, briefly but hard, upon the lips.

Those lips parted in astonishment as Sir Owen drew away. "I—I suppose I should ask you how you dare," she whispered.

"You, who dare so much, would ask me how I go about stealing a simple kiss?" His smile was mocking.

Antonia stared into his eyes, so full of humor now, and wished helplessly that he would kiss her again. "If not how, then why?"

"Now you wish compliments, madam," Sir Owen said with a grin. "If you must know, I've been looking at you all the evening, admiring your reserve, your careful control, even that proper hairstyle you affect. I've seen the real you, remember. I find these little parlor games amusing."

Antonia's spirits sank. He had seen her in her nightgown with her hair down. In her own eyes she looked much better this evening that she had in the middle of the night after being wakened from a sound sleep. It was the real Antonia, this Antonia here beside him, whom he found ungenuine.

"Sad, Miss Antonia? You must not think I intend to betray your secret. As long as it remains a simple secret. I mentioned earlier, and I repeat it now, I have no patience with traitors to the crown."

Antonia shook her head at him. Best to continue to pretend ignorance of all references to her sister's trade. "Sir, I don't know what you mean."

"Naturally you don't," said Sir Owen. She had not known gray eyes could burn so. "How endearing your innocence is. Pardon me again." And once more, his lips descended on hers.

Antonia was so far from being insulted that she would have kissed him forever, despite her proper upbringing, despite the fact that his only interest in her was as a curiosity. For this one moment she was grateful for his mistake, since it had brought her this delight. A famed smuggler might well be worth kissing, but the smuggler's mousy sister would be of no interest at all.

He broke away, muttering, "People are coming," and began a discourse on the orangery at his home estate as the Simpkinses, accompanied by two of the next-worst gossips in the parish, strolled casually by.

"Oh, Antonia, my dear," called out Miss Simpkins. "We're about to make up the card tables, Lady Hambrey says, and I quite depend upon you to partner me."

"I'm sorry, ma'am, she is already engaged to partner me in any scheme our hostess may get up," Sir Owen said with a heart-stopping smile.

Antonia struggled inwardly, though her public manners were all that could be wished. What was she to do with this gentleman? She might stalk away from him in high dudgeon. Or she might caress that endearing cleft in his chin and smooth the hair back from his forehead. A blond lock had fallen forward sometime during their kiss.

One thing was certain. If Sir Owen, as must be supposed from his lurking behavior the other night, were really working for the government in some capacity, it would be a measure of safety for Laura if he thought Antonia was the Lady.

Laura must get out of the country soon, though. If Sir Owen was going to be nosing about the neighborhood, the Lady's game could be up with a suddenness that would make one's head spin. This Antonia could sense. Sir Owen might be misguided for the moment, but he was highly intelligent. That showed in his face. He would not be misled for long.

5

As the Worthingham postchaise rattled through the night back to Easton Grange, Antonia laid out for her sister the events of the evening—some of them. She could not bring herself to reveal that Sir Owen had kissed her. That was a secret she would carry in her heart forever. But she felt honor bound to relay the hints he had thrown out—though one could hardly call them hints, they were so obvious—about the Lady.

Laura was astonished at the news that Sir Owen had somehow tied the identity of the Lady to their family.

"It's my fault," Antonia admitted. "That night of the smuggling, you'll remember you told me to blindfold him. Well, I did, but not before he came to consciousness for a moment and saw me. At the time I didn't think it signified. I didn't think he'd remember me."

Laura's laughter seemed to echo around the interior of the coach. "My dear, you may not have known it, but you've helped our cause immensely. Sir Owen is obviously working for the government, and you've set him off on the wrong track. From what you say, he ended the evening certain that you're the Lady, despite your denials. He'll never suspect me."

"I did think of that," Antonia said. "This is a measure of safety for you. It would be dreadful if your band was caught out just as you're about to leave the country."

"I do find his mistake amusing. You, the Lady! If he only knew how very wrong he is."

Antonia was in the mood to take offense, an unfortunate product of her knowledge that Sir Owen hadn't liked her for herself. She took Laura's remark to be a slur on her unadventurous nature rather than a tribute to her good sense, and fought down the unworthy urge to say something sharp to her sister. Only after mastering this inclination did she continue the subject at hand. "But there's one unfortunate side effect to his suspicions. If he thinks I'm the Lady, he'll be watching our house, and he may just as easily uncover your operations."

"There is only one solution to that problem," Laura said decidedly. "He is bound to follow you. I could tell, Antonia, that he admired you, aside from any suspicions about your activities. He'll go wherever you go, and that, my dear, is why you must go to London."

Antonia gasped. "London! But I have no desire—what would my reason be?"

Laura's expression was mischievous in the light of the carriage lamp. "The same as my reason was, long ago. You are long overdue for your season."

Antonia spent a night plagued by worries and hardly closed her eyes. She didn't take kindly to the idea that she must leave the comfortable rural solitude of Kent for an extended visit to the metropolis. A London season had always been at the bottom of her list of wishes.

She had traveled up to town with Laura for that season years ago, and what she had seen then, from between the banisters on the schoolroom floor at Lady Pomfret's, had not inclined her in society's favor. Laura, as an accredited beauty, had attracted the worst as well as the best of the crop of *tonnish* bachelors, and giggling young ladies by the score had also come to wait upon her, hoping to bask in her reflected glory. Antonia, with the unforgiving eyes of thirteen, had seen it all, or as much as she wanted to. She had come back from her London visit as sure as ever Laura had been that society was not for any sensible person. Now, years later, the thought of spending months surrounded by the frivolous beau monde did not appeal, not when she could make herself useful at home where she belonged.

"But you really ought to marry if you can," Laura pointed out the next morning. In her new character of prospective bride, she seemed to wish, most kindly, that Antonia could be as happy as was she. "And here's a prime candidate in Sir Owen. You may see much more of him in town than if you both remained here. There is such a quantity of social life in town, I'll say that for the place."

"Oh, Laura." Antonia was setting painstaking stitches in her brother Monty's latest shirt and pricked her finger at the thought of Sir Owen's kiss. A sober night's reflection had convinced her, though she had really needed no convincing, that no part of the handsome baronet's fascination had involved her, Antonia. "You're being absurd. I assure you Sir Owen feels no sort of attraction to me. He's fascinated by the Lady, and I am not the Lady."

"But he thinks you are." Laura's eyes sparkled. "When you go up to London, there he'll go, too, chasing after you. He'll be bound to think you're in town to transact business with the distributors or some such, and he'll follow you about from mantua makers to morning calls, wondering when and how you're going to transact your business. You'll lead him such a dance! I wish I could be there to see it."

"But you won't," Antonia said, hitting upon another point that troubled her. "And one day quite soon you'll disappear for good, won't you, without a word to me or Monty?"

"I suppose I will," Laura said with an unexpected touch of sobriety. "But it can't be helped. The sooner Jean-Baptiste and I can get away, the safer he'll be. Meanwhile I can keep up with the operations here. I really do hate to leave the men, though I think Thomas Vale can be trained to take my place. If only Vale weren't so restless. Sometimes I wonder if he won't disappear altogether and leave me in the lurch."

"In my opinion, you wouldn't be unfortunate if he did. That man does make me feel he's hiding something."

"But who of us is not hiding something? I expect he came to this part of the country to get right away from some other part. He's a thief, perhaps, or a highwayman. But I see only what I can use. He's extremely intelligent. I can't trust anyone so well with the thinking part of the operations. There are many men who can carry two barrels overland if the need arises, but few who are savvy enough to find a good hiding place for the same two barrels."

"I don't want to hear about it," Antonia said.

Laura's smile, as she bent over her book, was vaguely mocking.

"Laura." Antonia could not remain silent for long. Like it or not, this was not simply a typical morning at home, she sewing, Laura scanning another novel from the Margate circulating library. She voiced a thought that had been troubling her for some time. "Where am I to say you've gone, once you have gone? What am I to tell Monty?"

"I've been thinking that over. You must tell Monty the truth, of course, as soon as you feel he's old enough to understand. And as for the world—you may give out that I've run away to marry an American. True enough, for Jean-Baptiste will be an American someday. Scandalous enough, too, for people to reason that I would disappear without a trace." Laura paused in her recital. "There's only one thing that worries me. I do hope even such a mild *on-dit* as this will be won't hurt your propects, my dear."

Antonia shrugged. "I don't think it will be such a minor thing when the greatest beauty in Kent runs off to parts unknown. But I don't see why it would reflect on me. And you shouldn't worry over me. I don't have any prospects."

"Haven't we just been discussing a very charming one?" Laura said. She was smiling; the thought that her disappearance would be a lasting shock for the countryside evidently pleased her. "And in London there will be many other gentlemen, and, unlike your sister, you may think well enough of some one of them to marry. But with a sister who has eloped to America—"

"I wouldn't marry any man who thought that much of the

world's opinion," Antonia said in scorn. "And I expect to
meet no other kind in London. You did not, and I have much
less to hope for than you did."

This seemed unanswerable, and Laura didn't contradict
her sister. She went back to her book. "Shall I read aloud?"

"You're in the middle of the story."

"It's a translation of *Manon Lescaut,* the French book we
read with Mademoiselle Bluet in the schoolroom. You know
the story quite well."

Antonia did. "Are you certain you want to go to America,
Laura? Manon's journey there didn't work out well."

Laura laughed airily. "Heavens. You say you are not
superstitious, Sister. Do me the favor of not seeing signs and
portents in everything we do."

Antonia crooked an eyebrow. "Well, it was worth a try."
At any rate, she was glad to leave the subject of a London
visit, at least for a while.

Later they talked around again the topic of Antonia's future
plans. Antonia held to her position, or thought she did. But
into the debate had crept a certainty that Antonia would,
indeed, be going to London soon.

By the time the day was over, another letter had gone off
to their godmother, Lady Pomfret, this one hinting that
Antonia, rather than refuse her godmother's annual invitation
to London for the season, would be likely to accept if such
an offer were issued. The letter also canceled the request
for a chaperone.

Antonia watched the window in vain all day, both hoping
and fearing that Sir Owen Longfort would play a call, and
dreading what she would say to him if he did. Laura's advice
was to play his game, not to say anything incriminating, but
not to protest too much when he didn't believe her denials
about the smuggling involvement.

But Antonia had no chance to practice her wiles. He didn't
come, and word filtered down from the stables that he and
the other gentlemen of Lord Hambrey's house party had spent
the day hunting. Laura called that a poor excuse, and to
Antonia this was one more proof that any interest he had

had in her, even in the person of a mysterious lady smuggler, had died a quick death.

The second day after the dinner party dawned bright and cold, and the sisters set off on an early ride to the Haunted Wood to see Jean-Baptiste. Antonia's head turned this way and that in her nervousness. She was certain she would encounter Sir Owen.

Instead, she and Laura had an undisturbed ride. Antonia then spent a half hour chatting with Old Hannah about the healing arts while Laura and Jean-Baptiste made loving noises in the corner.

"Laura tells me you have taken up her identity," Jean-Baptiste said, in a teasing tone, when Antonia went up to bid him good-bye.

Antonia was a bit provoked that he, as well as Laura, should think it ridiculous that her quiet and prosiac self should be thought to have a more adventuresome side. She merely smiled in answer to the Frenchman's sally.

"We both think it best if you go to London as soon as possible," Laura said.

"I hope you don't mind if I wait to be invited."

"That's precisely the problem. Jean-Baptiste and I have been discussing it, and we think the element of surprise will intrigue Sir Owen. If you leave suddenly, as though there is urgent business in town, he'll be certain you're the Lady. We think you should go up with the mail this very night."

"What!" Antonia couldn't believe her ears. "Lady Pomfret might take it amiss to have me dumped on her doorstep."

"Why so? She's very courteous. And then, don't you see, Sir Owen would be out of this neighborhood, leaving Jean-Baptiste and me in freedom," retorted Laura.

"Has it ever occurred to you," Antonia said, "that if Sir Owen is interested in the operations, others might be, too? That he may only be one of a group?"

Laura shrugged. "He was on his own that night. And his group, if he has one, will hear that you're the Lady. They won't keep watch on me.'' Her eyes shone. "Not that it matters. I delight in outfoxing the revenuers.''

Antonia knew that to be the truth. "I suppose there's nothing to hold me here. The bailiff has the spring planting well in hand. Mrs. Abercombie is an admirable housekeeper, and you will still be here to look out for things.''

"Until I leave,'' Laura said, exchanging a glance with Jean-Baptiste. "And when I do, Antonia, I shall take care to drop clues in the opposite direction of the one I take. You will probably hear from the neighbors gossip that I've gone off to Scotland.''

A distressing thought struck Antonia. "My heavens! If I go to London tonight, I may never see you again.''

"True,'' Laura said matter-of-factly. "You must see to it you marry a man with an adventurous spirit, Antonia. One who will bring you to America to see me.''

"And our many children,'' Jean-Baptiste added with a grin. "I wish a large family.''

"If you're hoping that might slow Laura down, sir, you must be advised, you're likely chasing moonbeams,'' Antonia told him with a wry look. "Now come, Laura. If you're really set on this plan, I should be home and packing this very minute. I have masses of lists to leave for the servants, and there are Monty's new things. Oh! If I'm really to be in London, I can go and visit him at Eton.''

"There! Didn't I say going to London would be precisely what you need?'' Laura said. They took leave of Jean-Baptiste, Antonia wishing him Godspeed on his eventual journey, Laura bestowing upon him a passionate kiss, while Antonia averted her eyes. Old Hannah, meanwhile, was silent over her knitting in the chimney corner.

Antonia flew through the rest of the day, scarcely thinking of Sir Owen in the bustle of packing, sending a servant to secure a place for her on the mail, making out those multitudinous lists without which, she was convinced, the household staff would dissolve onto the floor in a kind of indecisive puddle.

When evening shadows fell, Laura drove with Antonia into the town, where the younger Miss Worthingham took her inside seat on the mail coach and, with a suddenness that seemed ludicrous, found herself waving good-bye to her sister through the window. Would she ever see that face again? Suddenly Antonia forgot about all the ways that Laura had ever irked her, and simply yearned to stay with her as long as possible. She knew, though, that there was no turning back at this stage of the plan.

"Beautiful girl!" exclaimed the merchant sitting next to Antonia as he stared out the window. "Never seen the like."

"My sister," she said with a touch of pride, and settled down as best she could to a nap surrounded by the snores and wheezes of her fellow passengers.

Lady Pomfret's tall house in Curzon Street was silent when Antonia alighted from the hackney coach onto the flagstones. The jarvey threw down her baggage with a snarl; she had discovered she was not lavish in her notions of vails, but her embarrassment at this knowledge was nothing compared to her resentment of the coachman's manner.

"I would have given more to a kinder soul," she told the man sweetly, then stepped back as he glared, cursed at her, and whipped up his maltreated hack.

As the clopping of hooves retreated down the cobbles, the quiet of London, in the moment before it would awaken to noisy life, overcame Antonia. She stood on the steps of Lady Pomfret's house, enchanted by the stillness. The sky above the chimney tops was showing a bit of color and a determined morning star. The street looked fresh and clean in the wake of a night rain. Somewhere, far away, a cock's crow could be discerned.

That sound, so reminiscent of the country, brought Antonia back to life. She lifted the knocker, wondering if the servants would believe her story. What was her story exactly?

Several knocks were necessary; they seemed to echo in the silent street. Antonia began to be nervous. The knocker was on the door. Lady Pomfret had to be in town, didn't she?

A full five minutes passed before a sleepy individual, a middle-aged footman in rumpled livery, came to the door and stared at Antonia in surprise.

She smiled and stated her business in a rush. "Good morning. I am Lady Pomfret's goddaughter, Antonia Worthingham. I've come to pay her a visit."

Gaping, the man stood aside to let her in and then scrambled down the steps to gather her baggage.

It occurred to Antonia that she had passed the portals too easily. "Tell me, my good man, why did you let me in at once with not even a question?" she asked as soon as the footman had stacked all the bags neatly and closed the door. She might have to speak to her godmother about him. She held back a smile, realizing that it would be quite unusual to complain that a footman hadn't been rude and surly.

"Recognized you, ma'am," said the man, ducking his head. "A little girl you was, but remember you, I do."

"Oh." Antonia looked more carefully at him, and a memory rushed back to her of the kind, if stuffy, footman who used to accompany her and little Monty to the Green Park of a morning during Laura's season. Monty's nurse had been too aged to like the duty . . . "Charles!" Antonia cried, holding out her hand. "It's so good to see you."

Solemnly the footman shook her hand.

"And now, what do you suggest I do?" she asked. "It's too early to rouse the household, and I won't wish Lady Pomfret to be disturbed. Perhaps I might rest in the morning room?"

"You'll be wanting your bed, ma'am, all respect," Charles said. "Housekeeper will take you to it. Walk into the drawing room, please, and I'll fetch Mrs. Addins."

Charles seemed to be quite sure of himself, and Antonia was too tired to contradict him. The word "bed" had acted as a soporific, and she was barely able to make it to the sofa of an elegant drawing room before she dozed off, only to be shaken awake a few minutes later by Mrs. Addins, the ancient housekeeper, and shown upstairs to a comfortable bedchamber.

Antonia had no time to look around at the elegant hangings, the pretty French furnishings, the thick carpet so unlike the serviceable matting in her room at home. She struggled with the hooks and tapes of her clothes in a desperate race against Morpheus, and lay down in her shift.

Soon London stirred, and the Pomfret household, prematurely awakened, went noisily about the duties of the day. The young lady in the guest bedchamber knew nothing of this. She was having a dream that featured a man with light hair and an intriguing cleft chin.

6

The Worthingham butler loomed at the door of the Easton Grange drawing room. "Sir Owen Longfort," he said in tones of icy disapproval. He stepped aside to let the visitor enter, but this courtesy carried with it a perceptible bad grace.

Miss Worthingham rose from her chair and went to meet the baronet, as the heavy footsteps of her servant retreated into the distance. "You must excuse Barrows, sir," she said with a welcoming smile. "He is very proper and thinks it daring in me to receive male visitors by myself."

"By yourself, ma'am? But—" Sir Owen looked about the room. "Oh. I see your sister isn't in."

"Do sit down, Sir Owen," Miss Worthingham said. "I know you're disappointed to find Antonia from home, but I must insist you make do with me for a little while. If nothing else, I can ask you your intentions."

"My intentions, ma'am?" Sir Owens obeyed the lady's instructions, hoping that his expression did not betray his alarm at such a question. Intentions, indeed! His thoughts lingered on the kisses he had stolen from Miss Antonia. Had she confided in her sister? If so, he had better be ready to explain himself.

"My intuition tells me that you find my sister—shall we say intriguing?" Laura Worthingham said with a wise nod.

Sir Owen shifted uncomfortably in his seat, telling himself that this young lady's playful manner did not have to be laden with double meaning. She might even be unaware of her younger sister's career as a smuggler. Yet he could tell that Miss Worthingham was toying with him; and he wasn't altogether displeased that he had been found out in his partiality for her sister.

"I find her enchanting," he said in a frank tone, looking Miss Worthingham right in the eye. Her eyes, he noticed, were nothing like Antonia's. Almost the same color, yes; the darker violet-blue might be quite appealing to the less discriminating. But there was something extraordinary in the shape, the expression of Antonia's eyes that was missing in her sister's.

"Enchanting, forsooth! Do you indeed?" Laura Worthingham clasped her hands. Was this gesture mocking? Sir Owen couldn't tell. "Then I expect you'll be disappointed, sir, to hear that my sister is gone."

"Yes, you've already told me that—"

"Gone to London," she elaborated.

Sir Owen committed the social impropriety of staring. "To London? But isn't this rather sudden, ma'am?"

"Oh, Antonia is quite impulsive," her sister said with a bland smile. "Nothing like me. I'm the most sedate of creatures, but Antonia? She is always shocking me with her dashing schemes."

"And so she's gone to London." Sir Owen knew that Miss Worthingham's account of her sister's temperament didn't mesh with the facade the young lady presented to the neighborhood. Was he being led down the garden path? "A short visit, I presume?"

"Presume nothing of the kind, sir," Laura said. "She is gone to do the season. High time, for she is long out of the schoolroom, and our trustees were beginning to be insistent. Our papa's will, you see, demands that each of us have a London debut."

"The beau monde has sorely missed you since your own season, Miss Worthingham," Sir Owen said politely. He was careful to use no such terms as "long-ago" or "distant."

"I am a relic," Laura said with a laugh, surprising him again. "I do hope my little sister has better luck than I, and

finds someone she can bring herself to accept.'' She looked
at Sir Owen significantly.

He smiled. ''In answer to your unspoken questions,
ma'am, yes, I will soon be leaving for London. This very
day, I think. And, yes, I do hope to encounter your sister
there.''

After a few more pleasantries, Sir Owen took his leave.
Laura watched him out of the room, waited a few minutes
until she heard the front door close, and rang the bell.

''Well, Barrows,'' she said when the butler entered, ''what
do you think? Was I too subtle?''

Barrows, as Laura knew, had softly returned as soon as
his heavy tread had receded a good distance for the benefit
of their guest, and had been listening at the door during the
interview. This was one of his most useful talents as a butler.
''Never you fear. He's hooked, Miss Laura,'' said that
worthy, bowing.

''I hope he is,'' Laura said. ''For more reasons than one,
I hope he is.''

Antonia rose in the afternoon of her arrival at Lady
Pomfret's, and found all her clothes put away in the wardrobe
of a delightful bedchamber. She could now recognize the
room as the one Laura had had during that season so many
years ago, when Antonia and Monty had been consigned to
the nursery floor.

A tug at the bellpull eventually produced an elderly
maidservant bearing a tray of tea and toast; she was followed
by another rickety serving woman, perhaps five years her
junior, who carried a can of hot water. Antonia denied any
necessity for one of them to remain to help her dress; indeed,
the idea of asking either aged female for assistance seemed
most improper. She would have to have a dresser if she were
to stay here, but she would set about hiring someone younger.

The maids had said that Lady Pomfret was sitting in her
boudoir, and thither Antonia took herself as soon as she had
consumed the tea and toast and hurried into a muslin gown
that seemed to have stood the trip better than the rest of her
things. Her hair she left unbound; she expected to meet no

one but her ladyship, and though she was not in general approving of her own looks, she quietly enjoyed her wealth of hair very much when it was down about her shoulders.

The boudoir hadn't changed. Antonia remembered with great exactitude the pretty jewel of a chamber, done in tones of peach and silver. On the long chair lay a slender, white-haired woman with a fine-boned, lovely face that three quarters of a century in a most perplexing world had failed to fade.

"Little Antonia!" The lady held out a hand and smiled in genuine pleasure. "Grown up at last, and so lovely. But do tell me now, dear, did I misread your letter? It arrived only this morning, and I'd swear you wrote you were still fixed in Kent. Yet here you are."

Antonia realized that she and her letter must have traveled to town by the same coach.

"Godmama, suddenly it became so dull at home that I couldn't bear it." She was glad Lady Pomfret didn't really know her. Antonia Worthingham would never behave in so flightly a manner as she was about to claim. "I decided, in the wink of an eye, that I wanted to come to you."

"Does this mean you're willing to enter society?" asked Lady Pomfret eagerly.

"I suppose it does." Antonia bent to kiss the older lady's thin, expertly rouged cheek. She sat down on a fragile chair beside Lady Pomfret's and thought grim thoughts. The decision had been made so quickly, but that did not lessen its impact. Here she was, about to launch onto what she had for so long successfully avoided. She felt no great resentment toward Laura for pushing her into this step; she had had the power of refusal, and she had not used it.

Her ladyship withdrew a delicate quizzing glass and surveyed Antonia. "If I'm not mistaken, child, you'll pay for the dressing if you do but wipe that rebellious expression from your face. What eyes you have! I'm so glad the barouche was just relined in blue. Now the first thing we must do is notify your trustees that you've arrived, at last, to honor your father's wishes for you."

Antonia took a deep breath. It was best to be aboveboard

with her godmother from the very first. "I must warn you, ma'am, that I'm not here to shop for a husband. I wish—I suppose I merely wish to see a little more of the world. But you must not hope to arrange a match for me."

Lady Pomfret shook her head. "Laura's sister through and through, aren't you? Absurd, I think it. It doesn't hurt any woman to marry once. But from my point of view, my dear, what does it matter whether you are here to get a husband or no? The chief business of a season is pleasure, and with you here, I'll be able to make the most of this year's festivities. I'll give a party for you—why should I not? And we'll be invited everywhere once it's known I have another Worthingham beauty on my hands." Her ladyship's fine dark eyes shone with the delightful possibilities awaiting her.

"A Worthingham beauty? But, Godmama, I'm barely passable," Antonia exclaimed.

"How can you say that when your color rises so prettily?" Lady Pomfret contradicted her, smiling. "Do you think that because you've always been compared to Laura in the past, it will be so in the future? Laura isn't here, my child. And all things considered, that's no bad thing. Now would you bring me my desk, dear? I'll get the note right off to whatever your solicitors are called, and ask one of them to wait upon me here. As I remember the terms of the trust, there is to be no expense spared." She winked. "There's no need to be as dismayingly honest with your solicitors as you were with me, Antonia. They may as well think you are here to 'shop for a husband,' as you so charmingly put it."

Antonia, in a daze, went to do her godmother's bidding. "Failing and Failing. That's the name of the trustees' firm," she said docilely. She could feel that her life was about to take a different turn.

In the next couple of days, Antonia's suspicions were confirmed. As expected, her first duty was a spirited round of the shops in the company of Lady Pomfret, who was as avid a shopper as she was a party goer. This was no hardship to Antonia, fresh from her years of scrimping. Mr. Failing of Failing and Failing had been most odiously hearty and generous in the matter of a dress allowance and pin money. It had been all Antonia could do not to snap at him to raise her housekeeping allowance, but she decided, quietly, to do this for herself. She could falsify a few bills or simply send one in for a dress that did not exist and transfer the money down to Kent.

This worthy resolution formed, she entered wholeheartedly into her godmother's plans and visited mantua makers, shoemakers, glovers, and milliners until her head began to spin from the unaccustomed effort of buying so many charming nonessentials for herself. Luckily, since Antonia was of a greater age than most debutantes, no one proposed to rig her out in innocent white for all her costumes, or tried to press upon her more frills than she thought tasteful. She was more satisfied than she could have imagined with her new things.

Town was thin of company, Lady Pomfret informed her charge, but Antonia could not have guessed this from the crowds, which seemed to be everywhere one turned in London, and had to take the statement on faith. Though the two met many of her ladyship's acquaintances when out on the rounds, they accepted no invitations. That, Lady Pomfret said, must wait until Antonia was ready to burst upon society in all her glory. Antonia had to giggle at this image, but she agreed demurely. The longer she could delay the frightening debut, the better she would like it.

Antonia and Lady Pomfret began a good-natured argument about the younger lady's hair as they rolled down Conduit Street one day in her ladyship's chariot. Antonia had made her observations of the most fashionable young ladies, and was leaning toward cropping her beloved light brown hair, a decision that surprised and pleased her, since it was the first daring idea she had formed in her life. But Lady Pomfret wouldn't hear of such an abomination.

"Crops are for those whose faces would come alive if freed of all that hair," said Lady Pomfret firmly. "But you, dear Antonia—you have no need of such a miracle. You are quite sweet as you are, with perhaps a thin fringe and a few curls about your temples. And I've been thinking you might wish to wear your hair unbound on some occasions, merely to cause a stir.''

Antonia considered this idea. The thought that she could cause a stir, even in one of her delightful new outfits, was totally foreign to her. Not for nothing had she spent all her twenty years entering rooms after Laura. But she easily gave up the idea of cutting her hair. She was relieved, really, that Lady Pomfret had not immediately said such a change would be the very thing.

''And now here we are in the umbrella-maker's,'' Lady Pomfret said as the carriage slowed. ''You must have a white parasol, and a rose-colored one, and of course something sensible for the rain, since nothing will stop you walking out in all weathers.'' She and Antonia descended, talking happily about this and that, and entered the establishment.

Antonia came to a stop just inside the door and felt her face color to what she knew must be a most vivid hue. Lady Pomfret, still chatting, was halfway across the shop floor before she noticed that Antonia wasn't following her. Her ladyship turned, a question in her eyes, and Antonia scurried to come up with her. She offered no explanation for her odd turn and began, in a determined manner, to pick and choose from among several pink parasols a fawning clerk was laying out for her inspection.

Lady Pomfret let her gaze travel casually around the shop and said, in a low voice, ''Don't look now, Antonia, but I see two people whose acquaintance you must make. They're across the way. A handsome couple, wouldn't you agree?''

Antonia was forced to turn, much against her will, in the direction her godmother had indicated. There, looking every inch the town beau in a flawless morning coat, close-fitting pantaloons and Hessians, stood Sir Owen Longfort. Hanging on his arm was a delicate blond creature in a celestial blue walking dress trimmed with swansdown, a delightful beauty who put Antonia in mind of a fairy princess.

''They look so much alike,'' Lady Pomfret continued with

a fond glance. "She is precisely the friend you should have, dear Antonia."

Antonia had seen them the moment she had walked into the shop, of course, and had immediately jumped to the conclusion that this lady on such intimate terms with Sir Owen must be the female who had writtten him that embarrassing letter. But Lady Pomfret's words confused the issue.

"Are they relations?" Antonia asked with more interest in her voice than she would have wished.

Lady Pomfret didn't answer, merely hailed the couple when the gentleman, his bored expression testimony to a less than entranced attention for the umbrella the lady was examining, found his gaze upon them. He immediately said something to his companion, and they both crossed the shop to Lady Pomfret's side.

Introductions soon made clear that the lady with Sir Owen was his sister, Miss Elizabeth Longfort, and that the pair of them had known Lady Pomfret since they were in leading strings.

"Miss Worthingham and I met recently down in Kent," Sir Owen said with a special smile for Antonia.

She felt, somehow, that something much more intimate than a smile had just been exchanged, and hoped that the other two ladies hadn't noticed.

"You don't say. I thought she looked as though she recognized you but couldn't place the name," Lady Pomfret said.

The gentleman looked disconcerted, and the next smile he directed to Antonia was even more brilliant.

"I called you over anyway, young scamp, not because I think you a proper acquaintance for my goddaughter, but because she and Eliza will be the greatest of friends," continued Lady Pomfret.

"Oh, will we?" burst out Eliza, with a giggle.

Antonia, seeing the spark of intelligence in gray eyes that could probably look as vacuous as they pleased when the situation called for stupidity, was immediately intrigued.

"You will indeed," Lady Pomfret affirmed, "and you'll

start out the project by coming home with us to take a nuncheon. How is your dear mama?''

"Perfectly well, my lady, so long as she doesn't have to shepherd me to all the shops. As you see, I've pressed my brother into service."

"And a fine thing, too, if you ask me. A gentleman can't spend too much time fussing over ladies' fripperies. Gives them an idea of what we put up with for their sakes."

Sir Owen laughed. "Come now, Lady Pomfret. You are too knowing to propagate the amusing fiction that ladies dress for gentlemen. Your efforts are all for each other. Admit it now."

"I admit nothing, sir, and for that thrust you may consider yourself uninvited to nuncheon. We mean this to be a ladies' coze, and you are most certainly not welcome."

He bowed in good humor, but Antonia thought he looked genuinely disappointed.

"Is the Hambrey's house party broken up so soon?" she found herself saying; the first full sentence she had dared since he had come near her.

He flashed her a look full of meaning. "No, the Hambreys are still entertaining, but I was obliged to leave early, Miss Worthingham. Urgent business called me to town. I'm sure you know the sort of thing I mean."

She laughed, trying for as silly a sound as she could manage. She must have succeeded, for he looked surprised. "Business? What should I know of business, sir? I've come here to do the season with my godmother, and for no other reason."

"But of course. And your sudden departure? No one in the neighborhood seemed to know your intention."

Antonia settled down to the business of convincing him that she was indeed the Lady, though of course, as the Lady, she would be trying to hide that identity. "I cannot flatter myself that the neighborhood finds my activities such engrossing entertainment," she said, batting her eyelashes. Perhaps a contrived effort to misunderstand him would turn the trick.

"You do yourself too little credit, ma'am," he said. His

sister and Lady Pomfret were looking on at this exchange with evident amazement. "I honor you, Miss Worthingham, for your modesty."

This caused more sharp looks from his sister and Lady Pomfret. Antonia did her best not to look conscious but was, she feared, only half-successful. Sir Owen parted from the ladies, leaving his sister in their care. She would be driven home in the Pomfret carriage after her visit in Curzon Street.

"Now do tell me, dearest creature," Eliza Longfort said as soon as she, Antonia, and Lady Pomfret were settled in the carriage and on the way to Lady Pomfret's house, "what was the meaning of that strange conversation you had with my brother? So you've met before?"

"We met very briefly," said Antonia, ignoring the first question.

Miss Longfort took the hint and confined her further questions to the most obvious. "And don't you think him handsome?" she said in the unmistakable tone of a fond sister. One day, Antonia knew, she would be asking some young lady that same thing about her brother Monty.

"Oh, yes, he's quite good-looking." She was relieved to be able to state her honest opinion without exposing herself. If the man were the greatest quiz in nature, she would have to tell his sister he was handsome.

"And quite a reputation with the ladies," Miss Longfort continued with satisfaction.

Antonia gave a start, thinking of that letter.

"Too sure of his attractions, if you ask me," Lady Pomfret contributed. "That's why I set him down." Her expression was not severe, but rather exhibited the same tolerant affection Miss Longfort was showing. Sir Owen did indeed have a way with the female of the species.

By the time they reached Lady Pomfret's house, the young ladies were calling one another by their Christian names and making plans for future walks and rides. "You see," Lady Pomfret said as the three walked into her Chinese saloon, where she had told the butler to deliver a tray of eatables, "I said you would be great friends, and so you are already."

Eliza laughed, a charming, sweet sound that matched her

looks. "Do you know, my lady, I believe you knew that, because you see in your goddaughter some of the traits you disapprove of in me."

Lady Pomfret's eyes grew wide. "I disapprove of you, my dear Eliza? How can you say so?"

Eliza undid the strings of her bonnet and shook out her head of flaxen curls. Her hair was several shades lighter than her brother's. "Madam, never tell me you now think it's quite the thing for a young lady to reject her class."

"You aren't rejecting it at the moment," Lady Pomfret pointed out, while Antonia wondered mightily what this was about. "Here you are, about to sit down to break bread with a pattern-card of the decaying aristocracy you are so pleased to rant about."

Antonia looked eagerly at her new friend. "Why, this is beyond anything great. Are you some sort of radical, Eliza?"

A perfect pair of dimples flashed as her new friend responded, "Hardly that. I'm not wise enough—or stupid enough, depending on whom you talk to. But it can't have escaped your attention that I'm past my first season."

Actually, it had. Antonia would have sworn that Eliza Longfort was no older than eighteen, and so she protested.

"Twenty-one," Eliza said with a sigh. "And I've been trotted through the marriage mart for three years now without success. For one reason only, my dear. Society is composed of nothing but fribbles. I intend to rise above its silly limitations."

"Oh," said Antonia, totally at sea. "Do you?"

"Yes," Eliza answered. "By marrying someone who shares my ideals. And as I've met no such person, and there is no chance of my encountering such a person in our circles, you see me in a state of single blessedness. Am I wrong, Antonia, to feel that you have somewhat the same ideas on matrimony? You're not just out of the schoolroom either, and there must be a reason such a pretty girl as yourself isn't yet married."

"I have no objection to matrimony," Antonia said, "but I would object to selling myself to the highest bidder, which—forgive me, Godmama—seems to be the usual practice here in town.''

Eliza nodded in approval of such sentiments.

Lady Pomfrets' laugh rang out, and she clasped her ringed hands in delight. "Revolutionaries indeed! I look forward to quite a season. And have no fear, Antonia, I don't intend to play slave trader.'' Her eyes twinkled. ''But why do I think the two of you will be married by the summer?''

"I don't intend to be,'' Antonia said, thinking of Sir Owen. That intriguing man would never care seriously for a smuggler, and would care less than nothing for her if he knew she was *not* a smuggler.

"Nor do I,'' Eliza said with a firmness quite belied by her ethereal, frivolous appearance.

"Have it your way.'' Lady Pomfret smiled wisely and turned to give orders to the servants, who were just bringing in the meal.

Her ladyship had an air of such mystery, such power, that Antonia and Eliza exchanged a worried glance.

7

Lady Pomfret, unlike the common run of elderly dowagers, might not have set herself up to be a matchmaker, but Antonia had not been in London many days before she found out the reason why her ladyship indulged in no such activity. Lady Pomfret had far too many suitors of her own to need to promote the romances of others.

Antonia had been too young to notice this phenomenon on her earliest visit. Lady Pomfret was an elderly female, but she was a most unusual one. Through no evident effort of her own, she collected men; men who were aging in relation to her own advancing years, but men nevertheless. The gouty, the hearty, the frail, the robust: walking under their own power, or wheeled to her side in Bath chairs, the most eligible bachelors of an early generation spent their days at Lady Pomfret's dainty feet.

Her ladyship was one of those women, infuriating to most of their sex, who had grown up to be a beauty and never left off being one. She had been the toast of her long-ago season, when the Marquess of Pomfret had carried her off as the prize she had been, and now that the title of Incomparable was going to ladies who could have been her grandchildren, she contented herself with the faithful adoration of members of her own generation.

Antonia spent several bemused mornings watching as Lady Pomfret received her court. She soon picked out the favored gentleman. Disbelief had stopped her from hitting on him at once as the cavalier of Lady Pomfret's preference, and only Eliza Longfort's laughing confirmation of Antonia's idea had convinced her that she had guessed aright.

Mr. Aloysius Daingerfield was not titled, as were most of the other men who flocked around Lady Pomfret; nor was he handsome, as more than one contender could still claim to be, though having surpassed the biblical lifespan of threescore and ten. Mr. Daingerfield was wealthy beyond expression, that was true, but at her age Lady Pomfret could hardly be said to need more in the way of money than the great plenty she evidently enjoyed. And, what was more, she was not on the catch for Mr. Daingerfield. They had known each other forever, she informed Antonia when the young lady couldn't help asking if her godmother had matrimonial plans. They had known each other long enough to consider all thoughts of matrimony absurd.

What Mr. Daingerfield did have, besides an amusing mode of dress that incorporated most of the excesses of the present day with one or two old-fashioned affectations such as red-heeled shoes, was the ability to amuse Lady Pomfret by the hour. Even Antonia could listen to him forever as he recounted the glories of the French court in the days before the parvenu Bonapartes had defiled it; the best way to mend a mainsail, remembered from his yachting days; the varied menu he had last encountered when dining at Carlton House.

Antonia soon accepted Mr. Daingerfield as a more or less constant fixture at her ladyship's dinner table and their future escort of choice for the wealth of *ton* engagements, which Lady Pomfret promised would begin very soon.

While waiting for the season to commence, Antonia settled into her new life. She and Eliza Longfort formed a partnership and spent many mornings riding, and more afternoons reading and talking, while the whole town readied itself for the rites of spring.

Quite often Sir Owen would join the girls on their ride. He called several times at Pomfret house, and though he and Antonia had no opportunity to speak together beyond the most casual of pleasantries, she could somehow feel that he was watching her, waiting, no doubt, for the Lady to make a move that would give her away.

Antonia began to look forward to her encounters with Sir Owen. In his eyes, at least, she was something special, someone out of the ordinary run of young ladies. She had never seriously craved Laura's great beauty, but she had wished more than once that a tiny bit of Laura's flamboyance had been vouchsafed her. Now, by the merest accident, she could borrow a little of her sister's aura.

"Mr. Daingerfield says we should accept this one," said Lady Pomfret one morning at the late breakfast table, passing Antonia a gilt-edged invitation card from the stack she had been sorting through. "A splendid way to begin, he says."

Antonia scanned the card and shrugged. "I must trust that he knows what we should do. I have no idea if the Featherstones' ball is a major event or no."

"Oh, it isn't the ball itself, but the ballroom that Mr. Daingerfield recommends," Lady Pomfret said earnestly. "Quite the most charming place, and it will be splendid for that *grande toilette* of yours that just came home from Madame Hélène's."

Antonia laughed. "We're choosing to accept an invitation because the decor of the house goes with my gown?"

Lady Pomfret looked as severe as her lovely face permitted. "My dear, you are the one, I thought, who had such a clear idea of the absurdities of society. Can you name a more sensible reason to choose a ball?"

Antonia agreed and gave over.

On the night the Featherstones' decor was to be pressed into service in the launching of Antonia, Mr. Daingerfield was in the Curzon Street drawing room to meet the ladies when they came down. "Ravishing," he exclaimed with his ordinary enthusiasm on viewing Lady Pomfret. Her ladyship was turned out in silver-gray satin trimmed with pearls, and a lovelier foil for her silver-white curls and blooming, if enameled, complexion could not be imagined.

Mr. Daingerfield, a compact, somewhat paunchy individual in a plum-colored coat of too freakish a cut to please Antonia, impressed the younger lady, as always, by his dignity and air of self-possession. He was well-known to be an arbiter of fashion. And how correctly, indeed, he seemed to judge the foibles of the modish set, much though he could not escape them in the matter of his own person.

"Will I do, sir?" Antonia asked hesitantly, pausing beneath the chandelier for his inspection. She knew that if he commanded her to run upstairs and change, she would do it without question.

Mr. Daingerfield whipped out a quizzing glass and eyed her, a thorough going-over from the top of her head to the toes of her slippers. "You will do, my dear Miss Worthingham," he pronounced at length.

Antonia heaved a sigh of relief.

"The hair, Daingerfield? You are certain about the hair?" Lady Pomfret asked. "You know we are taking a little risk there."

The quizzing glass was lifted once more, and Antonia held her breath. "Perfect," said Mr. Daingerfield.

The ball dress designed for Antonia by the first modiste in London was a diaphanous cloud of white net, scattered with brilliants, over a slim gown of light blue silk. Slippers of silver tissue peeked through beneath the hem. The daring feature of the costume, besides the low neck of the gown, was Lady Pomfret's personal achievement and a source of much pride to her. Her ladyship had decreed that Antonia was to wear her light brown hair unbound, held back at the temples with two diamond-and-sapphire combs from Lady Pomfret's ample collection of jewels. "You will never be lost in the crowd," Lady Pomfret had promised, and Antonia's new maid, a haughty middle-aged dresser with definite ideas of her own, had grumbled and muttered as she left her young mistress's hair practically in a state of nature.

To Antonia the question of her hair was nothing compared to the question of whether she would acquit herself well at her first London ball. Sir Owen was to be there, though he so infrequently attended society parties; Eliza had let that tidbit slip. Would he seek Antonia out? And if he did, would their encounter be at all more satisfying than the very public conversations they had had since she had met him in town?

When Antonia saw the Featherstones' ballroom, she had to smile. The entire setting might, indeed, have been designed with her ball gown in mind. Hangings of pale blue silk, mirrors framed in heavy silver filigree, and crystal chandeliers ornamented the vast place. Having spent a half hour on the staircase trying to gain the entrance, Antonia was prepared to see a crowd. But, she thought with a perceptible quaking of her shoulders as her name was announced after Lady Pomfret's, she was not prepared for a crowd to see her. She scanned the room, desperate to see Eliza's friendly face, but could distinguish only a sea of strangers.

Lady Pomfret took one look at Antonia's expression, nudged her with her fan, and whispered, "Buck up, my girl." Then in a normal tone, she spoke to Mr. Daingerfield. "Sir, do see if you can get me a good place in the dowagers' ranks. I'll want an unobstructed view of the floor for Antonia's triumph. I don't mean to play cards at all tonight."

"A sacrifice indeed, my dear," exclaimed Mr. Daingerfield.

"Heavens, Godmama, you aren't curtailing your enjoyment of the party for my sake?" Antonia demanded.

"No," Lady Pomfret said. "Truth to tell, my luck has been out lately, and I'll welcome a chance to watch the dancers. And to see your triumph," she repeated in a determined voice.

Antonia nearly choked at the idea of a triumph for herself. She was torn between amusement and fright, and was reaching out to take Mr. Daingerfield's plum-colored arm when a familiar, light-haired gentleman advanced through the crowd.

"Miss Worthingham," Sir Owen Longfort said with a bow. "How lovely you are this evening." To Antonia's eyes, he was absolutely dazzling in his *corbeau*-colored evening attire. He turned from the suddenly blushing Antonia to Lady Pomfret. "My lady, I beg forgiveness for not greeting you first, but I was so much stuck by your charge's beauty that

I could not restrain myself. I hope you'll grant me the first dance with the young lady, madam?'' He turned back to Antonia.

"Go on, child," Lady Pomfret said with a twinkle when Antonia hesitated. " 'Tis what you're here for.''

With a deep breath, Antonia placed her gloved hand upon Sir Owen's arm. Were all eyes following her with envy? They ought to be. Sir Owen was certainly the handsomest man present.

They found places in the set, and Sir Owen smiled in an intimate manner. "May I say how much I admire your gown, ma'am. French, I take it?''

"Why, yes, my dressmaker is French," Antonia had responded before it occurred to her that he was making another touch at her supposed career of smuggling.

"My word," the gentleman drawled, "I had not supposed you went so far as Paris.''

Antonia caught herself on the point of explaining that Laura did not go over to the Continent at all; at least, she had never told Antonia about it if she had. Instead, Antonia murmured something about her modiste's Bruton Street salon.

"To be sure." Sir Owen looked wise. The music started then, putting an effective end to what was threatening to become an uncomfortable conversation.

Antonia was a graceful dancer, and she was quite happy so long as the country-dance lasted. She had the most charming partner in the room, and a gratifying number of stares came her way from other gentlemen, though whether these looks were of admiration or merely shock because her hair was unbound, she could not say. When she glimpsed Eliza going down the line and exchanged a look of greeting with her friend, she was more comfortable than ever.

Also, it had occurred to her that the overskirt of her dress was Urling's net, as British as she was, and that if Sir Owen reopened the subject of her gown, she would be able to hold her own.

When the tune came to end and Sir Owen offered his arm to escort her back to her godmother, Antonia was less than determined to defend her gown's honesty. There was Laura's safety to think of, and that depended on Antonia successfully masquerading as the Lady in Sir Owen's eyes. Would it not be better for her to pretend that her toilette had, indeed, come from Paris direct, that she, as the Lady, had somehow sneaked into the French capital herself to order it from the great Parisian modiste Leroy? She chuckled at the thought.

"What amuses you, ma'am?" Sir Owen asked. "Have I done something cloddish that I don't realize?"

She glanced up at him. "No, you're being a perfect gentleman—for a change." The last words showed a touch of daring quite foreign to her ordinarily, and she was rather proud of herself at the thought.

He looked genuinely puzzled for a moment; then his eyes lit in amusement. "Oh, you're referring to the liberties I took at Lord Hambrey's. I deeply regret, Miss Worthingham, that we're in far too public a situation for me to repeat my mistake. A most pleasurable mistake, was it not? I assure you that I'll be as much a gentleman as you're a lady."

She fancied double meaning in his last words and looked alarmed. It was one thing to keep him uncertain, to feed his suspicions ever so slightly, but if he were to accuse her publicly of smuggling, she would be in a fine fix.

"Never fear, my own lady," he murmured into her ear, "your secret is safe with me. You have taken to heart, I trust, my warning about treachery."

Antonia's eyes grew wide. On the night of the Hambrey's party, she had forgotten to tell Laura that Sir Owen had made some warning remarks about betrayal of the crown. His kisses, later on that same night, had driven the incident from her mind.

His remark about her gown took on a new, sinister meaning. He evidently suspected her—suspected Laura—of trafficking with the French in serious ways. Perhaps of being a secret Bonapartist.

It wasn't fair. Laura might be planning to marry a former French spy, but she was as English as Antonia and wouldn't think of betraying her country. Antonia resolved to write to Laura at once to relay this new line of thought. How would she phrase the warning in subtle enough terms? It wasn't out of the question to suppose that Sir Owen or some government agent would have her letters intercepted and read, if she was thought to be the Lady.

Antonia gave Sir Owen an icy look. "My gown," she said distinctly, "is of British net, sir." Then she removed her hand from his arm and walked away. He did not follow her.

Lady Pomfret welcomed her goddaughter to her side, where she had been chattering with a plumed dowager of daunting aspect, and said, "What did you do to Longfort, dear? He's stalking away looking most sober. Ah, well, it's no matter. As I foretold, Antonia, the line is forming. May I present you to the Earl of Depton as a most suitable partner?"

Antonia smiled at the long, thin young man, whose receding hairline made him look touchingly vulnerable. She gave him her hand, satisfied, not only with the earl's evident admiration, but with the thought that high-and-mighty Sir Owen would see that Miss Worthingham could get a partner without relying on him.

The evening began to fly by in a dazzling succession of bright lights, varicolored silks, and faces, mostly friendly, which Antonia slowly began to match with names. She met a patroness of Almack's, and, to Lady Pomfret's gratification, was promised a voucher. She was presented to Mr. Brummell, whom she had had a great curiosity to see, and he made a most fortunate remark about her hair, which had several ladies of less unstructured coiffures hurrying to the retiring room to remove the pins from their topknots.

Most satisfying of all, though everyone remembered Laura Worthingham and many made references to her, nobody seemed to be measuring Antonia against the forbidding standard of her sister's beauty. It was as Lady Pomfret had said: Laura was not in town, and the *ton*, remembering only that a Worthingham beauty had once charmed them, was quite ready to set up another.

Antonia sent her partner of the moment away to procure her a lemonade, and leaned against a Corinthian column to catch her breath after a particularly spirited reel. She had been too busy to think of Sir Owen, she told herself in determination. She didn't even know if he were still at the ball, she further congratulated herself, letting her eyes rove around the crowded room in quest of a certain blond head.

"Champagne, madam?" asked a voice near her ear.

Antonia whirled around and beheld a footman in the Featherstone livery, politely proffering a loaded tray. She shook her head and turned away.

The footman cleared his throat. "Madam, if you please."

She turned to him again and was about to say something very sharp when she took a good look at his face. The strong lineaments, the reddish hair, were unmistakable. "My God!" she gasped. Her sister's right-hand man in the smuggling gang; Lord Hambrey's groom. "What are you doing here?"

"The most expedient way, ma'am, to speak to you," Vale said. "You had better take some champagne, and it would be well if you were to meet me in the south corner of the conservatory in a quarter of an hour."

Antonia stared and did not take a drink off his tray. "Why should I?"

Vale shrugged. "You may not care to." He smiled. "I know the Lady—your sister—thinks nothing of her reputation. But she might care very much if she and her band went to prison for her shady activities at dark of the moon."

"Keep your voice down, you wretch," Antonia whispered in a panic. "I'll meet you. Fifteen minutes." She watched him walk away.

Here was the answer to the question of why Vale had always made her uncomfortable, she was thinking as her erstwhile dancing partner approached, balancing two glasses of lemonade, and began to talk. Where was the conservatory, and how was she to get there without putting a period to her reputation?

The young man thought her a fine listener and was in a fair way to being besotted when Antonia broke into the middle of his account of his latest purchase at Tattersall's to say, "Do excuse me, sir. Urgent business. Thank you very much." And, having thrust the lemonade glass into his hand, she was gone, dodging her way among the fashionable crowds in a tearing hurry.

A woman of mystery as well as a dashed pretty girl! The sprig looked after her in fascination.

8

Sir Owen Longfort had scarcely taken his eyes off the young woman since she had arrived at the ball. Antonia Worthingham was a delightful mystery. A ruthless smuggler at dark of the moon, she did not hesitate to dance among society's finest in her other guise of respectable young lady.

Her admirer's confusion was growing by the minute. Miss Worthingham *was* respectable in all ways; he would swear to the sweetness of her disposition and the strictness of her moral principles. He didn't even find it hard to reconcile these principles with smuggling. The Lady was by tradition in the business only to help her people.

One troubling question did remain, though. How could a band she led be involved in the treasonable activities all evidence pointed to? How could she be concerned, even indirectly, in the passing on of information that must lead to the death of British men in the sorts of bloody battles young English ladies could not imagine in their wildest nightmares?

There was one possibility. She did not know what her men were up to. Sir Owen devoutly hoped this would turn out to be the case. He watched closely as the waiter, who had been talking to Miss Antonia Worthingham, separated from her.

Where had he seen that servant's face before? Since the fellow had been talking to Miss Worthingham with every appearance of familiarity, it followed that he was known to her from before. A man of Lady Pomfret's unaccountably decked out in the Featherstone livery? No, that worthy female was known to employ only those who had passed the half-century mark, and this man was young. That reddish-brown hair seemed as familiar as the narrow features, but Sir Owen couldn't remember where he had seen it before.

He stared harder, searching his memory, and had the sudden impression of horses in a particular stable. Of course! A groom. Lord Hambrey's groom. Sir Owen had noticed the man in particular because his speech was much more cultivated than that of his fellows.

Now what would a groom of Lord Hambrey's be doing in the Featherstone colors, talking to Antonia Worthingham as though he had known her forever?

The answer came in a flash. The man must be a smuggler, must be the Lady's liaison between town and her motley band of spy landers. Sir Owen's brow darkened. He would have to watch Miss Worthingham very carefully indeed, and he would watch this footman, too.

On the thought, he lost sight of the man. He blinked. One moment the suspicious groom/waiter had been offering his tray of beverages to a lady in pea-green satin, the next he was gone. Proof, if any were needed, that the man was an expert at deception.

Sir Owen sighed and began to circulate through the ballroom. Miss Worthingham was talking to a harmless young man who would have no choice but to return her to her chaperon when they had finished their lemonade. She might be the Lady, but this evening she was a young woman at a ball and had to behave as such. Much more important to keep close watch on her minion, who was bound by no such strictures.

Antonia tiptoed into the conservatory, hoping she had not been seen. The stuffy retainer who had told her which doors to go through had seemed quite shocked that a young lady would ask the way to this place.

One step inside and she knew why. The conservatory was the resort, and probably the notorious resort, of dallying couples. Their dark shapes and soft whispers could be made out here and there as Antonia, whose sense of direction was remarkably good, nearly felt her way to the south corner through a tangle of tropical plants and vines. Her anger was building. How dare Vale lead her into this compromising situation?

The groom was there before her, waiting between a wicker chair and a flourishing pineapple. "Well?" Antonia asked in a furious undertone. "What is so important that I must risk my reputation to see you?"

Vale actually smiled. "It's quite simple, ma'am. I wish you to find me a post."

Antonia's eyes widened. "A post? You mean Lord Hambrey let you go?"

"Not exactly," said Vale. "I let him go. My patience with the country was running out. Now I have a fancy to see a bit of town life, ma'am. And you must help me."

"Why?"

"For the reasons I stated earlier. Refuse, and I tell the world about your sister's business." His dark eyes gleamed in what Antonia thought a sly manner.

"Tell me the reason you really left Kent, and I'll consider your petition," Antonia said with a toss of her head. Her heavy hair shifted and reminded her of Mr. Brummell's kind compliment. She was newly aware of how much she had been enjoying herself before this creature had shown up to spoil everything.

Vale folded his arms and leaned against the brick wall of the south corner. "I see no reason not to be candid. It's Miss Worthingham, ma'am. Your sister. She will be leaving the country, so she says, and she has some maggoty notion that I would make a splendid leader for the gang."

"I know she thinks so." Antonia didn't mention how very far she had been from agreeing with her sister on that point. "It would seem to me that leader of the free traders would be a most challenging post for a man of your abilities."

Shaking his head, Vale answered, "Too tied down. I joined the gang as a lark, and happy I was to help your sister with this and that. But I can't do it forever. Not my idea of a life, ma'am, and I wasn't so dishonest as to pretend to Miss Worthingham I could stick it out in the Thanet.'' That section of Kent where Antonia's home lay had been an island once. It retained some of the isolated qualities of its ancient condition. Antonia could understand that a newcomer would take ill the prospect of devoting himself to a close-knit community that did not admit him.

But she was still confused. ''So you decided to come to London. I understand that. But with Lord Hambrey's reference, why must you come to me for help?''

''Hambrey wasn't so eager to give a letter to a man who was leaving him within the hour, ma'am. Once I'd decided, I had to be off. It's the way I am.''

''That will certainly be a fine recommendation to any employer I might find for you,'' Antonia said. ''And you expect me to get you a post—where? I have no connections in London.''

''You've a most important one, ma'am.'' Vale's grin was more insolent than ever. ''Lady Pomfret. She must need a new groom. One hears the men she's got have one foot in the grave.''

''Well, that might be true, but nothing unusual in her household,'' said Antonia, willing herself not to smile. Charles, the middle-aged footman, and Antonia's new abigail, who admitted to fifty, were indeed the youngest members of the Pomfret entourage.

''Sounds to me as if she'd be up for a change. She might wish to try someone who could lift a saddle without suffering a palpitation,'' Vale said. ''Come, ma'am, don't begrudge an honest man a little sight of town life.''

''An honest man? You would call yourself that when I know what you've been doing?'' Antonia rolled her eyes. ''I never did trust you.''

''You didn't?'' Vale seemed genuinely surprised at this and not at all pleased. ''Because I was an outsider, ma'am? The men of Kent don't trust a foreigner, that's true.''

''As a woman of Kent, I never knew what to think of you,''

Antonia said. "I meet many outsiders, even down in the country, but you—I simply don't think you're what you seem to be."

Again he looked startled. "Why is that?"

Antonia hadn't expected to be begged for information on this point. "I don't know what to tell you."

"Pity." Vale shrugged. "I'd like to know. You'll be getting me that post, then, Miss Antonia, ma'am? I'll call in the morning to take it up."

"You're rather high-handed, Vale," Antonia said. "Heaven only knows if I can convince my godmother she needs a groom."

"Trouble here, ma'am?" asked a familiar voice. Antonia turned and saw Sir Owen moving from behind an orange tree. How long had he been standing there? How much had he heard?

A warning glance from Vale decided Antonia against telling Sir Owen that she was being harassed. "Everything is fine, Sir Owen," she said with a nervous smile. "I'm merely arranging things with my godmother's new groom."

Sir Owen directed a searching look at Vale. "You're leaving the Featherstones, are you? Lady Pomfret must think you very valuable if she'd hire you out from under their noses. But I think she would prefer that this young lady not deal with you in a situation that wagging tongues might interpret as too private."

Vale shrugged and turned on his heel.

"Wait a minute." Sir Owen spoke in a clipped tone.

Vale looked back. "Sir?"

"Watch yourself," said Sir Owen. He glared at the man, and Vale walked away, his swagger betraying that he was not at all intimidated.

"Shall we leave here, sir?" Antonia said with some urgency. "I'd hate for you and me to be caught together. This is much too private a place. You're right."

"I merely didn't like to think of you loitering here with that fellow," Sir Owen said. "But now—I'm reminded of another conservatory, another night." They had been whispering the whole time, and now he leaned closer to Antonia, tantalizingly close.

She jumped back, alarmed at her own wishes.

He smiled. "Don't worry, my dear, I did promise you that I would be as much a gentleman as you were a lady. And it's clear to me that you're every inch a lady."

Antonia glared at him, sensing the satire in his tone. Double meanings again. She was growing tired of them.

"Do you care to tell me what that scene with the servant was really about?" Sir Owen asked in a gentler voice. His eyes promised understanding. "I happen to know already that you make it your business to find employment for the people of your neighborhood. Lady Hambrey fairly sang your praises. And you've helped at least one servant since you've been in town."

"What can you mean?" Antonia asked. She had been in the habit of aiding many villagers to find positions, mostly in domestic situations, but that was no more than the duty of a daughter of the Grange. And in truth, she had always believed that the people she could find respectable positions for would not have to turn to smuggling.

He smiled. "My sister Eliza has a loose tongue. Your new abigail is the person I'm referring to."

Antonia swallowed. Drat that Eliza! Antonia hated to have her actions talked about. Yet she could hardly have kept the situation a secret; it had been through Eliza that she had heard of Steelman's plight and hired the woman . . .

"It was a kindness, ma'am, that I won't soon forget, and I know the person most concerned will not. You have saved a woman from poverty or worse—"

"I beg you not to speak of it again, sir."

"Your modesty intrigues me, Miss Worthingham," Sir Owen said. "And I stand ready to help you with any problem concerning this footman—or this groom, whatever he wants to call himself."

Antonia chanced to look into his eyes and was sorely tempted. She would lose her mystique and put Laura in grave danger if she so much as hinted at the truth to this man. The strong wish to murmur all her worries into his coat front was alarming. So was the secret hope that he would yet take liberties.

One thing she was certain of: they must get out of this near-privacy and back to the lights and people, and at once.

Giving him a short no in answer to his question, she took his arm for the walk back to the ballroom. This was a dilemma she must solve for herself.

In the coach going home, Antonia mentioned that she knew of a former groom of Lord Hambrey's who was in town and wanting a position. Would Lady Pomfret consider the man? "I'm sure he's very efficient." Antonia did not care to recommend Vale more strongly than that.

Lady Pomfret exchanged a glance with Mr. Daingerfield. "I'll take a look at him, but I've no need of a groom."

"Oh, do say you'll take him, Lady Pomfret. It's most important." Antonia's voice held an honest note of panic that made the older pair look even more curious. Clearing her throat, she rephrased her plea. "That is, he is a former employee of my neighbor's, and I know he'll be suitable."

"Antonia," Lady Pomfret said, "is there something you're not telling me? Is this man a friend of yours?" Her eyebrows shot up, and she looked shocked. "Can you have lowered yourself to a groom?"

Antonia's genuine horror-struck gasp must have helped to put that suspicion to rest in her ladyship's mind. "By no means, ma'am. I would never—I don't even like him."

"Then, why, young woman, are you making a cake of yourself over his affairs?"

Antonia shrugged. "I suppose I'm a meddling spinster already. I consider him my responsibility because he's from my parish. I'm so used to finding jobs for the men who live near us at home."

"That sounds plausible," Lady Pomfret said, "and I've already had an example of your charitable way with servants' problems—that new abigail of yours—but I'd dare swear there's a little more to this new start. Wouldn't you, Daingerfield?"

The old man looked in Antonia's direction. His lined face, in the light of the carriage lamps, was keen as ever. "I would swear this young woman is completely blameless, whatever the story."

Antonia relaxed somewhat, but she still wished she might throttle Vale rather than see him safely employed in her godmother's house.

The ladies of the Pomfret establishment didn't rise until late the next morning. When Antonia appeared at the breakfast table before Lady Pomfret was down, Dunn, the ancient butler, coughed discreetly and told her, his expression impassive as only a long lifetime of practice can render a servant's visage, that there was a person eating his head off —begging Miss Worthingham's pardon—in the kitchens.

Antonia's memory of the evening before was confused, for many reasons, and she puzzled for a moment over Dunn's words, wondering how they could possibly have to do with her.

"Name of Vale," the butler elaborated.

"Oh." Antonia sighed deeply. So the problem of Vale hadn't gone away overnight. She had hoped that perhaps his admitted volatility would lead, before morning, to a pressing desire to see the Scottish Highlands. "I will see him as soon as I finish my breakfast, Dunn. And has her ladyship rung for her dresser yet?"

The butler indicated that her ladyship had done so. Antonia dismissed him and Charles the footman, preferring to serve herself. As she nibbled on a muffin, she wondered what Laura could be doing to replace the capable Vale. Was Laura still in Kent, for that matter? How difficult it was always to keep in mind that Laura could disappear at any moment, forever. She hadn't answered Antonia's last letter, but Antonia would write her again, immediately, with news of Vale's treachery.

Antonia narrowed her eyes in thought. She must remember to find a way to include in the letter her suspicion that Sir Owen Longfort considered Laura's smuggling ring to be trafficking in forbidden secrets. If only Sir Owen knew Laura.

The thought of her as a traitor was almost as ludicrous as the thought of her as a plain spinster.

Antonia caught herself. What had Laura to do with this line of reasoning? In Sir Owen's mind, she, Antonia, was the traitor to the crown. How could he think such a thing of her? Anger flared. She was almost glad, for the moment, that she was hoaxing him.

Lady Pomfret came in before Antonia had finished with her meal. Her ladyship was quite willing to see the new prospective groom. "Vale!" she exclaimed when Antonia told her the man's name. "Something havey-cavey about this one, I'd say."

Antonia agreed so strongly that she didn't question her ladyship's unusual reaction to Vale's surname.

Later, suitably fortified with kippers and toast, Lady Pomfret led the way to a small office under the staircase that was her usual resort when interrogating or otherwise browbeating her staff. She had told Dunn to bring Vale to meet them there.

The ladies arrived first and settled themselves, Lady Pomfret in the one armchair the simple room boasted, Antonia on a hard chair near the writing table. They both directed suitably severe looks at the door.

A diffident tap at the barricade produced from Lady Pomfret a harsh "Enter!" and in came Vale, his hat in his hand. He made a servile bow, but somehow he didn't look as if he meant it. This, at least, was Antonia's opinion.

"So." Lady Pomfret took a long look at the man, then rose from her seat and advanced toward him. "You have precious little respect for those you think to serve, sirrah, and though I do sympathize with someone in your sad situation, you'll not get my help until you choose a different name. No, I don't care about Miss Worthingham's wish to perform an act of charity. Another name you must have."

Vale and Antonia both looked at the lady in wonder.

"Yes, I see it in the lineaments and that peculiar red-brown hair," Lady Pomfret went on. She had stopped just inches from Vale and withdrawn her lorgnette, through which she proceeded to examine him. "Who is it?" she asked. "The old duke himself? His brother Claude? That one was always a loose fish. Whoever's by-blow you are, my good man, you'll have to stop using the family name. It's unseemly. It's unheard of. It's—did your mother really dare to give you that name? The hussy."

Instant understanding lit Vale's face. "I assure you, my lady," he said with another bow, this one a sweeping and courtly gesture, "my mother would not have dared to give me the name unless I had every right to it. Fitz-something would be usual for a bastard, would it not? Rest assured my mother would have held to the established pattern."

Antonia was following this exchange with difficulty. "Could one of you please tell me what this is about?"

Lady Pomfret spoke in an indignant tone. "This insolent puppy is a by-blow of the house of Taverton, quite possibly of the duke himself. He looks just like them. And here he comes sporting not only the family face, but the family name. Disgraceful, I tell you."

Vale gave her ladyship just time to finish this diatribe before he said quickly, "Miss Worthingham, Lady Pomfret errs in one particular. I am not a bastard of the house of Taverton. The duke is my father, true, but I'm quite legitimate. At least I was led to believe so."

"Your given name?" questioned Lady Pomfret crisply. Antonia was speechless with the implications of his confession.

"Thomas, an' it please your ladyship."

Lady Pomfret did some reckoning on her fingers. "Such a confounded number of sons. Heir and a spare is one thing, but heir and a cricket team is quite excessive! That's what Dr. Johnson said once of Taverton's brood. But poor Lucia—she was the duchess, Antonia—she never could say no to Taverton. You'd be the twelfth boy." Again she addressed herself to Vale.

He nodded.

Antonia found her voice. "Why in heaven's name would you work as Lord Hambrey's groom?" she burst out. "As the son of a duke, you could . . ." She hesitated.

Vale smiled, an ironic smile. "You have it, Miss Worthingham. I could—what? Nothing much. My father has no taste for the professions and had us all educated up to no useful purpose. My two eldest brothers had property secured to them and can busy themselves with that. The rest of us are completely dependent on the duke. Some of my brothers have gone into the army, true, and we have one sailor, but I'm afraid I imbibed my father's Whiggish politics along with my nurse's fairy tales and won't support the war. And my only other choice, toiling in some clerkship or the church, holds little appeal for me. When I reached my majority I decided to see the world, to work with my hands as I'd always loved to do.''

"Extraordinary," Lady Pomfret murmured. A gleam of something like admiration had come into her eyes.

Antonia, too, was quickly revising her opinion of Thomas Vale. "I can hardly believe it." She thought of how surprised Laura would be to hear that she had had a duke's son working for her gang.

"And I haven't been home in all that time," Vale stated, as though he were very proud of the fact.

Lady Pomfret was looking thoughtful. "I'd not heard anything about your odd way of spending your time, lad. Lord Thomas, I suppose we should style you."

"No, if you please. I left my title behind long ago. And it's likely my family doesn't know what's happened to me, though I told them why I was leaving and what I intended to do." He smiled. "So many things have changed in the last seven or so years."

"How the devil did you manage to find jobs working as a menial?" Lady Pomfret asked. "You even use the name"

"Nothing easier, my lady. I've been in the country all the time. By taking care to stick to counties far from my home, I've managed nicely. I'll admit that I don't volunteer who I am, but if anyone had questioned me in the past—and your ladyship is the first one who's done so—I would have told the truth. I don't believe sons of the aristocracy should be useless burdens upon society. That's all. I have no elaborate wish to hide, and so I don't. Vale is my name, and I'm not ashamed of it.''

"Yet you—you needed my help to get a post in London."
Antonia spoke up, choosing her words with care. She had
nearly used the word "blackmail," and it would never do
to make Lady Pomfret curious about the real reason Antonia
was helping Vale.

"I had a fancy to return to London," said Thomas Vale,
"and here I'm known. I've asked at one or two places, but
I don't disguise my accent; I don't hide my name. No one
is willing to employ a son of the house of Taverton as a
servant. And I have picked up no other trade than that of
groom, though," and he drew himself up, "I made a capable
waiter last night. Your ladyship might use me in that capacity
whenever the need arises."

"Young man," Lady Pomfret said, "you must go home."

"That I can't do. Will you help me?"

A long moment of silence passed, while Lady Pomfret
tapped her lorgnette against her nose and stared at Vale. "I
can use a groom who can keep up with Miss Worthingham
on her rides. My sources tell me that Miss Elizabeth Longfort's groom, who accompanies them, has been left in the
dust most mornings, and I must see that the young ladies
are looked after at all times."

Antonia squirmed; she ought to have known her hell-for-
leather gallops with Eliza would not remain secret.

Thomas Vale's smile was most attractive. Even Antonia,
who still did not like him, could tell that. "You won't regret
this, my lady. I'll serve you well."

"And leave me at a moment's notice, as you left Lord
Hambrey, I'd wager," Lady Pomfret replied. "Well, go
about your duties. Who knows? Perhaps it will become the
fashion to have a duke's son mucking out one's stables.
Though you may be sure I won't bruit your identity about,
you have already found out that word spreads fast in town."

Grinning, Vale shook her hand and Antonia's, then left
the room quickly.

"Whisked away before I could change my mind," Lady
Pomfret muttered. "Do you know, Antonia, there is something to admire in that young man."

"There is?"

"He's a younger son with no chance of inheriting the title. He might have become a fribble, a rake, a drunkard by now. Instead he's learned to respect himself and his abilities. Such a man would be a rare catch for some lucky young lady."

Antonia caught her breath. "You aren't suggesting that I—"

"By no means, my dear. If the spark were there, I would have seen it, and I did not."

"But he couldn't be a catch exactly, could he? I must assume he's penniless if he's been working for his bread all these years."

Lady Pomfret tossed off this problem as a mere bagatelle. "Pish, tush, he would be given a handsome allowance if he'd but reveal himself to Taverton."

"I imagine that was always the truth," said Antonia thoughtfully. "He must not have wanted it."

"Men change," Lady Pomfret said. "We shall watch his career with interest. Antonia, do see about ordering him some livery. There's not been a man of his strapping size working here since the reign of the second George."

Antonia took care of the errand quickly and ran off to her room, where she spent most of her remaining free time composing a long, crossed letter to her sister: a jumbled and vague epistle that sought to mingle an account of her first ball with Vale's blackmail of her, and Sir Owen Longfort's suspicions of Bonapartist activities among the smugglers.

She did not see how Laura would ever make sense of all of this, but she hoped that the warning about the pro-French activities would stand out, though she had couched it in such ambiguous terms. She must never forget that someone— perhaps even Sir Owen—might read her letter before it even got to Laura.

For this reason, she didn't mention her dance with Sir Owen, nor that she had found him the most agreeable of partners. She gave not a hint that he had nearly kissed her, nor that she would have welcomed the improper salute. He was puffed up enough in his own conceit, she suspected, without her giving him even more to preen himself over.

9

"Nay, Miss Laura, ye'll take him out in the morning dew at his peril." Old Hannah bustled up to her cottage door where Jean-Baptiste, leaning upon Laura's arm, was preparing to take the first walk since the accident which had injured him.

"I insist, Hannah. He can walk on his leg now. It must be used if it's to grow stronger." Laura's eyes flashed. In them blazed the pique of a spoiled beauty as well as centuries of outraged feudalism. Who was this old crone to be telling her, the Lady, what to do?

Old Hannah stood right up to this. "Hold there, missy. Be ye sayin' my potions ain't done him good?"

"She is certainly not saying that," put in Jean-Baptiste with a polite inclination of his head. "Nor am I. You have saved me, *ma bonne femme.*"

The good woman nodded firmly. "You see, Miss Laura, the man knows what's good for him. No wanderin'. Not yet. And do ye forget he's in hidin'? Lor' bless us, it's full daylight."

Laura sighed. The truth was she wished to discuss her sister's latest letter away from what she suspected were a pair of sharp ears; though Hannah, to be sure, pretended deafness when it suited her, Laura didn't believe that she missed very much. "A breath of air, then," she suggested.

"We'll step outdoors for a breath of air, and we'll stay hidden in the trees."

Hannah began another invective on the perils of air, but at this suggestion Jean-Baptiste, who hadn't been that enthusiastic over the prospect of a walk, did perk up. A sunbeam had struck his face that morning as he viewed it in the shaving mirror, he said, and he had been struck by his own lurid pallor. "For but a moment, Hannah," he finished with a pleading look.

"A moment, then," was Hannah's gruff answer.

"She likes you," Laura said when she and her fiancé emerged into the lovely spring morning. The wood was a velvet green. Birds twittered loudly, and rustlings here and there in the clearing signaled the friendly presence of small animals. Laura's trained ears kept guard for any sound more substantial than the hopping of a rabbit.

"The Old Hannah? Yes, she likes me well enough. Now," and Jean-Baptiste, letting go of Laura's arm, eased himself onto a fallen log and motioned for her to join him, "what do you wish to speak about?"

Laura sat down close beside him and clasped his hand. "I was too obvious, wasn't I? It's simply that Hannah has eyes at the back of her head and more ears than she admits to. I heard from my sister again."

"And?" Jean-Baptiste's free arm went around Laura's waist.

"Antonia and I are quite subtle these days in our messages to each other. But I was able to pick out some startling information from this letter of hers."

"Does this baronet Sir Owen now suspect she is not the Lady?" Jean-Baptiste asked in some alarm. "Your safety, *ma chère,* must be our first priority. We'll be off this very night . . . never mind my leg—"

"Heavens, dear Jean-Baptiste, nothing so serious as that," Laura said with a pretty toss of her head. "As far as I can make out, Antonia is still leading Sir Owen a merry dance. But she has found out from him something that disturbs me very much. There is a rumor, it seems, that my men—that I—have been landing spies."

"Shocking," her lover murmured with a rueful grin.

Laura appreciated the joke, but she was earnest in her defense of her operations. "We didn't land you. We may have saved you and hidden you here, but we didn't bring you. I land spies! It's an insult to everything that the Lady stands for."

"This I know. Who better than I?" Jean-Baptiste agreed.

"Then you will help me?"

"Help you? How?"

Laura's face set in determination. "I cannot prevent what is said about me. But I do wish that you, Jean-Baptiste, would keep your eyes and ears open. I know Hannah has dealings with many people."

"She may. But not in front of me. I hide from the world, you remember."

"But you can listen behind doors, can't you? Oh, I know I'm only shooting out arrows at random, but I must leave nothing to chance. I've informed my Gentlemen to be on the watch, too."

"But why, dear love, since it is as you say? You cannot help what is said about you. You and I know you are no traitor to your country. What more is needed? We shall be gone soon."

"My reason is quite simple," Laura said with a proud tilt of her head. "I will find who is maligning me, and I will have my revenge."

"Ah, will you?" Jean-Baptiste said with a detached interest. "And if you have no time for this before you and I are gone from here?"

"I will find a way," Laura said. "No one makes a fool of me."

The same spring day that had greeted Laura and her lover was breaking over the green expanse of Hyde Park; yet the shadows of night gave place here with a bad humor, leaving their traces in strips of fog. Sir Owen let his gaze wander over the peaceful scene. At this hour no one was about. He was no early riser by preference, and he was thinking of his bed with nostalgic longing. He felt a large yawn escape him.

"I know why you and Miss Worthingham choose this hour," he said to the diminutive figure by his side, who had giggled at his lapse, "but it never fails to amaze me that I do."

Eliza gave him a wink. "I can tell you why you do if you really haven't guessed, brother. Antonia is delightful, is she not? I'm glad you don't come with us often all the same, lazybones. We ladies simply must gossip together some of the time."

"I don't see any sign of Miss Worthingham," Sir Owen said, casting another comprehensive look around, "and so I'll snatch this moment to talk to you as a stern brother should."

"Oh, a brotherly lecture," Eliza said with spurious delight. "What is it this time?"

"It's Cavenham, Eliza. Mama is wondering why you don't look more kindly on him. Such a suitable match. You would be marrying up—oh, consider that I've said all the usual things."

Eliza's eyes flashed. Viscount Cavenham was a recent acquaintance. Already he was so particular in his attentions that any mother's heart must flutter at the possibilities. Certainly the mama of a baronet's daughter, who could not look nearly so high in the ordinary course of events, would be rubbing her hands in glee. "Yes, Cavenham is perfection itself, drat the man! You know such talk can have no effect on me, and Mama knows it, too."

"Yes, I'll grant you that, but Mama is puzzled over this one," Owen warned. "Your other suitors have been easy to reject, on my part as well as yours. But this Cavenham fellow is handsome, intelligent, excellent manners, all the things a young woman must find irresistible. Do you really mean to say that you'll stick to your radical ideas and reject him solely because he's titled?"

Eliza sighed. "How little you understand my feelings, Owen. I would reject the commonest commoner of them all if I didn't feel the proper affection. And that can't be forced."

"Quite," said her brother. "Well, I may tell Mama that

I've delivered my message to you and urged you, as a responsible brother, to consider Lord Cavenham.''

"Indeed you may," Eliza answered with deceptive sweetness. "And now here comes Antonia; I hope you won't mention this matter in front of her. She feels quite as I do about such things, and she might . . ." She hesitated.

"Trying a bit of vulgar matchmaking on your own, Sister," Owen said, laughing. "Miss Worthingham might look on me with disfavor if I seem to promote a practical union for you, is that your idea?"

Eliza nodded with a smile just as Antonia came up with them.

She was wearing a dark blue riding habit that deepened the color of her eyes. A small hat with a curving plume perched on her braided hair. She looked wide awake to Sir Owen's eyes, and completely charming.

"Miss Worthingham, you light up the morning," he exclaimed. "How you can contrive to look so perfectly fit at such an hour is a mystery to me."

"Perfectly fit? A backhanded compliment," Antonia said with a laugh. She was growing ever bolder in her dealings with Sir Owen Longfort. He thought her an intrepid smuggler. Thus she had no reason to be shy and retiring as her embarrassing attraction to him would dictate in ordinary circumstances. "Country hours become rather a habit after a lifetime."

"You must know Owen is never too free with his approval," Eliza put in. "That was quite a gallant comment for him."

"I assure you that is the case, ma'am," Sir Owen confirmed. "Can't remember the last time I paid my sister any compliment."

A general laugh followed this pronouncement, and Sir Owen's glance fell on the groom in the Pomfret livery who had ridden behind Antonia and was now waiting at a discreet distance. "A new groom?" he asked, quirking an eyebrow.

Antonia nodded. Then, fulfilling a certain promise she had made to Lady Pomfret, she said, "He's the very one you saw me speaking to at the Featherstones' ball, Sir Owen. He has turned out to be an amazing character. The twelfth son of the Duke of Taverton.''

''What?'' gasped Eliza and Sir Owen, almost in the same breath. Both of them stared at the groom, who touched his hat amiably.

Antonia said, directing her words to Eliza, ''Vale asked me for my help in finding him a post as a groom that night at the Featherstones' ball, and Sir Owen happened to see us talking. He worked for my neighbor in Kent, you see, and I have quite often found posts at home for the local people.''

Eliza turned her eyes from Vale and surveyed Antonia with a questioning look. ''He attends balls, yet wishes to earn his bread? Can he possibly carry that off socially?''

''He was at the ball as a waiter,'' Antonia said, a twinkle in her eye. ''I'm certain his social standing would improve if he were to go back to his family.''

''But he won't,'' Eliza guessed. ''He sounds—'' she learned toward Antonia and spoke in an undertone—''can he possibly have republican tendencies, my dear?''

''I very much fear he does,'' Antonia said. She noted the resultant spark of interest in her friend's eyes and wondered what Lady Pomfret could possibly mean to accomplish by stirring the fire in this direction. But so she had ordered; and Antonia felt honor bound to ''start the ball rolling,'' as Lady Pomfret had so delicately made her promise to do.

''You must come back to breakfast with us,'' Eliza stated. ''I wish to hear all about this unusual situation. I suppose it wouldn't be seemly for me to question the groom myself.''

''One of the most sensible judgments I've heard you make,'' Sir Owen said, glancing from Eliza, to Antonia—at whom he frowned—to Vale across the way. ''A duke's son,'' he added, and shook his head.

''That part is unfortunate, but he is interesting,'' said Eliza. ''Now shall we ride? I can tell my mare is wishing for a good gallop.''

The young ladies made a practice of riding out early precisely so that they might occasionally chance such unseemly behavior. Sir Owen, as the older brother present, had to give them one stern admonition, and then he was off with them, his fine Arabian leading the way. Antonia, mounted on a passable gray from Lady Pomfret's stable, had to admire the rippling muscles of Sir Owen's mount. She longed to see what it would do in the field. Her gaze locked on a pair of strong shoulders—not the horse's.

So intent was she on the sight of Sir Owen—though she told herself her attention was all for his charger—that she didn't notice that Eliza had fallen back until she turned to say something to her friend.

Eliza had dismounted and was talking to Vale, who had also gotten down and held the reins of both her horse and his. Antonia slowed her own mare and called ahead to Sir Owen.

"Well," that gentleman said, returning at once to Antonia's side, "so my sister isn't even waiting a decent interval. Tell me, Miss Worthingham, why did you feel compelled to blurt out that man's true identity when you might have guessed such an odd character would fascinate Eliza?"

Antonia sighed. "I knew you would be angry. But Lady Pomfret made me promise I would let both of you know about her new groom. And it would be no disgrace, would it, if Eliza forms a *tendre* for him? He's not exactly baseborn."

"*I* might think it a disgrace or not, as I like. My sister will go her own way no matter what her family tells her," Sir Owen said, his expression softening. Antonia could tell he did not blame her too much. "Lady Pomfret will have much to answer for, though, to my mother."

Though Eliza managed a short conversation with Vale and even went so far as to ask him to throw her back into her saddle, she still desired Antonia's presence at the Longfort breakfast table in order to ferret out even more about this strange new groom, Lord Thomas Vale—though he disdained titles, he had told her that, he also freely admitted he owned one.

Lady Longfort, a faded blonde with her son's cleft chin and her daughter's delicate features, held court in a beruffled

morning costume that revealed her taste to be frivolous and
her eye for color to be faultless. She listened, teacup poised
in mid-air, as Eliza prattled on about the noble groom she
had met in the park.

"And you would simply stare to see how handsome he
is," Eliza told her astonished mother. "The other Vale
brothers are nothing to him. Of course, they're all rather
old. He's not only the youngest, but the youngest by seven
years. His age is eight-and-twenty, and—"

"Heaven preserve us," Lady Longfort said. The teacup
rattled back into its saucer. "A groom."

"A duke's son, Mama," retorted Eliza.

Sir Owen was overtaken by a coughing fit. "No, it's too
much," he declared with a broad smile. "To think I'd live
to hear my radical sister extolling a man for his rank."

Antonia listened to all this in silence, toying with the
kidneys Lady Longfort had insisted she take and feeling quite
guilty to have upset the Longfort family to this extent. She
hadn't had to keep her promise to Lady Pomfret this very
morning, had she? On the other hand, Lady Pomfret herself
would have informed Eliza at the first opportunity of her new
groom's lineage and ideals. What did it matter what day the
information came out?

Eliza was fuming at her brother's remark. "I do not extol
anyone for his rank, Owen. I merely admire the stand he's
taken. Why, he told me, Mama, that he would disdain to
take an allowance from his father. He's always worked for
his bread, ever since he reached his majority. And since his
talents lie with horses, he has become a groom. I think it's
splendid! He said himself that he might otherwise have
become one of those dreadful gentlemen who do nothing but
hang about Newmarket and Tattersall's."

"Haven't I heard you mention once or twice in the past
that becoming attached to someone at first sight is the stuff
of sentimental novels?" Sir Owen asked, looking at the
ceiling innocently.

Eliza was indignant. "Nobody is attached to anyone,
Brother. If the gentleman was a bit attracted, I'm sure I
cannot help that." With evident satisfaction, she surveyed

the upper half of her face, which she could just glimpse in the sideboard mirror.

"He attracted? Mama, may I be excused? I don't want to listen to such stuff before noon." Sir Owen made as if to rise.

Antonia had never seen him in such a joking mood and watched him, intrigued.

Lady Longfort said, "You will oblige me, Owen, by staying by me while I talk sense to your sister. Elizabeth, you cannot be thinking of a groom—no matter what noble family he's been disowned from."

"As you say, Mama," Eliza said in a mild tone, casting down her eyes.

"And I rely upon you, dear Miss Worthingham," continued her ladyship, turning to Antonia, "to do all you can to put temptation out of my daughter's way. You know her high spirits. You can ride out with another groom."

"Yes, ma'am," Antonia murmured, for she could hardly contradict her hostess.

"Not fair, Mama," Sir Owen said. "Miss Worthingham has told us that this particular groom was hired by Lady Pomfret expressly to keep up with the girls on their rides. The other grooms in her ladyship's employ are not exactly in the prime of life, and ours has lagged behind them constantly."

Lady Longfort sighed and cast an imploring glance at Antonia.

"I'll do my best to follow your wishes, ma'am," Antonia felt bound to say. Looking at Eliza's rebellious face, she could tell already that her best would be insufficient. She considered mentioning to Lady Longfort, frankly, that since Eliza was bound to seek Vale out, she might as well do it where Antonia could chaperon them. Perhaps she would find the words when she and Lady Longfort could be more private.

Lady Longfort was thanking her young guest. "I know you'll do what is proper, my dear. You must understand, I wish only for Eliza's happiness. And he sounds a strange young man indeed, his occupation aside."

Since Antonia agreed with this statement, she nodded

rather vigorously, provoking a displeased look from her friend Eliza.

Sir Owen had eaten his breakfast rather quickly, and he now rose, saying, "I'll leave you women to talk over the latest dress patterns in an atmosphere unsullied by my masculine presence. Your servant, Mama. And yours, Miss Worthingham. You, Eliza, seemed to have picked out a servant of your own already."

And he was gone, leaving Antonia to giggle nervously. She had decided she found this levity at his sister's expense rather appealing.

"Brothers!" Eliza exclaimed, turning a pretty shade of rose.

"As if we could possibly talk over the fashions at a time like this," Lady Longfort said with a sigh.

"Sir Owen seems to be in a good mood this morning," Antonia ventured.

"Odd, that," Lady Longfort said. "I thought he was turning surlier and surlier at breakfast, like his dear papa, but how glad I am that I was mistaken. Much more comfortable for his wife, when he marries, not to have her head snapped off at the table every morning."

Antonia developed a sudden interest in her plate of kidneys to avoid what she believed was a significant look from the dear lady.

"Of course, one may always breakfast in one's room," Lady Longfort went on. "I used to do that myself. I was avoiding the issue, my strong-minded daughter would tell you, Miss Worthingham, and I will admit to that, but so much more comfortable than dearest Sir Malcolm's company."

Eliza, apparently seeing that the center of embarrassment had been transferred from herself to Antonia, was good enough to ask her mother if she might have long sleeves on her new evening dress—a question that sparked a spirited debate for the rest of the meal.

Sir Owen, still smiling in self-congratulation at some of the quips he had directed at his sister, went directly to his study to look at the morning post. He was strangely content at the mere idea that Miss Antonia Worthingham was under his roof, and this added to his good humor.

A highly scented note, placed directly on top of the pile on his desk, attracted his attention, and he broke the seal eagerly.

The contents both surprised and intrigued him. He would have to go out of town shortly, that much was sure. But why had his superior changed the meeting time?

A glance at the calendar on his desk followed, and his lips made a firm line as he counted days. He would be gone at dark of the moon.

Most unfortunate, for he had been looking forward to observing Miss Worthingham carefully during this delicate time. The Lady was reputed always to be with her men when they picked up and transported the cargo. If that were the truth, Miss Worthingham would have to arrange a flying visit home at some time during the days in question. He had been looking forward to following her if she did so, to catching her and making her admit everything to him.

He wondered idly what his superiors would do if he were to run right now to inform them that he had the Lady breakfasting in his own house. The answer came easily. Nothing. They would do nothing. There was that age-old problem of hardcore evidence. Without proof—without being caught with the goods—the most hardened and obviously guilty smuggler could not be touched. And to catch the Lady with the evidence, one would have to go to Kent.

Sir Owen's usefulness in that part of Kent was over, as Lord Hambrey had informed him at the house party on the day after he had been hit over the head; the day after he had first glimpsed the Lady in question. Miss Antonia Worthingham would certainly be on the lookout for him, and so it was best he stay away. Those who remained in Kent would be watching every nook and cranny on the coast, keeping track of every fishing smack and pleasure craft. He was not really needed down there, would be a burden if he insisted upon going, and apparently—he tapped the perfumed letter—he was needed elsewhere.

Still, it was a shame. He would have liked to be in on the

capture of the Lady. He planned, naturally, to plead for mercy on Miss Worthingham's account and perhaps see her put into his custody. That was a solution rife with suggestive possibilities.

But somehow he had a feeling that his kind plans would be unnecessary. She would emerge victorious once again. The Lady had never done anything less.

10

Sir Owen's orders were always the same when the perfumed letter arrived. The missive might say anything at all, and usually did, for female passion was thought to be a certain trick to avert the eyes of any who might intercept Sir Owen's private papers. Whenever the letter came, Sir Owen was to proceed to the agreed-upon place—selected at the last meeting—for new orders.

This time Sir Owen had his valise packed with a certain sense of injury. He never knew how long he would be gone on these jaunts, and he didn't like to be out of town at dark of the moon. But he knew his duty and did it, without hesitation, leaving London with the most plausible of excuses to his family, engaging a bedroom at the small hostel in Hampshire where his man should contact him.

And he waited. Luckily he had brought his favorite steed, and the environs of Alton had some charming rides, for nobody arrived, nobody sent word; and nobody tried to attack him or trick him, his first thought after he realized that the message was probably a mistake or a lure. After several boring days, Sir Owen returned to London, fuming and ready to speak very harshly with his superiors.

He arrived at his home in Mount Street after his mother and sister had already departed for a musical party. He dressed to join them, not out of any great desire to hear a crowd of amateurs banging away at some unfortunate instruments, but in hopes that Miss Antonia Worthingham would be there. The moon was waxing again. Sir Owen was most eager to see if he could trace, in the lovely, quiet features of Miss Worthingham, some hint that she had just had an exciting run.

Or—depressing thought—would she be absent precisely because the excise men had caught her at last? Sir Owen ruined a cravat in trying to tie it quickly and finally had to let his capable valet do the honors.

The musical party at the Skeffings' was a squeeze. Sir Owen made his way through the candlelit, overly stuffy rooms, trying to act as cool and casual as he did not feel, and searching every corner of every room for a certain head of light brown hair, or, at the very least, the regal white curls that signaled Lady Pomfret.

Lady Longfort and Eliza were part of a gay group that did not include Antonia or her godmother. Discouraged, Sir Owen waved, but did not approach them. He retreated to a secluded corner with a glass of punch, a pinkish brew that he never would have taken under more normal circumstances, but had absently accepted when a footman proffered a tray. Now he tossed it back and winced. Suitable for ladies, all right. Listening to the opening strains of a Clementi study sawed out by an out-of-tune violin belonging, he would wager, to some lord's supposed prodigy of a daughter, he wondered how soon he could decently take his leave.

A hand in a kid glove caught him—slap!—across the face. Sir Owen blinked in astonishment.

Facing him was a lady he had known for years, since before her marriage. She was a gorgeous creature with cropped raven hair and flashing dark eyes. She was clad in a low, filmy dress and a wealth of diamonds.

"Lady Cyril," Sir Owen said with a crooked smile. "It's been a long time."

"You monster," hissed the lady. Her full lower lip was trembling. "You beast. How dare you?"

Sir Owen was about to query, delicately, what exactly he had dared, when Lady Cyril Bromley's next words enlightened him.

"I poured my heart out to you, confessed my deepest feelings, and you scorned me by your silence! Scorned them—the delicate sentiments of a lady of quality."

Who happened to have an elderly husband at home, Sir Owen added to himself. The knowledge came to him all in a rush. Lady Cyril had written the letter that he had assumed called him to the country on official business. Hers had been those passionate words he had barely scanned, thinking they were merely the usual code.

Could this be true? She had indeed been batting her eyes at him lately. He had hardly noticed, for he had been so busy watching Miss Worthingham that many another intrigue might have passed him by. Now he felt a very fool not to have known.

"You didn't sign your name," he said helplessly.

"Do you think I would put myself in the power of chance to that degree?" Lady Cyril demanded, her impressive bosom heaving. "What if some blackmailing servant should have intercepted it? How foolish do you think I am?"

"I'm sorry," Sir Owen said. He looked into her provocative eyes and read hurt there. "I was a beast. You're right. I must beg your pardon. I misunderstood the letter."

She blushed red as her carmined lips. "You misunderstood *that*? Then what does it take, sir? I've never heard anything so ridiculous."

Sir Owen remembered the prose as being rather warm. Had she asked for a meeting? He thought back over the rambling phrases. No, merely a response. She had signed herself with a scrawled initial he had thought was his superior's deliberate illegibility; usually not even initials were signed.

"My very dear lady," he said in a soft tone, "I admire you greatly, but I'm not in the market for—that is, I cannot begin a liaison at present. I have other interests. I should have written you to say so. Please forgive me."

"Other interests?" Lady Cyril looked a little less wounded. A speculative gleam came into her eye. "Are you about to step into parson's mousetrap, then, Sir Owen? If so, I can wait for another season or so. *We* can wait." She looked him up and down as boldly as any female ever had.

Sir Owen realized he had accidentally said the perfect thing. Naturally, if he were contemplating matrimony, he would be keeping his behavior as circumspect as possible in deference to the lady of his choice. A refusal of Lady Cyril in such circumstances would be no reflection on her attractions, and thus he didn't tell her that she had guessed incorrectly.

With a flourishing gesture, he kissed her gloved hand. "My lady, you are condescension itself."

She gave him a strange look and turned away.

After such an interview, which he was aware reflected badly on himself for several reasons, Sir Owen grew restless. He left his secluded spot and wandered through the rooms again. He spotted Eliza, now chattering with several female friends.

"Tell me, Sister," he said softly, drawing her a little aside from the clutch of females, "is your friend Miss Worthingham here tonight?"

Eliza let her eyes sparkle mischievously at him. "She is gone out of town for a few days, Owen. I'll be sure to let her know, when she returns, that you asked after her. What a very sweet coincidence. She asked after you when you disappeared last week, too."

"Did she indeed?" Sir Owen hardly stopped to be flattered by this knowledge. His mind worked busily. So Antonia Worthingham *had* run down to the country! He wouldn't be surprised to hear that the Lady had safely brought her load in once more. In fact, he realized in surprise, he was hoping he would hear that very thing. Not for anything would he have her arrested, caught, clapped into irons . . . though they would surely not go that far with a woman . . .

"You look like a lost sheep, Owen," Eliza said. "Don't worry. She is due back tomorrow or the next day. Something about seeing her brother, I believe it was. Or did she say her sister?"

"I look forward to waiting on her," Sir Owen said, and he patted his sister on the shoulder and told her to go back to her gossiping.

"Thank you," said Eliza. "My schoolmates are all so interested in Thomas Vale! The story of his birth is going about town already, you see, and I have a firsthand report."

"You've spread much of the story yourself, too, I'd wager."

"By no means," Eliza said, eyes wide. "Thomas doesn't want it bruited about. There is a difference, he points out, between not lying in response to a direct question, and taking advantage of one's birth. I think Lady Pomfret is the one who spread the story."

"Thomas, is it?" Sir Owen was less than pleased; the noble groom was still not his favorite. He supposed his disapproval was rooted in the fact that he would swear the fellow had been menacing Antonia Worthingham in some way.

Eliza had the grace to blush. "He and I both believe that Christian names are the only titles possible between kindred spirits."

"Oh, Lord," Sir Owen said. "I wash my hands of you."

"Good," retorted Eliza, and turned away to her friends.

Sir Owen decided to go on to White's, or at any rate to escape from this party before another female said something he did not wish to hear.

Antonia was having a solitary moment in her pretty bedroom the next morning, reading a letter from Laura. This was Antonia's first news from home since she had arrived in town. Trying to decipher the cross, she turned the letter this way and that. She thought she could make out that Laura thanked her for the warning, and that things—which Antonia interpreted to mean the smugglers' usual affairs—were going nicely. Laura seemed to indicate that the latest load had been safely landed, and to thank Antonia for the information on Thomas Vale. Not that she was surprised; she had always known he was out of the common way. No ship yet for foreign parts—called in the letter a post chaise to Canterbury, the agreed-upon code—but her "dear friend" was healing nicely and, it was to be hoped, would be quite himself before they moved.

Antonia felt tears start to her eyes. She was so very glad

that everything was well with Laura, and more than anything, she was happy that Laura was still in the country. If only Laura would change her mind about Jean-Baptiste and stay in Kent.

But Antonia knew this to be a vain hope. Laura had never loved before, to Antonia's knowledge; having taken the step, she would throw herself into it as heartily as she had into every other activity of her life thus far.

A tap came at the door, and Antonia's abigail entered. "If you please, Miss Worthingham, a gentleman has called."

Antonia blinked, dashed away something from her eye, and looked up. "Thank you, Steelman."

"Oh, ma'am, begging your pardon for the liberty, but is anything amiss? May I serve you in any way?"

"No, thank you," Antonia said. "I was simply reading a letter from my sister, and I grew homesick for Kent. The spring there is so very lovely," she improvised.

"So one hears," Steelman said with a sympathetic shake of her head. "The garden of England, it's called."

Antonia sighed deeply.

"Now, speaking of spring, since it is that handsome Sir Owen who's called, wouldn't you wish to wear your jonquil muslin?" Steelman suggested with a knowing smile. "It's the exact shade of the flower."

Antonia had discovered that her new abigail, being of motherly age, was determined to fulfill that role for Antonia insofar as she was allowed. "Handsome or no, I'm sure he deserves something better than this old thing," Antonia agreed with a disparaging look at the venerable cambric she had brought from home.

Steelman bustled around, dressing Antonia efficiently, doing her hair over, though it didn't look mussed to Antonia's eye, and even dusting a little powder under her young mistress's eyes. "A credit to my skill, that's what you are, Miss Worthingham," she said at the end of her labors.

Antonia smiled. "I'm lucky to have someone with your powers."

"Oh, ma'am," said the abigail, "I'm the lucky one. I'd be out of work today if it weren't for you."

"No, I'm sure someone else would have taken account of your fine qualities and given you a position."

Steelman shook her head. Antonia had hired her when her reputation had been under a cloud. Accused of petty thievery by her last mistress, Steelman had been acquitted due to the near-miracle of a truthful witness. But she had found herself, all the same, without any prospects. No one would hire even an innocent servant who had been involved in a scandal.

Truth to tell, if Steelman had been a pretty young abigail rather than a middle-aged plain one, she might have had better luck. What grim days she had passed in her sordid little room, reflecting in gloom that her fingers were too slow for sewing, and that if she were to give up her principles and come upon the town no one would buy her favors. She had gone near distracted. All that had changed when angelic Miss Worthingham, on hearing society gossip about Steelman's plight, had sought her out on purpose. The very least she could do in return was to turn the young lady out a pattern-card of fashion.

Antonia, thus prepared by loving hands for the assault on Sir Owen's heart, descended to the drawing room in a bit of a flutter. Sir Owen would not see her alone, of course. She assumed that Lady Pomfret was downstairs. But on entering the room, she saw only the baronet.

"Don't jump and look about you, Miss Worthingham," he said, advancing to meet her. "Your butler says Lady Pomfret will be with us shortly."

"Oh, I feel perfectly safe with you, of course, Sir Owen," Antonia said.

"Do you?" His lips curved in what Antonia chose to think a suggestive manner.

"Yes." She sat down and motioned him to do likewise. How very large and masculine he looked surrounded by the delicate Chinese decorations of the room. And had his hair gone lighter in the sun this early in the spring? Antonia cast down her eyes to her hands, which were clasped in her lap. She mustn't stare, no matter how much she admired this man's looks, no matter how strongly she was drawn to him.

"I'm just back from a jaunt out of town," Sir Owen declared.

"Yes, your sister told me," Antonia said. "So am I, as it happens."

"Ah, is that indeed the case? Do tell me, ma'am: how is the weather down in Kent? I found some fine days for riding in Hampshire."

"I wasn't in Kent," said Antonia in surprise.

"Oh. Of course." Sir Owen gave her a look full of meaning, a look that she didn't quite understand.

"I was down at Windsor and Eton," she elaborated. "My old governess lives there, and I took the opportunity to visit her and also to look in on my brother."

"Of course," Sir Owen repeated.

Antonia glanced at him sharply. And suddenly it came to her: dark of the moon had just passed. He thought she had been down in Kent bringing in a load of brandy, laces, and tobacco, as Laura had undoubtedly been doing.

"Of course," she said quietly. She was rather vexed that she could not elaborate on her trip to Windsor, since Sir Owen would assume every word was a lie. She had been looking forward to telling him how her brother had grown, so much that the shirts she had made him had been too small, and how her governess, Mademoiselle Bluet, had turned into a staunch royalist of the *ancien régime* since Bonaparte had had the gall to divorce his Josephine and marry the Austrian archduchess. Antonia had laughed at the change in the staunch Bonapartist who had taught her her irregular verbs, but Mademoiselle Bluet had reminded Antonia, in her practical fashion, that she had been a royalist before and would probably be a Bonapartist again.

"Sir Owen," Antonia said with a resigned smile, "you can be rather trying at times."

"You do me too much credit, Miss Worthingham."

Lady Pomfret came in then, a delightful sight in lavender sarcenet. "Antonia, I must speak sharply to you," she said with a smile, holding out her hand to Sir Owen. "You ought to have left the door open or sent for your abigail."

Antonia and Sir Owen both apologized nervously for the oversight, and Lady Pomfret, nodding and tapping her gold-headed cane upon the floor, was free to draw her own conclusions.

Shortly on her ladyship's heels came the first of her own morning callers, an elderly bishop distantly related on Lady Pomfret's mother's side. He was clutching a nosegay of violets that contrasted oddly with his serious clothes and even more serious face. This pompous but infatuated cleric did much to dispel any romantic tension that might have been present between the young people.

Sir Owen stayed for as long as possible, helping Miss Worthingham to wind the yarn for some socks she was thinking of sending down to the cook at Easton Grange (who complained of chilblains in the warmest weather), and talking of idle matters while Lady Pomfret entertained the bishop. Sir Owen put forward the suggestion that Antonia and Lady Pomfret might enjoy a real excursion of some sort with his mother and sister; he asked Antonia for a dance at Almack's. Antonia accepted all his offerings with pleasure.

Yet she watched him warily, not at all certain what he really wanted from her. All questions of her own identity aside, and what effect knowledge of her boring real character would have on his admiration, she knew him to be a shocking libertine, not at all the sort of man she wished to take seriously. That letter, after all!

He had kissed her. He thought her to be an adventurous female. And he had the habit of libidinous relationships with women. Could it be possible he wanted her to be his mistress? No, he would surely not go that far with a respectable young lady. Perhaps he only wished, for sport, to make her fall in love with him. Men often did engage in such mental games; Eliza and the other girls Antonia had met had harrowing stories to tell.

He must not know how well he was doing. She set her jaw firmly and gave him a look that appeared to startle him very much, coming as it did in the middle of his description of the Tower Menagerie, which he would be happy to take her to see.

Did this complacent baronet really think that Antonia Worthingham would soon be scribbling him embarrassing letters? He would wait long for that day.

11

Every day Antonia reminded herself to be on her guard. Her heart was in some danger from Sir Owen, and she must not let it be captured. In self-defense, she began to observe him closely at every gathering they both attended, hoping—or fearing—to see some quality of his that would disillusion her.

Those who seek to find fault usually do, Antonia's mother used to warn her; still Antonia felt justified in her suspicions when, one evening at a rout, she saw Sir Owen chatting with an alarmingly sophisticated and beautiful lady who was hanging on his every word.

Eliza was standing near Antonia and saw the direction her friend's gaze had taken. She was most obliging. Without even being asked, she identified the beautiful lady to Antonia, in a whisper, as Lady Cyril Bromley, who had a reputation as a free-and-easy matron.

"She is lovely," Antonia said. "She reminds me of my sister." From Antonia, there could be no higher praise.

"She is ravishing, isn't she?" Eliza agreed easily. "I'd wager she wonders why Owen doesn't notice her. The poor thing has been flinging herself at his head for weeks, ever since she broke with that foreign marchese. Oh, you will please forget I told you that last bit. We young innocents aren't to know any of that sort of thing."

Antonia found it difficult to imagine a glorious creature

attired in the most elegant and décolleté of white satin gowns as a "poor thing."

"I see you're frowning," Eliza said. "Don't think harshly of Owen, I pray. As that lady has no doubt found out, married women aren't in his style."

"What kind are?" These words came out in a rush, and Antonia regretted them before her voice had died away.

Eliza's eyes danced. "Why, I scarce know what to tell you, for you won't stand to hear of the way he sings your praises. He is an eligible bachelor and not bad-looking; I suppose that's the beginning and the end of it. The ladies come to him."

"Oh." Antonia knew exactly why the ladies came to him: the energy apparent in his every movement, the intelligent spark in his eyes, the handsome face and strong physique. She swore once again that she wouldn't become one in the long line of Sir Owen's conquests. Lady Cyril, from what Antonia could tell from across a room, did look unhappy under her sparkle. Sir Owen must have used her to his heart's content and tossed her aside in a cruel, libertine fashion. Never mind that the lady, as a fast matron, was presumably up to anything. Was any woman's heart ever safe in the duel between the sexes?'

Antonia was suddenly overcome by a wish that she had stayed in the country where she belonged. She would never fit into this brittle, sophisticated society, and so she had known beforehand.

"Don't be sad," Eliza said, giving her friend's arm a squeeze. "My brother is a good person; I will give him that, though he can be remarkably satirical when it comes to my problems. Now do come with me. I see my old friend Alicia Montaigne over the way. I'll introduce you. She is quite the most spirited creature; thinks nothing of taking the most terrifying jumps. Owen can't bear her."

"But I thought he liked spirited women, unusual women," Antonia said in surprise.

Eliza giggled. "I forgot to mention that the most terrifying jump from his point of view was the one Alicia tried to take into Owen's arms. She made him her goal all last season, and, as I've said, she's quite spirited. She must have played every trick in the book to make him notice her. But it didn't serve. Now she's quite happy and betrothed to Lord Bentish, and she and I can be comfortable again. I do hate the strained atmosphere when one of my friends falls in love with Owen.'' Eliza paused and gave Antonia a sidelong look. ''You see, he usually isn't the one to do the chasing.''

Antonia took this as calmly as she could. If Eliza thought her brother was ''chasing'' Antonia, she was correct, in a way. But it was probably his duty, if he served the government, to chase a smuggler.

Antonia followed Eliza across the room and was soon being introduced to the spirited Miss Montaigne, who turned out to be a pretty redhead with the easy and charming manners Antonia envied in girls who had had a season or two.

''My dear, I confess that this time last year I would have been terribly jealous of you,'' Alicia said with a twinkle in her eye after the young ladies had exhausted the preliminaries of fashion and gossip and the unbearable boredom of the present rout party.

Antonia tilted her head in query.

''For your influence on my brother, she means,'' Eliza put in with a little laugh.

''Eliza! How can you?'' Alicia, seeing Antonia's stricken look, appeared to forget that she had brought up the subject and squeezed Miss Worthingham's waist in sympathy. ''Let us turn the subject like good girls. Antonia—may I call you Antonia?—is much too modest to admit to anything. Perhaps that's her secret.''

Antonia suffered herself to be cosseted a little, though she felt she was believed under false pretenses to be a maidenly creature who had captured Sir Owen's attention by her shrinking ways. How she did long to tell both the girls that her charm for that gentleman had nothing to do with herself, everything to do with a dashing lady smuggler who was nothing like Antonia.

She noticed from across the room that Sir Owen parted from the beautiful Lady Cyril with an easy grace and a sort of finality visible even at a distance. Was his reluctance in this instance only because the lady was married? Or did it have something to do with his feelings for Antonia—for the Lady?

"We've got it, Longfort," said Lord Hambrey. The baron was making a flying visit to town and had run into Sir Owen at the club one morning. They had retired to a private room and were taking the opportunity to discuss, over a companionable bottle, certain events on the Kentish coast. "At last there's proof that the smugglers are bringing in the Frenchies," Hambrey elaborated. "We caught one of 'em at last dark."

"Caught one? A smuggler?" Sir Owen's voice was sharp.

"No, a Froggie spy." Lord Hambrey's craggy face lit up in remembered pleasure. "I was in at the capture. Does one's heart good to be back in action for a change. Got him as he was walking up from the beach, and demmed if the coward didn't confess right off that it was the smugglers who landed him."

"Is that so?" Sir Owen spoke mildly, but he felt his world come crashing down around him. Antonia Worthingham had obviously been down in Kent at the last dark of the moon, though she had told him that Banbury story about Windsor. She had helped land a spy. She was despicable. He must hate her now, as a traitor to the crown.

None of this made any sense when taken together with her known character, her kindness, her seeming determination to do what was right. How could a young lady who, only the day before, had protested against the cruelty to the animals in the Tower Menagerie and asked if there were somebody she could speak with to ease their plight, flippantly land spies and not care if her country were done irreparable damage?

Sir Owen resolved to tell Antonia, point-blank, what was happening in her gang. She didn't know. That was the explanation. She couldn't know.

"Convenient, wouldn't you say, that this Frenchman came up on the beach just where you would catch him, and blurted out without a qualm that the smugglers had landed him?'' Owen said as an idea struck him.

Lord Hambrey leaned forward in his leather armchair. ''What are you saying, man? That there is some question about our information? We've caught them redhanded.''

''That's the problem,'' Sir Owen pointed out. ''You haven't. If I wanted to, I could pretend to be a Frenchman and go down to the coast, wash myself up on the shingle and say the Lady's Gentlemen helped me in.'' He was reaching for a solution, he knew that, but his belief that Antonia was not, could not be guilty of the atrocity of aiding the French made him throw out ideas virtually at random.

''You could. That's so,'' Lord Hambrey said. ''My boy, do you really think we haven't considered that angle? If there are rival gangs in the area, for instance, what better way for one to discredit the other than by this sort of accusation? The information seems clear, though, and that's all we're saying at the moment.''

''When I was down there nosing about, I found no sign of rival gangs,'' Sir Owen felt bound to say. ''Then again, I always had the feeling that the country people I talked to were on to my own game. That I was being led in circles to protect their Lady and her men. It's a closed community down there, but I don't have to tell you that. It's your home.''

Lord Hambrey smiled. ''There doesn't breathe a man of Kent who would open his heart to the big house. I'm as foreign as you in those parts, though I was born there.''

''And what is your move now?'' asked Sir Owen.

''We wait, of course. Nothing to do but wait until next month and try even harder to catch them at it, with the goods in their hands and the spies in their boats. It's the only way, as you point out, that the law will let us take them.''

''I'd like to be with you for that,'' Sir Owen said.

''Why not? You deserve to be in at the finish, since you laid the groundwork. See you keep out of sight, and you shouldn't be any threat to our safety. What attracts you, my boy, or need I ask? Is it the mysterious Lady whose face you were so taken with that night?''

Sir Owen shrugged. "You might say so. I must be a romantic at heart."

In the days that followed, Sir Owen made every effort to stick close to Antonia Worthingham without making his attentions so particular as to cause gossip. He tried once or twice to lead up to a direct question about the smuggling, but never accomplished this. His careful arrangements were at fault.

So unparticular must he seem in order to protect her reputation that he could not justify getting her alone at any time. He only saw her in groups of people, at excursions, picnics, and such outings that he organized with an energy that astonished his mother. He who had never lifted a finger to arrange one of her parties was now leading troupes of young people from Astley's to Hampton Court with what seemed a sincere enjoyment.

In avoiding gossip, he was notably unsuccessful, and the tattlers soon had it that Miss Worthingham had caught the heart of the elusive baronet.

Lady Cyril Bromley smiled serenely and waited her turn. A man with the sophistication of Sir Owen could hardly be satisfied for long with the Worthingham chit.

Lady Pomfret, though she was no matchmaker, made happy plans for the bride gifts she would give and the delightful wedding gown she would have Madame Hélène design for Antonia. She and Lady Longfort had talked the situation over privately and were agreed that the young people were ideally suited, though they could not come to terms on the fabric for the gown.

Mr. Brummell himself, urged by a friend, deigned to place a line on the subject in the betting book at White's, since he knew his remark in favor of Miss Worthingham to be her sole claim to notice by the ton, and thus considered her a sort of protégée.

Antonia heard the rumors along with everyone else, though by a more indirect route, and kept her own counsel. How delightful if it were all true! But she knew why Sir Owen seemed to be pursuing her, if the gossip-mongers did not. He was eager for any chance to observe the Lady.

"How I do admire that large hat, my dear," Lady Pomfret said to Antonia one day when that young lady entered the drawing room attired in an aquamarine walking dress with rose-colored trimmings.

The hat in question was lined with aquamarine and sported rose ribbons. "Thank you, Godmama. I hope he—that is, I'm glad you like it." Antonia smiled, passing her hand a bit nervously up and down the very rose parasol she had bought on the very day she had first encountered Sir Owen in London.

"And where is the excursion to be today?" Lady Pomfret asked. "Thank heaven Lady Longfort can lend her countenance this time. A hand of piquet and a quiet coze here with Mr. Daingerfield will exactly suit me."

"I hope you haven't been tired out by all this dashing about on my account, Godmama."

"By no means, my love. My losses have been a bit heavy, to be sure, but that's only because the play is so confounded high nowadays at the better parties. I wanted you here with me so I'd have the excuse to go out, did I not? I'm simply in need of a tiny repairing lease this afternoon," Lady Pomfret assured her.

"I'm glad to hear it. And in answer to your question, today we're going to the Summer Exhibition at Somerset House."

"Does Eliza go with you?"

"Yes, though she hardly ever seems really to be there lately, wherever we are. She's thinking of Thomas Vale, and there is a limit to the social occasions a groom may attend. Especially a groom who would cause Lady Longfort a palpitation if he appeared."

Lady Pomfret chuckled. "Has he come to the point?"

Antonia was shocked. "Ma'am, he's a groom. He could never propose matrimony. How would they live?"

"Never tell me the chit is penniless. The last baronet was a very careful man."

"But someone with Vale's pride would surely not live off his bride's money."

"It sounds to me," Lady Pomfret said, "as though you've been discussing this with him."

Antonia, though embarrassed, was ready to admit to having meddled. "Well, I did try to talk to him once. Eliza is my friend. I couldn't help asking Vale whether he would not consider going home or finding a less menial position."

"And he sent you to the rightabout?"

"Yes, and with justice," Antonia said, flushing at the memory. "I was interfering quite like an old spinster."

"Don't worry about it, my dear," was Lady Pomfret's advice. "Love will find a way. That young man must come about if he's to have Eliza."

"But, ma'am, that's why I spoke to him," Antonia said. "Eliza, for her part, is quite ready to throw her cap over the windmill and live in a hovel. Though she, it is true, sees nothing wrong in making use of her dowry."

They were given no chance to continue this interesting discussion. The doors opened, and Dunn announced that the Longforts were waiting outside to take up Miss Worthingham.

"Have an enjoyable outing, my dear," said Lady Pomfret with a pleasant nod, and Antonia, rose ribbons fluttering, hurried out to the Longfort's barouche. Sir Owen was waiting to hand her up into the open carriage, and he took the seat beside her. He then endured some good-natured joking from his sister. When last had Sir Owen Longfort, of the Four-Horse Club, suffered a mere coachman to take the ribbons?

Antonia was put to the blush, for Eliza was now pointing out that Sir Owen must have a particular interest in not driving, and Lady Longfort was smiling at Antonia in a manner most maternal. They were both kind but doomed to disappointment. Sir Owen's admiration was not a simple matter.

They were to meet Alicia Montaigne and her betrothed at the gallery, and once the teasing stopped, they had quite an enjoyable drive through the busy streets in the sunshine. Lady Longfort was in particularly high spirits.

Antonia wondered why, when they alighted in the Strand, Eliza drew back and gave an annoyed little grimace at first

view of Miss Montaigne's party. Antonia could see nothing
to disgust in the pretty Alicia, clad becomingly in yellow
and accompanied by not one, but two good-looking
gentlemen.

"Dear Cavenham," Lady Longfort said, holding her hands
out to one of the gentlemen. He kissed them with the freedom
of a close connection.

Antonia understood immediately. She had never happened
to see Lord Cavenham, but she had heard stories from Eliza.
So this was the latest unbearable wretch who was out to
capture Eliza's hand.

Five minutes' observation convinced Antonia that Viscount
Cavenham was handsomer than Vale, better-mannered, and
much cleverer. There was no understanding the ways of the
heart—especially Eliza's. Cavenham took care to make the
whole party laugh any number of times, testimony to his
exquisite address and quick wit. With Eliza on one arm and
her mother on the other, he led the way up the stairs of
Somerset House and through the gallery.

Crowds of people had chosen this day to come out and
see the paintings, and it was slow going through the rooms,
even slower if the promenaders actually decided to stop and
look at a picture. Antonia and Sir Owen, who were walking
together, found themselves separated from the rest of the
party at one point.

"I didn't arrange this on purpose," Sir Owen murmured
into Antonia's ear, "but since we do have a moment's
privacy, what do you say I show you my favorite painting
of the exhibition? We're about to pass it by. Cavenham has
no taste for the sea pictures."

Antonia murmured her acquiescence, and Sir Owen helped
her to the front of the group that was looking over a painting
of a small boat, tossed on stormy night seas and manned by
black-clad sailors.

" 'Bringing in the lugger', the program calls it," Sir Owen
said, rattling the pages he had paid sixpence for at the door.
"Does it bring back memories, ma'am?"

"Of course it does. I'm from the coast, where smuggling
activities are legion," Antonia said sweetly.

"I meant, ma'am, more intimate memories," said Sir Owen.

Something snapped in Antonia. Tired of fielding his endless hints, she decided on the spot to take him up on them. He never let a meeting between them pass without making some allusion to her supposed wild career as a smuggler, and the strain of parrying his hints was beginning to be less than amusing.

"Why do you say such things to me?" she asked in a soft voice, for though technically alone and unchaperoned, they were in a sea of people. "Do you wish to provoke some sort of confession? I sobbing out my terrible secrets on your understanding shoulder?"

His violent start gave her to think that he had expected something of that very nature.

Antonia shook her head. "I'm sorry. I can't oblige you." She began to excuse herself through the press of people back to where there was a clear walkway.

Sir Owen followed her. "I'm the one who's sorry, ma'am," he said as he hurried to keep up with her energetic stride in pursuit of the others of their party, "I've been most unfair."

"That you have." Antonia whirled and glared at him. "And you will cease baiting me at once. Is that clear?"

"Your wish is my command, dear lady," said Sir Owen. He was staring in a most piercing manner, a strange light in his eyes. "But though you find the thought of sobbing on my shoulder so distasteful, do keep in mind that I am always here for you if there's anything you'd like to say, at any time, on any subject. For instance, are you quite confident that you, here in town, know everything that your associates in the country may be up to?"

"Oh!" Was there no end to his accusations? Antonia turned away, furious with him, and stalked off to the others.

Tapping her foot, feeling rather than hearing or seeing that Sir Owen had come up right behind her, she toyed with the idea of being the most blatant smuggler he had ever encountered. What must she do to give that impression? Leave empty brandy casks scattered about the house? Wear obviously foreign lace on her gowns? One thing she must not do: however tempted she might be, she could never confess to the crime. That would be fatal.

Then a thought occurred to her. Why not confess? Unless she could be caught in the act, there would be no use in prosecuting her.

Such musings were dangerous. Antonia shivered. What was she coming to? She must remember that leading Sir Owen a dance did not include grabbing him by the the cravat and telling him she was the one he sought. It was a lie, for one thing. For another, such a point-blank confession, coming from her, would surely provoke an even closer watch on the Kentish operations and thus on the true Lady. At all cost, Laura must remain safe.

No, Antonia must go on as she had begun. She would continue to couch her supposed smuggler's identity in ambiguity, tantalizing Sir Owen with the occasional remark, keeping silent when he asked direct questions. Then, someday soon, she would be able to go home. Laura would be off to her new life in America, Antonia would be at Easton Grange with whatever dreary chaperon she could come up with, and the smugglers would have no Lady.

Antonia felt a certain grim satisfaction at the thought of Sir Owen, when that day arrived, crouching in bushes and nosing about for news of the Lady, who no longer existed.

12

"Another excursion, Eliza?" Antonia looked curiously at her companion. The young ladies were gossiping together in Lady Longfort's morning room. "Where does your brother wish to be off to this time? There is scarcely any place left."

"He means to take a large party on a picnic down to Windsor," Eliza said. "He even talks of making it an over-night trip. I convinced him those of us who wish to ought to go on horseback. It's only twenty miles or so. It should be great fun."

"Why, that does sound intriguing," Antonia said, thinking of her brother Monty. She would manage at least to speak to him for a short time, if not to get him leave to go out for the day. Perhaps Sir Owen could speak to the headmaster down at Eton.

Despite this happy plan, Eliza's news of yet another excursion brought Antonia some pain. She was spending too much time in Sir Owen's company. He was watching her, looking for her to slip her guard in some way. Meanwhile, she was fast succumbing to his charms. Did he know that? Depressing thought; she would not like to believe him cruel. *Why does he continue to torment me?* she asked herself, though her words to Eliza were all of Monty's delight at a day's holiday, and the pleasant rides around the castle, and whether or not Vale could be put into the entourage.

"I don't see why not," Eliza said on this last issue, setting her chin. "He never gets to go anywhere."

"His choice, remember," Antonia said.

Eliza sighed deeply.

Lady Longfort drifted into the room just then, in trailing draperies and a voluminous, lace-trimmed morning cap. Her ladyship, though she appeared betimes each morning, could not be considered awake until sometime in the afternoon. She greeted Antonia in a pleasant if sleepy voice. Having lowered herself into a deep chair, she yawned once, then gave her daughter a decidedly unlanguid look. "Well, Eliza, you seem grave. I suppose you've been mooning over that dreary groom."

"Duke's son, Mama," Eliza said tightly. Antonia knew what it must cost her friend to use Vale's title, which she disdained as much as he did, as a bargaining point with her mother.

Lady Longfort gave her daughter a pitying smile. "My dear, I've done my research on that young man, and he refuses to be anything but a groom. His family has been notified that he is in town and what he's been doing, and he won't have anything to do with them. He's an undutiful son as well as an ordinary workingman. No good can come of such an attachment."

All these words were spoken sweetly, but they had the hint of steel behind them.

Eliza's eyes widened. "He's refused to speak to his family? No, I didn't know that. I was certain it was the other way about."

Antonia, who had expected that this tidbit would merely raise Vale higher in Eliza's eyes—surely being an undutiful child was one of the first duties of the truly republican aristocrat—was surprised at Eliza's next words.

"Family is important," she said. "It matters."

Lady Longfort nodded in emphasis. "Precisely my point. Think how unhappy you would be without us, dear Eliza."

"Don't tempt me, Mama," Eliza returned, at last in her ordinary joking tone. She stood up. "Antonia, it's such a lovely day. What do you say to a short stroll? I know you and your abigail walked here, but you aren't tired, are you?''

"Eliza!" admonished Lady Longfort. "You are quite impossible. What can the poor child possibly answer to a question like that?''

"But I'm not tired, ma'am," Antonia said, wondering what Eliza could be up to. "I'm used to long country walks.''

Eliza smiled sunnily. "Let's go and put on our bonnets. You will excuse us, Mama?''

The bustle of putting on outdoor things and collecting Steelman, Antonia's maid, from the lower floor where she had been enjoying a cup of tea in the housekeeper's room, kept Antonia from asking any personal questions. Once they were outside and walking along the pavement of Mount Street, though, she felt quite justified in asking where they were going.

"Cavendish Square," Eliza said. She looked determined and rather martial, not at all like someone who had decided on a spur-of-the-moment promenade in the spring air. "Isn't it warm for this time of year, though? Everyone is remarking on it.''

Antonia was not to be dissuaded. "Why Cavendish Square?''

"I'll tell you when we arrive," Eliza said. "Let's enjoy the day.''

"Certainly." Antonia paused, though, and turned back to her maid. "Will Cavendish Square be too great a distance for you, Steelman?''

"By no means, ma'am," responded the abigail, "I hope I know my duty.''

Eliza looked stricken. "Oh, I didn't think. The two of you have come a long way already. Mama was right.''

"We haven't come anything like a good distance. Why, in the country this wouldn't be a third of a way to the village," Antonia said. "And I'm sure Steelman would be frank with me; wouldn't you?'' She addressed the last words to the maid.

The town-bred Steelman nodded stoically.

The three made their progress north, crossing Oxford Street and passing many fashionables of their acquaintance, to whom they gave cheerful greetings. As they neared Cavendish Square, they suddenly found themselves pushing through a crowd.

"Stay back, mum," shouted a helpful citizen, touching Antonia's arm as she stepped down to follow Eliza across a street.

Steelman soundly whacked the fellow on the rib cage with her ever-present umbrella.

"I say!" The man's eyes darkened in anger, and Antonia, reaching for Steelman's arm, murmured an apology and was thinking of making a run for it when they were joined by Eliza.

"Thank you for saving my friend from danger, good sir," said that young lady, smiling at Steelman's victim. He nodded and moved a distance away from them, looking much mollified by such attention from a fashionable beauty. Turning to Antonia and the maid, Eliza explained, "They have this street roped off. I didn't remember."

"Oh." Antonia was about to question Eliza further when a great shout rose up from the surrounding populace, and the street was suddenly filled with elegant carriages, each pulled by a team and driven by a man in distinctive costume.

For Antonia there was only one man, one equipage. She had immediately picked out Sir Owen Longfort and his famous chestnuts. Was it only her imagination, or did he catch her eye? On the chance that her impression was real, she lifted her hand in greeting.

"Why didn't you warn me?" she said to Eliza. "Only think! I've seen the Four-Horse Club set out on the way to Salt Hill. My brother will be thrilled." She was more than a little thrilled herself.

Eliza shook her head. "You don't understand, my dear. I forgot it was Thursday. I didn't bring you out to see this, though it was rather exciting, wasn't it?" She grinned. "Did you see Owen? I always tell him the striped waistcoat and spotted cravat are too ridiculous."

"If we didn't come to see him—to see the club," Antonia demanded, "why are we here?"

Eliza took her friend's arm. "Let's get on with it."

They entered Cavendish Square proper. Eliza paused to look about at the great houses all around them.

"Yes," she said, nodding toward one of the more massive of the residences, "that is the one." She took off toward it with a sure step, Antonia and Steelman following her.

The house was one with an ornate entrance portico and a daunting flight of steps. Eliza led the way and firmly lifted the knocker.

A liveried footman, evidently chosen for his great height, answered the door.

"Miss Longfort and Miss Worthingham to see His Grace," Eliza said, staring the fellow down in her most regal manner, though he was nearly twice as tall as she.

Antonia nearly fell back a step in her surprise, then wondered why she had not realized that something like this was about to happen. She raised her eyes to the large, engraved *T* in the stonework above the door, and studied the ducal crest that surmounted the letter. This was the residence of the Duke of Taverton. Vale's father.

Meanwhile Eliza was answering questions and dealing with the footman most capably. No, they were not expected. Yes, their mission with His Grace was of the utmost importance. "Does the name Lord Thomas Vale mean anything to you, my good man?" Eliza asked when the footman hesitated. "We bring news of him."

This statement, grandly uttered, had the desired effect. The footman stood aside to let them enter, then led them past a line of other retainers and down a vast parqueted entrance hall adorned with statuary in niches. Paintings with mythological themes ornamented silk-covered walls, and the ceilings were vaulted and heavily tenanted by plaster cherubs.

The ladies were taken into a small but elegant reception room. There the footman left them, saying he would see that the duke was informed. Steelman remained in a chair in the hall.

In this house, Antonia wagered, a series of perhaps ten retainers would pass the information along, one by one, until finally, in some gilded chamber at the center of the great house, the message would reach the duke. She had the sudden, unworthy image of a worm at the heart of a nut.

She glanced at Eliza's determined profile. "What do you mean to do?"

"Do? Why, nothing. But I mean to say a great deal," was Eliza's stern answer. The solemnity of the ducal abode seemed to have drained all humor from her. "Poor dear Thomas," she said, looking about her.

Antonia also saw the opulent furnishings, the grand tapestries that decked even this small sidechamber of Taverton House. At first glance nothing aroused her pity. Then she imagined a child trying to fit into all this magnificence. Thomas Vale, she had heard, was the youngest of his family by seven years. He would have grown up virtually alone.

There was little time for such musings, and less for conversation, before the door opened and a tall, forbidding old man entered with the aid of an ebony walking cane. His clothes looked more suitable for shooting birds in the country than receiving town visitors, and he wore a startling wig of bright red hair, done in a queue. His brown eyes looked out from behind a pair of square spectacles.

Eliza and Antonia both rose and curtsied deeply. Antonia, who had noticed before that Eliza never curtsied in company and was constantly chastised for that idiosyncracy by her mother, knew the situation must be serious indeed.

"Who are you?" the old man said. "And what have you to do with Lord Thomas Vale?"

Eliza rose and looked him in the eye. "You must be the duke, sir." To Antonia's amazement, there was a hint of reproof in her tone.

"I am," came the gruff reply. The admitted duke made his way over to a massive, gilt-and-plush chair and sat down heavily, propping one foot on a stool.

Though no invitation had been issued, Eliza sat back down. Antonia followed her example, not wishing to be the only one left standing.

"Well?" the duke repeated. "Who are you?"

Eliza smiled and inclined her head graciously. "I am Elizabeth Longfort, a friend of your son's."

"And she?" Taverton pointed his stick at Antonia.

"I am Antonia Worthingham, a friend of Miss Long-fort's," Antonia said.

"Don't suppose you're lightskirts, come to blackmail me?" the duke next said, quirking an eyebrow.

"No," Eliza told him, "we are not." Antonia turned a deep shade of scarlet.

The duke sighed, and a little smile was visible for the barest moment on his craggy countenance. "No, I don't suppose you are. Never do get any excitement around here. So. Shall I guess who you are, Miss Longfort? A friend of my son's? That would mean you're in love with him, at the very least."

"Yes," Eliza said. Her color now matched Antonia's hectic flush.

Antonia looked on, fascinated. It was as though she were attending a most interesting play, and sitting on the stage at that.

Taverton leaned foward. "You look to be a young lady of good family. What are you doing attaching yourself to a groom?"

Eliza straightened her spine. "I have no respect for the artificial ranks of society, Your Grace," she said, apparently not recognizing what a contrast her courteous address made to her pronouncement.

Antonia noticed, but managed to hold back a nervous giggle. Her eyes met those of the duke for the merest instant, and she knew he had noticed, too. Antonia returned her gaze to her lap at once.

"Or perhaps, young woman, you're not attaching yourself to a groom so much as to the house of Taverton," the duke said to Eliza.

Eliza visibly fumed. "Sir, I have but this instant told you I care nothing for rank. What I care about is Thomas. You and the rest of your children are his family. He is alone in the world but for me; and how unnatural that must seem to him, for he has eleven brothers and a sister. He must be reconciled to you for his own happiness. I care about that, sir, and I care very deeply."

Silence reigned while the duke's eyebrows climbed into

the crevices of his forehead. "Do you, begad," he said in a gentler voice than he had yet used.

"Yes," Eliza said. She bowed her head, then raised it. Antonia could see that a few tears were glistening on her friend's cheeks. "I assure Your Grace," Eliza continued, "that I would not choose to expose myself before my friend Miss Worthingham. I am only putting her through this uncomfortable scene because I have no choice. I could not come here alone. But I wish she could be spared the embarrassment of watching me beg you, from the bottom of my heart, to receive your son."

"A pretty speech, young lady," Taverton said, peering over the tops of his spectacles.

"Not intended to be," muttered Eliza, looking down.

Antonia was sensible of a great wish to be out of the room, but propriety made her keep her seat; propriety as well as a perfect ignorance of how she would get herself unobtrusively out the door.

"Tell me now," the duke said, "do you mean to marry my son?"

"Yes," Eliza said, "if he will have me. And no, in answer to your unspoken question, I am not here to beg you for an income. I have quite a little fortune on my own account, and we must live on that and his groom's pay. What I wish for Thomas is the comfort of knowing his relations again."

"I see." The duke leaned back and took a long look at Eliza. Suddenly he met Antonia's eyes. "And what do you think of this, young lady?"

"I—I had no idea my friend's attachment had gone this far," Antonia said honestly.

"I'm sorry." Eliza turned to her. "I haven't told you because there's nothing official. Perhaps I ought not to speak. Thomas has not talked of marriage. But I have made up my mind, you see."

The duke's barking laughter suddenly filled the room. "Miss Longfort, you're a rare 'un," he exclaimed. "You've made up your own mind, indeed! That's rich."

"You may find if you examine your friends' situations, Your Grace, that it is usually the woman who instigates even a marriage supposedly arranged by the parents. I have found that to be true in my circle,'' Eliza said. ''And I have no patience with the false posturings of society. I will speak my mind.''

''You have done so,'' the duke agreed, smiling at her.

''You approve, don't you, Your Grace?'' Antonia burst out; then, astonished at her freedom, she lapsed back into embarrassed silence.

Taverton gave a ponderous nod of his peruked head. ''I'm not the one marrying, though. And I will tell you this, young lady.'' These words he spoke to Eliza. ''I sent a letter to my son when I found he was in town and was told the full story of his disappearance. It was returned unopened.''

''What? Why, it's infamous,'' Eliza cried. ''You held out the olive branch, and he refused?''

''Olive branch? As it happens I did. But he had no way of knowing if that letter disinherited him or offered him a fortune,'' the duke said. ''Unopened, I say. Not even the courtesy of a reading. My last son, young lady. He's learned the manners of a groom, if nothing else.''

''Oh, don't judge the whole profession by your son. I know some very courteous grooms,'' Eliza said thoughtfully. ''Thomas, sir, doesn't appear to be one of them. Do not you worry. Let me handle this problem. Do you have the letter still?''

''Yes, I put it by for some sentimental reason,'' the duke said. ''You propose to take it to him, do you?''

''And force him to read it. Yes,'' said Eliza with a smile. ''Will you allow me that, sir?''

The duke laughed again and went so far as to slap his hand on his thigh. ''I'd like to be at that scene, young woman.''

The mood in the room changed rapidly to one of friendliness, even intimacy. The duke asked Antonia to ring the bell, and, when a servant responded, ordered wine and cakes for himself and the young ladies. He also told the footman to have his valet wait on them. While they looked for the arrival of this worthy, and the refreshments, Taverton questioned Eliza about her family. He had heard of Sir Owen and remembered her father, Sir Malcolm, as a force to be reckoned with in the Commons. He recalled Lady Longfort from her first season; he had danced with her. Antonia was content to sit by and watch her friend's triumph.

The duke's valet, an effete-looking young man, came in presently and was forthwith ordered to fetch a certain letter contained in a certain box in His Grace's private closet. The man bowed and went immediately to do his master's bidding.

Wine and sponge cakes arrived, wheeled in on a cart. The variety of liveried retainers seemed to be endless.

"Will you do the honors, Miss Worthingham?" Taverton asked.

Antonia managed to pour out the wine and place cakes on precious Sevres plates without disgracing herself. The servant handed them around, then departed soundlessly.

"Here's to you, Miss Longfort," the duke said, raising his glass to Eliza. He drained it in one draught. "And to you, Miss Worthingham, her courageous companion in this adventure."

The girls smiled and raised their glasses to His Grace. They quietly munched sponge cakes.

In a remarkably short time the valet was back, bearing upon a silver tray the letter that had caused so much discussion already. The duke took it and dismissed the man with a nod. The instant he and the girls were alone in the room again, he rose from his chair, stalked over to Eliza, and dropped the letter in her lap.

"There, young lady." Turning on his heel, he went back to his chair. "And now let's drink to luck in your enterprise."

"Thank you, Your Grace," Eliza said demurely. She put the letter away in her reticule, then raised her glass again.

Very soon the visitors took their leave. Taverton gave them both his hand in parting and called them brave girls. "Come again and see me," he offered, "no matter what happens."

Antonia was delighted with this attention, which she took, of course, as a compliment to her friend. She could not picture herself visiting the duke again, whatever the circumstances.

When they were out on the street, she praised Eliza for

her bravery more fulsomely than the duke had done.

"I am sorry I had to drag you into that," Eliza responded, "but as I explained, I couldn't go alone. Mama would have had fits. Besides, I wanted the duke to think me a very proper young lady."

"And aren't you?"

Eliza smiled wickedly. "How many proper young ladies do you know who announce their marriage plans to the young man's father before announcing them to the young man?"

When Antonia and Steelman arrived back in Curzon Street, Antonia found a letter from Laura on the tray in the hall. Dispensing with Steelman's services, she hurried to her room.

She took off her bonnet and spencer and sat on the bed in her favorite tailor-fashion to break the seal. The sheet was crossed and recrossed. Luckily Antonia was quite able to decipher her sister's scrawl.

She had not read two sentences before she realized that this letter must be written for a particular reason. Never would Laura, in person, chatter on about dress patterns and new lengths of muslin, so it followed that she would not do so in a letter. She never had before, yet here it was: a sisterly request for some shopping commissions while Antonia was in London. Stockings, gloves, velvet ribbons, corsets, all were mentioned in tedious detail. Then Laura apologized for being so short of time and drew the letter to a close, with her love.

Antonia scrutinized the postscript, a hastily scribbled note: *Only fancy,* Laura wrote, *the servants say the dreadful smugglers succeeded again; even that they landed a French spy who was caught and confessed. Did you ever hear anything so ridiculous?* All questions of muslin aside, this was obviously the real meat of the letter.

Antonia folded the sheet up again into the neat package Laura had made, and tapped it against her cheek, thinking. What was Laura's message? Heaven forbid—had Jean-Baptiste been captured?

Antonia had to find out. But how? Then she remembered Sir Owen and his mysterious trip out of town at dark of the moon. Why had she not thought of it before? He hadn't been to Hampshire any more than she had. He had evidently gone down to Kent. His activities there she did not like to imagine, but he had not caught the Lady. Laura's letter was proof of that. He might have seen Laura from a distance and mistaken her for Antonia, for he had definitely accused Antonia of lying about her own trip to Windsor.

But whom had he captured down in Kent? There was no way of telling if Laura's letter was a plea for help on Jean-Baptiste's account, or merely a way of saying that Antonia's previous warning to Laura had been taken to heart: that the real Lady was now aware of the machinations of Bonapartists in the area and would be on her guard.

Antonia resolved to get the information out of Sir Owen one way or another. She would somehow manage a moment alone with him at their next meeting, which was to be the excursion to Windsor.

And in addition, she thought with a smile, she would fulfill all Laura's commissions and more in the matter of clothes. With her own season's dress allowance, she could afford to buy her sister's wedding clothes. How Laura would laugh, whether she had expected the presents or not.

Antonia rose and rang instantly for Steelman. She would miss nuncheon, but Lady Pomfret understood about shopping. Antonia had to go out to the shops immediately. She needed not only the things for Laura, which must be sent down as soon as possible lest Laura disappear to America before they should arrive, but a new hat suitable for the dark blue riding habit she was planning to wear to Windsor.

The Lady was attractive and dashing at all times. A new hat would be just the thing to remind Antonia to play her part well.

13

The unseasonable heat continued. The night before the proposed ride to Windsor, Eliza sent a message over to Antonia informing her that Lady Longfort had decreed it to be no sort of weather for the young ladies to go on horseback. Antonia sighed over this, or rather over the jaunty shako hat she had bought to wear with her habit, but soon moved on to optimism. She had been wondering how she would be able to present an elegant, let alone an alluring appearance dressed in dusty broadcloth after a twenty-three mile ride in the grueling heat. Besides, Eliza's note urged her to pack her habit in hopes of a short ride on hired horses when the party reached Windsor.

The excursion was to be overnight, and Sir Owen had booked rooms for the group at the White Hart. Young Montgomery Worthingham's tutor had given him leave to spend the day with his sister's party, thanks to the influence of ex-Etonian Sir Owen.

Antonia settled into Lady Longfort's barouche with a lighter heart than she had expected to bring to the outing. Still on her mind was the subject she must somehow open with Sir Owen: had Laura's Jean-Baptiste been the French spy captured down in Kent? Since no further communication had arrived from Laura on the subject, Antonia was inclined to think no, but somehow she had to be sure.

"Have a delightful trip, dear girl," Lady Pomfret called

from the open drawing-room window. She was waving her handkerchief. Mr. Daingerfield could be seen just behind her, and he lifted his hand.

"It's a mystery to me why those two don't marry," Lady Longfort remarked as the carriage rolled down Curzon Street.

"Not everybody has to marry, Mama," Eliza said. She sat next to Antonia facing backward.

"I know, child. But that particular pair is so constant in their friendship that I wonder they don't wish to."

Antonia often wondered about this herself, but even after nearly two months of observing the older couple, she didn't have any clear opinion. Mr. Daingerfield was always mild and never encroaching; yet he seemed in some undefinable way to look on Lady Pomfret as his own. She, in her turn, was no less kind to anyone who visited her than she was to Mr. Daingerfield, yet there was no doubt whose opinion she valued most.

This last was no answer, of course. Lady Pomfret might defer to Mr. Daingerfield, but so did Antonia, and so did his gentleman rivals to Lady Pomfret's favor. Mr. Daingerfield's quiet attitude of inexhaustible knowledge on almost every subject seemed to bring out respect in all people.

"Well," Antonia said, "I suppose we'll simply have to trust that my godmother knows her own heart."

This sentiment brought an approving nod from Lady Longfort and an impish smile from Eliza, and Antonia concentrated on the trip before her as the carriage turned into Piccadilly, heading for Hyde Park Corner. The journey was to last most of the day, allowing her stops to bait the horses and take a leisurely luncheon.

The party in the open carriage was a merry one. They stopped at Alicia Montaigne's house in Richmond, and she settled into place next to Lady Longfort with happy greetings for the ladies. Antonia had now met Alicia several times and grown to like her very much. The gentlemen, who were all riding horseback, included, besides Sir Owen, Alicia's betrothed Lord Bentish; a middle-aged military man called Captain Hervey who, Lady Longfort whispered mischievously, had been asked along for her; and Lord Cavenham, Eliza's hopeful swain. A closed carriage completed the procession and contained the baggage, Lord Cavenham's man, and Lady Longfort's dresser, who was to "do" for all the ladies.

Antonia happened to get a sight of this carriage as it pulled ahead of them—the better to have the baggage unpacked by the time of the gentlefolks' arrival at Windsor—and thought the coachman driving it looked familiar. She took another quick look at the man's back. Surely that was Vale.

She gave Eliza a sidelong glance. No wonder she seemed so carefree this morning despite the unwelcome presence of the amiable Lord Cavenham.

The ladies passed a pleasant morning chatting of this and that. Giggles and some small excitement enlivened the coach's trip over Hounslow Heath. In broad daylight and surrounded by so many gentlemen, they were scarce in any danger of the highwaymen said to haunt the place.

"And how does your sister do, Miss Worthingham?" Alicia asked, so quickly on the heels of the story of some knight of the High Toby that Antonia jumped. At least, she had been thinking in relief, Laura had never gone in for highway robbery.

"Why, she is very well." Antonia was subject to a slight fit of coughing.

"We were talking earlier of people who ought to marry," Lady Longfort said. "Now there, young ladies, is a female who didn't wed simply because of the wide choice that confronted her. Such a beauty! How many offers did she have, Miss Worthingham?"

"I don't remember, if I was ever told," Antonia said. "I was still in the schoolroom during her season. Although," she added with a smile, "she's had no fewer than ten offers down in the country. Those I did count, because it seemed so exciting to me. Nothing bores Laura most than false protestations of love, though."

"False?" Alicia inquired in surprise.

"Why, yes," Antonia said. "Laura always felt, and so do I feel, that men who offered for her because of her looks and no other reason were to be scorned. Love cannot be based solely on a female's beauty."

"I agree completely," Eliza said. "Your sister is very wise. How I wish I could know her."

"Well, dear, perhaps she will come to town again someday," said Lady Longfort. "Though when I knew the child during her season, she always looked to be wanting something more important to do."

"Whatever do you mean, Mama?"

"She was bored by her season. I must say I did find it odd that she should find her fulfillment not in marriage, but in keeping house for her father when her great-aunt Harriet died," Lady Longfort said. "Why, Antonia, my dear, what's the matter?"

"Not a thing." Antonia, who had succumbed to another sharp cough, cleared her throat. Great-Aunt Harriet, the last Lady, had officially kept the fires burning at Easton Grange after Mrs. Worthingham's fatal fall from a horse when Antonia was twelve. Aunt Harriet had been a heedless housekeeper, to be frank, for she had always had her head full of the smuggling operations, and the proper disposition of each load of brandy had been much more interesting to her than the great wash or the kitchen garden. This state of affairs had led to Antonia's early mastery of the housekeeping arts, and Laura had learned smuggling at her great-aunt's knee. Naturally the world would have assumed that Laura's had been the guiding hand of the family after Harriet's death, but Antonia had never quite realized that before.

"Wasn't Miss Harriet Worthingham one of Dr. Johnson's friends?" Alicia asked. "I met Mrs. Piozzi once, and how thrilled I was. I wish above anything that I were clever enough to be a bluestocking."

"Aunt Harriet used to write monographs on serious subjects, and she always treasured her signed copy of the *Dictionary*," Antonia said, smiling. "I quite admired her and wished to emulate her; but I'm no bluestocking either."

"I shall be," said Eliza. "Later. And I'll be a famous one, too. I think a woman should be known for her intellect and nothing else."

"How quiet it must be for you and your sister all alone out in the country. But that situation may change, of course," Lady Longfort said with twinkling eyes, still speaking to Antonia. She pointedly ignored her daughter's outburst, not to be done out of her hint to Antonia. When she had made it, she looked significantly at her son, riding near them on his magnificent stallion.

Antonia feigned interest in the other side of the road, hoping that Lady Longfort was not building her hopes on a match. The well-meaning lady was bound to be disappointed.

Luncheon at a little country inn was a merry meal, with much flirting to enliven the proceedings, though not from expected sources. Alicia and Bentish, as the engaged couple, seemed already to have sunk into the serenity of matrimony. Antonia was pleased to note that, though Alicia had once had a *tendre* for Sir Owen, there was no awkwardness between them now and that Alicia seemed truly attached to her baron.

Eliza's situation was less comfortable, as she resolutely paid no attention to Cavenham's charming efforts to draw her out. But Lady Longfort and Captain Hervey made up for any lack on the young people's part by flirting quite outrageously. As for Antonia and Sir Owen, they merely looked at each other—significant looks indeed, though, Antonia reflected wistfully, for vastly different reasons.

Her melancholy thoughts were interrupted by yet another peal of laughter from Lady Longfort and raucous bark from her military escort.

"Mama!" Eliza whispered when the ladies were walking back to the carriage. "I'm glad you brought along three chaperons."

Lady Longfort fluttered her handkerchief. "The captain and I understand each other. We're lending countenance to Owen's party, aren't we? And it didn't seem much of a party at all. We simply had to do something to liven things up. You young people were too boring for words."

Eliza and Antonia exchanged wry smiles.

As evening shadows fell, the group entered Windsor and

pulled up at the White Hart, where Sir Owen had bespoken bedrooms and a private parlor as well as a fine dinner. There was time to do nothing but eat the dinner, again in a spirit of companionship that traveling so often engenders, before all declared themselves too tired for cards and ready for bed. The gentlemen, the ladies assumed, would sit up late over their bottle.

Antonia was finding that traveling was a delightful activity when congenial people made up a group. She and Alicia settled down to bed in good spirits in the room they shared after a serious talk about important matters, from Alicia's hope for the next hunting season (Bentish had a box in Leicestershire) to the outfits they were to wear on the morrow. They were satisfied that excursions out of town were the best way to enliven a season.

Breakfast time found the party congregating in bright-eyed anticipation of what the day would bring. Later they were to visit the royal rooms of state. Merely to know that the historic castle was looming nearby was exciting.

Antonia noted the empty place by her side. "Sir Owen, don't tell me that you're bringing my brother here so early."

"He should be here any minute," Sir Owen told her with a broad smile.

Antonia was on her second cup of tea when the door did indeed open to admit Mr. Montgomery Worthingham, Esq, of Easton Grange in Kent.

"Monty!" Antonia stood up to embrace the boy, to his evident embarrassment. Her brother was a good-looking lad with her light brown hair and the deceptive fragility of one whose body was shooting up faster than his mind could comprehend. Hastily, she introduced him to the company. "You are even taller than you were two weeks ago."

"I say, Sister, let a fellow sit down and have some kippers."

"Two weeks?" Sir Owen looked puzzled.

"Why, yes," Antonia said. "I was sure I had mentioned —oh!" She stared at Sir Owen. Why had she not thought before that this excursion to Windsor must be intended to prove that she had not told the truth about her last visit? Her blank look turned to a glare before she could prevent it, and she cast down her eyes.

"Two weeks," Monty Worthingham was saying with a nod of his head as he sat down and began to heap a plate with toast, buttered eggs, and the kippers of his desires. The others watched in apparent fascination at the awe-inspiring sight of a growing boy and his breakfast.

General conversation broke out. "Well, Mr. Worthingham," Sir Owen said from across the table, "you must be delighted to see your sister again so soon."

"It's capital, sir, thanks. A day's holiday! And do call me Monty. Say, Sir Owen, you're the one who got me leave, aren't you? Thanks." Monty alternately shoved in food and talked with impressive control and great speed.

"It was only a couple of weeks ago that you saw her last?" Sir Owen pursued with a searching look at Antonia, who tightened her lips in annoyance.

Monty, at this moment too replete with kippers to venture any other answer, nodded.

"We'll go to see mademoiselle right after breakfast," Antonia told her brother. "Then I'm told Sir Owen has seen to hiring a horse for you as well as the rest of our party, and we're to go riding."

The boy received this news with much pleasure. "Have to go back to mademoiselle's, then, to change."

"Allow me to escort you to see, er, mademoiselle," Sir Owen offered politely.

Antonia met his eyes for a moment; there seemed to be some challenge in the gray depths. She tossed her head and devoted herself to Lord Cavenham. The viscount was on her other side, and, as his own breakfast partner was the uninterested Eliza, his lordship was really suffering for conversation.

Breakfast passed too slowly for Antonia's taste. She could sense that Sir Owen was watching her, and Cavenham's good manners, delightful as they might have been to some other young lady, didn't serve to divert her. But the meal eventually did end. Some of the party went out to walk about the narrow streets and look up at the castle. Antonia and Monty, accompanied by Sir Owen, took off across the bridge and soon reached the High Street of Eton.

Mademoiselle Bluet was Antonia's old governess, an émigrée of uncertain origins that were sometimes noble, sometimes plebeian, according to her political feelings of the moment. The lady had decided, when Antonia came out of the schoolroom, to make a change in her circumstances. She had a friend who was a dame at Eton, and was growing elderly, and had gone into business with her.

The dames of Eton saw to the lads' washing, fed them, and housed them. Antonia and Laura had been very glad, when it was time for Monty to go off to school, to be able to place him in the home of someone he had known for years.

Mademoiselle Bluet was busily employed in the small sitting room of her compact house. A small, round woman with black hair and eyes, she jumped up excitedly at the sight of Antonia, dropping her knitting. "*Mon Dieu!* Antoinette, *ma petite*. Oh—and who is this?" She looked up at the tall, fair-haired gentleman who was standing in the doorway, hat in hand.

Monty ducked past Sir Owen and sped up to his chamber, throwing over his shoulder a phrase about changing quick as anything.

"May I present Sir Owen Longfort. Mademoiselle Bluet, my former governess," Antonia said, observing the encounter with interest.

Mademoiselle, being a Frenchwoman, did everything but take out a notebook to jot down Sir Owen's merits. Her eyes were extremely sharp as she looked from her former charge to the baronet and back again.

"Antoinette," she said, smiling at the girl, "do me this small favor, if you will. I dislike to trouble Mrs. Black with the making of the tea, for she is napping in her chamber. Would you go and put the kettle on?"

Antonia nodded and left the room. She knew just where the kitchen was, and she saw no way out. If mademoiselle wished to speak to Sir Owen and ask him embarrassing questions, much better that she do it alone.

"Now I have you by yourself, monsieur," said Mademoiselle Bluet. So small was she that she appeared to have to put her neck out of joint to look at him. "What are your intentions, please?"

Sir Owen's eyes opened wide. "My intentions, ma'am? What do you mean?"

"I mean, sir, that you trifle with *ma petite* at your peril. Is that clear?"

"Perfectly," Sir Owen said. His smile was like a burst of sunshine. "May I sit down, ma'am?"

Mademoiselle Bluet grandly indicated that he was welcome to be seated on a remarkably spindly-looking Windsor chair. She took the armchair she had been sitting in before.

"She is a delightful girl, worth ten of her sister," the Frenchwoman said, glaring. "I do not mean to disparage her sister, you comprehend. It is that my Antoinette is so much more."

"So far we are in agreement, ma'am, though I fear to do Miss Laura Worthingham too little credit. I hardly know the lady."

Mademoiselle Bluet shrugged. "It is of no importance. Mademoiselle Laure will go her own way; she has no need of any of us. But Antoinette—she is special. Do you know, monsieur, have you any idea what the child has had to suffer in her life?"

Sir Owen hesitated. "Her parents are dead, that I know. I lost my father, and I can understand—"

"Bah!" said Mademoiselle Bluet. "You can have no idea of what she went through. First the mother, dead too soon, and from a silly accident. The old aunt lived with them, true, but less than useless, that one. I came to them, and all was well."

"I imagine it was," Sir Owen said in fascination.

"And next it was the father, drinking himself to death they say, but it is only whispers. And all the time Antoinette was holding the family together. Keeping the house, for the aunt would not, and the sister? Bah. *La pauvre* Antoinette. Being a *maman* to the little brother. And taking on the duties of lady of the manor. This girl, I tell you, is special. She has one quality, though, which you would not understand.''

The lady hesitated, and Sir Owen's mind leaped to the smuggling. This Frenchwoman could know Antonia was the Lady; she could even be a spy Antonia had once landed . . . No, that was ridiculous.

"Tell me, ma'am." He leaned forward. "What would I not understand?"

Mademoiselle Bluet looked the baronet up and down. "You will not understand when she will not believe you love her."

He stared and felt himself turn brick red. "She won't?" was all he found to say.

"She will not," the ex-governess affirmed. "Antoinette, you see, is used to taking care of things, of people. And not a soul, monsieur, excepting myself, returns her devotion. It is the way with people of that sort."

"People who take care of things," Sir Owen prompted.

"*Exactement,*" said Mademoiselle Bluet.

"Tell me something, ma'am," Sir Owen said. "Did Miss Worthingham visit you a couple of weeks ago?"

"In this very house she stayed, for we have a spare room," the Frenchwoman told him without hesitation. Then she peered at her guest suspiciously. "Why do you wish to know? She must be willing to tell you herself of her comings and goings?"

"Mademoiselle, tell me one thing more. What do you know of the smuggling on the coast near Easton Grange?"

The small dark eyes widened. "*Mon Dieu,* the bush you do not beat. What do I know? When it was I who was smuggled in myself, when I was escaping the Terror?"

This was not something Sir Owen had expected to hear. "How interesting, indeed exciting, ma'am. You were brought in from France by the Kentish smugglers?"

Mademoiselle Bluet frowned. "My lips, they are sealed till the day of judgment, monsieur. And it was long ago."

"Odd," Sir Owen murmured. "A change indeed. First bringing in émigrés such yourself, royalists, I suppose"— she nodded at his inquiring glance—"who were escaping your government's excesses. Now, though, who do they land from France? Would you happen to know, ma'am?''

"I have told you, monsieur, about the state of my lips," the lady retorted.

Sir Owen gazed at her in fascination. She would have been landed by the last Lady, for the Terror was twenty years ago. Antonia would have been in her cradle.

He fancied that the Lady and her Gentlemen had been opportunists over the years. When there were royalists wishing to escape France. the smugglers had landed émigrés—for a price, one must assume—but stayed within their country's prejudices. And now that the commodity in Frenchmen ran to Bonapartist spies, had they tossed all patriotic feeling aside in the name of pecuniary gain?

And what of Antonia's role in all this? He had hoped this excursion would make Antonia open her heart to him when he exposed as false her claim to have been in Windsor at last dark of the moon. A complication, however, was that her young brother and now this female were confirming the fact of Antonia's visit.

Riding boots clattered down the staircase, and before Sir Owen and Mademoiselle Bluet had the chance to exchange another syllable, they were joined by Monty Worthingham.

"Sorry it took me so long," the boy said with a grin. "Dashed coat barely covers my elbows, and I was trying to pull it about to make it fit."

He was right. He had outgrown the serviceable riding clothes almost past the point of decency. Sir Owen gave the matter his full consideration while Monty writhed under the gaze of a genuine man of fashion.

"Nothing to be done about it," Sir Owen said with a shrug. "Monty, come with me quickly. I'd wager there's a haberdasher here in the school, or a fellow Etonian who would be glad to sell or lend you some things. We'll go to the Christopher to inquire."

"I say, sir," Monty said, wide-eyed. "Can you do it?"

"Watch me." And Sir Owen nodded to Mademoiselle Bluet, took Monty firmly by the arm, and left the little house.

"We'll return within the quarter hour," he said over his shoulder.

"Ah, *un homme qui peut,*" the little Frenchwoman sighed, clasping her hands.

"A man who can?" Antonia appeared in the doorway to the kitchen, a loaded tea tray in her hands. "What do you mean, mademoiselle? And where is everybody?"

"You did not say, when you were here before, *ma chère,* that he was so very handsome."

Antonia shrugged. She didn't bother to pretend that she didn't understand her friend's meaning. "Laura would not agree with you. She doesn't think he's anything out of the ordinary."

"Taste in men is a personal thing," stated the ex-governess. "It is like clothes. Oh, that reminds me. Sir Owen has taken your brother to get him some riding clothes that fit."

"How kind of him," Antonia exclaimed.

"This I think to myself. And now, Antoinette, pour for us the tea and tell me much, much more about this gentleman of yours."

Antonia poured, but she felt bound to explain first off that Sir Owen was not her particular property. Her mingled exasperation and admiration made her description of his many good qualities sound confused to her ear. Mademoiselle Bluet frowned, nodded, and looked wise as Antonia admitted that the gentleman was most attentive.

What could she say? Even to mademoiselle, Antonia couldn't admit that Sir Owen was only attentive because he thought she was a renowned smuggler. Nor could she explain how she was regretting more and more that she was not that fascinating woman he seemed to admire so very much.

14

Antonia and Sir Owen chanced to find themselves comparatively alone a little later in the day. The young people of the party had gone on the expected ride to a particularly fine view that Monty Worthingham, in all the glory of a suit of riding clothes that fit him to a nicety, and all the importance of a very young man consorting with adults, had offered to show them. Sir Owen let his horse lag behind a little, Antonia followed suit, and it was done. They were as private as they had ever been, and with their official chaperon far away, enjoying an hour's flirt with Captain Hervey.

Antonia stiffened. How was she to open the subject of the French spy captured in Kent? This was her chance; would probably be her only chance to speak with Sir Owen in privacy.

"I've been talking to your young brother, ma'am," Sir Owen said. "He does nothing but sing your praises."

"How tedious for you, sir," Antonia answered with a nervous laugh.

"Probably a habit he picked up from your governess. Do you know, the two of them are so positive that you were down here with them a short time ago that I must apologize for doubting your word—which no gentleman would have done in the first place."

Antonia was shocked and even touched. "I'm glad you see the truth, sir." She took a deep breath. "Since you now

believe I was not in Kent, perhaps I could ask you something about what did happen down there.''

"You know I was not there myself," he said.

She shrugged. "You were not in town. Now, I wish to
know only one thing, sir. Was any capture made at dark of
the moon?''

He gave her a searching look. "As a matter of fact, ma'am,
there was a man captured. A foreigner who was landing and
caught coming ashore. I can say no more; but you, in your
position, can understand that I've already said too much."

Antonia nodded, trying to school her features into a lack
of expression. Thank heaven! Jean-Baptiste, in his injured
condition, would never have been caught coming out of the
water. He wouldn't stir from Hannah's cottage until the time
came to move on with Laura. Antonia's fear had been that
Sir Owen would tell her a capture had been made in the
Haunted Wood. "I shall not repeat what you have told me,"
she said, feeling generous in her relief. "You have my word
on it."

Sir Owen looked at her with a new respect, she thought,
or at least with surprise. "My dear Miss Worthingham, you
astonish me," he declared.

Good, she thought, but she said nothing, only gave an
enigmatic smile and rode on ahead. Scanning the road for
the rest of the party, she was just in time to see Eliza separate
from the others and go off down a narrow wooded lane with
a rider who, though familiar, hadn't been included in the
list of those invited to ride. Thomas Vale.

"Do wait for me, Miss Worthingham," Sir Owen said,
spurring his horse.

Antonia met his eyes as he rode by and could not doubt
that he had seen the same thing she had. She did wait, hanging
about beside the entrance to the lane and watching the riders
on the main road grow more distant.

A trio of disgruntled-looking equestrians returned back
through the wood before many minutes had passed.

"Well, Antonia, are you here to lend me countenance?"
Eliza said. Her face was very flushed, and she shot
murderous looks at her brother.

Vale merely nodded to Antonia. He was giving Eliza as well as Sir Owen a wide berth, and when he reached the road, he went down it in the opposite direction of the rest of the party, back to Windsor. He touched his hat in a mockery of respect as he passed.

Sir Owen said, "You had better pray our mother doesn't hear of that little display," and, giving Antonia a sympathetic look, he rode off after the others.

"I was in the middle of explaining to Thomas that he had to read his father's letter," Eliza said once she and Antonia had privacy. "Look, I still have it here in my pocket."

"Am I mistaken, or was Vale a little put out with you?" Antonia asked, trying for delicacy.

Eliza sighed. "He was. Called me an interfering minx. Then I called him a blackguard, and Owen came up with us."

"Oh, dear. Do you think you can make it up?" Antonia's anxiety was more for the Duke of Taverton and his letter than the squabbling lovers.

"My dear Antonia," Eliza said, "I am a stubborn creature, as you know. What do you think?"

"Vale hasn't a chance," Antonia said, smiling. Eliza smiled back with enough confidence to satisfy Antonia that her spirits were not permanently cast down.

The girls hurried their horses and soon arrived at the beauty spot. The company had dismounted, and Eliza and Antonia did the same.

Monty was in alt as everyone complimented him on his choice of the little bluff that looked down on the Thames and the pretty surrounding country. Spring was in full bloom, and Lord Bentish, an amateur botanist, amused Alicia and the others by identifying every tree in sight, however distant—though with what accuracy, who could say?

Eliza thrilled young Monty by attaching herself to him and asking him all manner of questions about school in an effort to leave Cavenham out in the cold. Cavenham, an old Etonian himself, turned the tables and joined in with a will. Soon the conversation among the three turned solely on cricket and excluded Eliza.

Antonia observed all this and thought it served Eliza right for being so cruel to poor Lord Cavenham.

"My sister, ma'am, is playing the fool."

Antonia turned. Sir Owen was standing beside her. His arms were folded and his gaze was stern; he was every inch the protective brother.

"Oh, I don't know that she is being foolish, if you are referring to Thomas Vale," Antonia said. "There are circumstances—well, it is not my business. Suffice it to say that Eliza has the situation well under control."

"You mean, I suppose, that she's determined to have him. Let's say that happens, Miss Worthingham. My sister's of age, and she may simply go off to be married at any time she likes. But what am I to do when my mother finds out her only daughter is living above your godmother's stables on a groom's pay?"

"I have every reason to believe the Duke of Taverton wishes to be reconciled to his son and approves his marriage to Eliza," Antonia burst out. Then she remembered that offering this information was hardly an example of minding her own business and flushed at her own audacity.

"Does he!" Sir Owen was surprised. "But knowing Eliza, that wouldn't change the fact that they will live in poverty rather than accept their families' help."

"You must know Eliza sees nothing wrong in living off her dowry."

"I am paying Lord Thomas the compliment of assuming he would object to it."

Antonia nodded. "You're right. Well, sir, how do you propose to remedy this?"

"I? Remedy what?"

"Eliza's love in a cottage. You must find a post for Thomas Vale, sir, one that your mother won't faint over."

Sir Owen gave her a rueful look. "My dear young woman, I've been doing nothing else lately. I have inquiries out to all the offices of government I can think of, and I've presented Lord Thomas with one or two ideas, but he laughs at me. The man simply likes to work with his hands."

"And horses. He likes horses," Antonia said thoughtfully. "I know! They might breed horses. That's quite a respectable occupation, isn't it?"

Sir Owen lifted an eyebrow. "Quite respectable, ma'am. And I wonder I hadn't thought of it before. You and I are to set them up on some suitable estate, then supply them with breeding stock? I had no idea your income stretched that far, even taking all your activities into consideration."

He was laughing at her, Antonia thought in irritation, and making another hit at the smuggling while he was about it. "I don't say either one of us must set them up in the business to that degree. I'll arrange it myself, sir. Don't worry." And she would, too. She would wager that the Duke of Taverton would be pleased to look out some small stud farm. He could—Antonia thought quickly—His Grace could say that taking over this as yet unknown farm would be a favor to him; that there was no one else he could trust. Yes, they would find a way, she and the duke.

"My dear, I really believe you'll do it," Sir Owen said, looking at her in bemusement.

"Why should I say I will, if I don't mean to?" Antonia demanded, opening her eyes wide.

"And I'm not to ask how?"

"Better if you do not. There's the slightest chance that I'll fail, and then I would be mortified."

"Somehow, Miss Worthingham, I doubt that you've ever been mortified. Such a life as you must have led already, and you so young. Will you tell me just one thing, ma'am, if I promise to let it go no further?"

"What?" Antonia looked up at him, her mind still half on her new project with the duke, and felt a sudden shock at how close together she and Sir Owen were standing. Looking about her, she was relieved that the others of the party were far off and had all turned in another direction for the moment.

"Do you operate a certain smuggling ring as the Lady?" Sir Owen asked, searching her face.

Antonia drew in her breath. So he had finally gone beyond hints and jokes, and meant to have the truth. Well, he would not get it. Laura's safety depended on the continuation of Antonia's masquerade.

"You look shocked, I see," said Sir Owen. "But are you really so taken aback?"

Antonia looked him in the eye. "What do you wish me to tell you, sir? That the ladies of my family have always led the Gentlemen? Since you will undoubtedly ask that question next, if it were true we would have nothing to do with traitorous activities. Plainly put, we would not land spies."

"Oh," Sir Owen said softly. Now he was the one to look shocked, as no doubt he must be. He would never have expected such plain speaking from anyone, Antonia thought smugly, though she had carefully kept her words in the conditional.

"You do remember, sir, that you promised this information would go no further," Antonia said. "I have done nothing but indulge in speculations with you. But I presume I have your word that you'll say nothing, your word as a gentleman?"

"You have it, ma'am," Sir Owen said. His eyes, which had looked so vague and confused, now lit up. "Shall we seal that bargain, Miss Worthingham, with a kiss?"

"Why should we do that?" Antonia stepped back.

He caught at her hand. "Because we've kissed once before, and it wasn't enough for me. To kiss the Lady to my heart's content has been my ambition ever since I woke one night from a certain blow to the head and saw your face looking down at me." He placed his lips ever so softly on the hand he held.

"You can hardly kiss anyone to your heart's content in front of all these people," Antonia said in a nervous undertone, glancing around again. Suddenly the aplomb she had put on to act the Lady deserted her, and she was only a jittery schoolgirl. The others were still occupied, thank goodness, but at any moment her young brother might run up to them, or Eliza might call out.

He smiled. "You don't object to the act, then, merely to the audience. I hoped it would be so."

"It isn't so. That is, I mean to say . . ." Antonia's mind was whirling. She was exhilarated from her near-confession of a smuggler's life. She was injured because Sir Owen said he wished to kiss the Lady, not her, Antonia. And she wished, more than anything else, to be taken in his arms and to be as abandoned as any Lady of legend could be. She looked at him, wondering if any or all of these emotions could be read on her face.

"We'll wait for another time, my dear," Sir Owen said. With a mischievous spark in his eye, he leaned over to kiss her on the lips, so briefly that Antonia couldn't believe that the feathery touch could affect her as it did, turning her knees useless and making her breath come fast and hard.

Grinning, Sir Owen gave her his arm. "Shall we go take another look at the view? I see Lord Bentish is helping Miss Montaigne to mount. I gather we're going then. I have a fancy to show you Salt Hill while we're out."

"Could you?" Antonia's eyes shone. "I—Eliza and I happened to see you set out with your club last Thursday."

"You did, did you?" He looked flattered.

Antonia wished the rules of conduct permitted her to tell him that she had been to Cavendish Square on purpose to see him in all his glory. She certainly would have done, had she known he was a member of the famous driving society.

They took a quick glance at the view of the Thames, for the others were indeed remounting. Sir Owen threw Antonia up into the saddle, very properly to any eye that might have been watching. He gave her waist what amounted to a caress though, and squeezed her hands before strolling off to his own horse.

Antonia gazed after him, wondering if she had ever been so angry, or so happy, in her life. What was to be done with such an infuriating man?

She lifted her chin. She would enjoy this strange flirtation, or whatever it was, as long as possible. When Sir Owen found out the truth about her, that would be time enough to think about being a proper young lady. When that day arrived, he would not wish to kiss her in any case. But now, while his excitement at actually being acquainted with the

Lady was infecting her, she would do whatever she wished—
within reason. Her reason, she knew, was in danger of
deserting her in the matter of Sir Owen. What luck that he
was every inch the gentleman!

Sir Owen rode a little behind Miss Worthingham on the
way to Salt Hill. What would he do when he caught her in
the act of smuggling? He was much relieved to hear from
her what amounted to an assurance that she and her men had
nothing to do with landing spies. He didn't know why, but
he believed her implicitly on that detail. There was some
sort of proof, too, in the calm way she had taken the news
that "a foreigner" had been captured at last dark of the moon.
She had been relieved, he could swear it. She had probably
heard a rumor that one of her Gentlemen had come to grief.

Next dark of the moon would find him watching her
closely. He smiled. Perhaps they might travel down to Kent
together? Meanwhile, he would spend all his energies in
getting to know what made her mind work. He had never
before had the opportunity to study the criminal brain.

Could smugglers, especially altruistic smugglers like the
Lady, really be called criminals? He didn't really believe
so. Yet anyone who operated outside the law owned that title.
Yes, she would bear watching.

Sir Owen grew quite lighthearted. He would have to keep
dancing with Antonia Worthingham at every ball, arranging
more outings to include her, calling at Lady Pomfret's
home—it would be a sacrifice well worth making. Perhaps
he could even talk Miss Worthingham into giving up the
smuggling life. A shame, in a way, to see the Lady vanish
from the Kentish coast, but more important to keep her out
of trouble. Sir Owen was beginning to discover that he cared
very much for Miss Worthingham's safety. Nobody who
flitted about on the seacoast at dark of the moon, evading
the riding officers, could be called safe.

For the first time he felt what amounted to irritation with
Antonia for being the Lady. She was so much what he wanted
in a woman. Did she have to be a notorious lawbreaker as
well? Dashed inconvenient. Such a lady he had admired as

a legendary figure; but he would not have chosen to attach himself to her.

Suddenly he was seized by a protective urge that nearly overwhelmed him. He spurred on his horse and caught up with Antonia. She was riding beside her brother. Both Worthinghams looked quizzically at him.

"Do you know, Miss Worthingham," Sir Owen said through clenched teeth, "that the riding officers are armed? That they do not hesitate to fire when the situation warrants it?"

Antonia nodded, giving a warning glance in her brother's direction. "We were talking earlier about—about officers, Monty," she explained to the boy.

"There are those who would not like to see y—to see anyone hurt," Sir Owen pursued, his voice intense.

"I will keep that in mind, sir," she retorted coldly.

"If you please, sir, won't you race me now? You said perhaps you would when we came to a straight stretch of road," young Monty put in, in a pleading tone. He seemed totally uninterested in any undercurrents that might have been present in his sister's conversation with the gentleman.

"Of course. I did say that. Ladies and gentlemen," called out Sir Owen. The four other riders paused and looked back. "Stand aside, if you will. Mr. Worthingham and I are about to give you a taste of what horsemanship is all about."

Antonia shifted her mare to the side of the road and looked on indulgently as her menfolk made a display of themselves. She found, without much surprise, that Sir Owen seemed to belong to her as much as Monty did—though in a different way.

This was inconvenient, certainly, and might be sad later on, but for the moment her feelings were a delightful novelty. She would treasure each sensation up in her heart. Someday, when she and her elderly duenna were sitting in the drawing room at Easton Grange, she would need all the happy memories she could recall.

15

A few days after her return from Windsor, Antonia, dressed in her finest walking things and followed by her abigail, was seen navigating the great stone steps that led from the door of Taverton House down to the pavement of Cavendish Square. Casting a glance back at the great door, Antonia nodded to herself. The plan would work. It must work.

She and Steelman began a brisk walk back to Curzon Street. The day was gray and cool, a welcome respite from the recent heat, and Antonia began to perk up, looking around about her at the stately buildings, the greenery in the middle of the square, the birds perched here and there on a spindly tree. Springtime might be more pleasant in the country, but London had its own charm, with life bursting whether there was space for it or not. "Shall we stop off at Grafton House and see about those ribbons?" Antonia asked her maid. "Or are you too tired?"

"Mercy, ma'am, there never was such a young lady as yourself for asking if a body is tired," Steelman puffed as she struggled along in Antonia's wake. "Ribbons is needed for your new bonnet. I say get 'em soon. One never knows when a new bonnet might be of use."

In the next moments, Antonia was indeed wishing that a new bonnet sat upon her head, for Sir Owen Longfort, in his smart yellow-wheeled curricle, was pulling up beside the pavement.

"How do you do, Miss Worthingham?" he called down with a smile. "Are you recovered yet from the excursion to Windsor? You look to be in fine fettle. May I take you up?"

Antonia hesitated.

"Do go, ma'am," Steelman whispered with an earnestness that Antonia recognized as a matchmaker's zeal. "I'll stop for the ribbons. I've got the sample right here by me."

"Perhaps I don't want to," Antonia murmured with an expressive, sidelong look toward Sir Owen.

"Nonsense, ma'am, 'course you do." Steelman smiled in her fondest and most maternal style. "I'll tell Lady Pomfret you'll be along. 'Twill be most proper. His tiger's with him."

Antonia didn't know what to do other than to accept Sir Owen's gracious offer. It was either that or stand quarreling with her maid for the rest of the day, while the baronet looked on in apparent amusement and fashionable passersby stared curiously.

"Delighted, ma'am, that you've overcome your scruples and will deign to answer my heart's desire," Sir Owen said. He leapt down to the pavement and offered Antonia his arm, sparing a wink for Steelman.

The abigail went on down the square, her step much jauntier than it had been a moment before.

Sir Owen saw Antonia settled in his curricle. When he had taken his place beside her, he said, "I admire your abigail, ma'am. She seems to have a most proper concern for your happiness."

"What do you mean, sir?" Antonia found courage to flirt a little now that she was surveying the world from the comfortable perch of a stylish open vehicle driven by a member of the Four-Horse Club. She was more than glad that she had ended up accepting the offer. What a fine pair of grays, too. She looked at their broad backs with pleasure, wondering if Sir Owen's politeness would extend to letting her have a turn with the ribbons. She didn't know if she could find the courage to ask.

Sir Owen grinned. "Your maid apparently thinks you

ought to drive rather than walk. Perhaps I mean nothing more than that.''

"Oh. Of course.'' Antonia kept her eyes on the street, the buildings of the square—anything but his laughing face.

"What were you doing at Taverton House?'' were his next words.

Antonia felt a flush overspreading her cheeks. "Do you remember, sir, the discussion we had the other day down at Windsor? About your sister and Lord Thomas Vale?''

He nodded, frowning a little.

"I said they might open a stud farm, and you joked that neither you nor I had the money to help them.'' Antonia judged that his frown betokened an unclear memory and hastened to recall the matter to his mind. "Well, I was merely going to the person who does wish most to help them, and who does have the money.''

"You went to see the Duke of Taverton, the greatest curmudgeon in the *ton*?'' Sir Owen said, sounding awestruck.

Antonia nodded.

"Ma'am, you do astonish me. You are intrepid, indeed. I never would have thought—''

"That I would have the courage?'' Antonia finished his sentence for him with a slight feeling of injury. Didn't he think the Lady would dare anything?

"Miss Worthingham, you must stop reading others' thoughts. It's most unsettling, especially when your guesses are less than accurate,'' the gentleman said. "Perhaps I was thinking that you wouldn't feel yourself responsible for Eliza and Vale to that degree. Silly of me, I realize. You would do as much for any creature you thought to be in need of your help.''

Antonia thought that this made her seem too insipid for words, and more put-upon than good-hearted, but she recognized his positive opinion of her even though it seemed to have taken an overly sickly tone. "Thank you,'' she said with a little sigh.

"And now, ma'am, where shall we go? The park? It's not yet the fashionable hour, but even so I might show you off to any number of people.''

She smiled her acquiescence. "But only for a short turn. I am expected at home."

"Trust me, it will be the shortest turn imaginable. Might I stop to pay my respects to Lady Pomfret afterward?"

Antonia had no reason to refuse him. So friendly was he, so charming, that she forgot everything except that she was with him and enjoying it mightily.

Their circuit of the park turned up several friends and acquaintances. Sir Owen slowed the curricle more than once to call out greetings. The sunlight gleamed on his light hair, his easy manners could not be faulted, and as for his driving style! His hands seemed hardly to touch the ribbons, thought Antonia in an excess of admiration. If only such an attractive man could like her for herself. If only she might consider this drive as a promising sign of courtship.

Well, nothing was perfect, and Antonia was soon playing the philosopher as the carriage tooled out of the park, down Park Lane and into Curzon Street. She had told herself more than once that she would enjoy Sir Owen's company to the full while it lasted, would flirt with him to her heart's content while she had the opportunity. What was wrong with her now? This touch of melancholy every time she was with him would soon turn Sir Owen from her even if he didn't find out she was not the Lady.

Lady Pomfret and four elderly gentlemen were taking wine in the Chinese drawing room when Antonia and Sir Owen entered. "Good day to you, Sir Owen," Lady Pomfret said with a sly smile. "So you've taken Antonia out to enjoy the day. Do sit and have some wine and recover your strength."

"Your goddaughter isn't that tiring, ma'am," Sir Owen said with a mischievous look at Antonia, as he bent over Lady Pomfret's hand. "I didn't give in to her obvious desire to take the ribbons."

"I never even asked," protested Antonia, blushing.

"You didn't have to. I saw it in your eyes."

"How attentive you are, Sir Owen," Lady Pomfret said. "Here, sir, would you like Madeira or burgundy or perhaps some cognac? Mr. Daingerfield always takes cognac in the morning." She nodded at her constant cavalier, who sat close beside her and was smiling beatifically. "And do ring the bell, Marquess," she ordered an old man who sat nearest that convenience, "and we will order some lemonade for my goddaughter."

"Don't bother, my lord, I will take a very small glass of wine," Antonia said, coming forward to the tray her godmother was presiding over. The marquess, who had not moved, gave a cough and relapsed into what she believed must have been a doze.

Besides the marquess and Mr. Daingerfield, a baronet and a new-made City knight, each of grandfatherly age, were sitting with her ladyship. Sir Owen placed himself beside the City man and made himself entertaining. Antonia took her wine and sat down near Mr. Daingerfield and her godmother, the spot which was, incidentally, also closest to Sir Owen.

"Your suitor is so very charming," Lady Pomfret murmured. "I've been trying to draw out that poor Sir Ralph, but he's been dumb as a post. Now look at him chatting away to Sir Owen as though they'd been acquainted for years."

"Sir Owen is not my suitor," Antonia felt bound to inform the lady.

"Then why, pray tell, is he haunting the house?"

"My dear, he is not here nearly so often as I," protested Mr. Daingerfield, exchanging an amused look with Antonia.

"You do not haunt this house, Daingerfield, you permeate it," Lady Pomfret said with a flirtatious smile. "I maintain that there's something going on between that gentleman and Antonia. Mind you, marriage is not in the question. The girl told me when she came to town that she had no wish to marry."

"That's so," Antonia said.

Mr. Daingerfield's eyes twinkled, and he opened his mouth to say something very clever, Antonia was certain, but he never had the opportunity. The superannuated butler pushed open the double doors at that moment and announced, in a creaking voice, "His Grace of Taverton."

Lady Pomfret's gentlemen visitors bristled with something like jealousy as Taverton, certainly the catch of the season in their age-group, entered the room leaning on his stick.

Antonia stared at the duke in surprise. He had changed his clothes since their interview barely an hour before. He now wore, instead of his old furze, an embroidered court coat, the like of which she had never seen before. His bright red wig sat proudly above his craggy face. He looked taller and more stately than ever.

Sir Owen was watching the proceedings with interest as Taverton advanced to Lady Pomfret, took her hand tenderly, and said, much to the apparent displeasure of Mr. Daingerfield and the other gentlemen, "Dearest Louisa! You grow lovelier with each passing year."

"You are most welcome in my home, Duke, with a manner like that," Lady Pomfret said with a pleased nod. "Will you sit down?"

"Thank you," replied the duke. "I've been thinking that it's time I got on a more intimate footing with you. All things considered." He gave her a look full of meaning, and the suitors put on angry expressions.

Lady Pomfret doubtless took His Grace's remark to mean what Antonia took it to mean, that, considering his son was sleeping above her stables, they were connected in spite of themselves.

"Now, do you know all the company?" Lady Pomfret got busy with introductions, and soon all the gentlemen who had been looking murderous were constrained to put on their most courteous manners to meet a duke.

"Sir Owen!" Taverton said when the comparative youth in the room was presented to him. "I know your sister, young man. Charming girl."

Sir Owen, to do him credit, took this revelation well and returned only a pleasant smile and some indefinite gratitude for the kind words.

The other gentlemen went back to sparring with each other for Lady Pomfret's attention as they saw Taverton pull up a chair between Sir Owen and Miss Worthingham. His Grace was posing no direct threat to their collective courtship of the marchioness.

Antonia looked curiously at the duke. He returned her look

with a measuring glance of his own. Leaning forward, he addressed her. "My dear, I wished to confer further on this scheme of yours that we talked over this morning."

Antonia blushed. "I've already confided it to Sir Owen," she said. "I felt that as Miss Longfort's brother, he should know."

"Quite so." The duke nodded ponderously and thumped his stick upon the floor. "The boy might have some ideas."

Sir Owen looked startled on hearing himself referred to as "the boy," but immediately asked, "What sort of ideas do you mean, Your Grace?"

Antonia and Taverton exchanged another look. "You know of your sister's start?" the duke then asked.

"She makes no secret of her, er, infatuation with Lord Thomas Vale, sir."

"And what do you suppose we must do, young fellow, to make them see sense?" the duke demanded.

Antonia hid a smile. "Young fellow" was at least as unexpected a title for Sir Owen as "the boy."

Sir Owen's expression was blank.

"We mean, Sir Owen," Antonia said, "that His Grace and I have decided upon a sensible means of support for Eliza and Vale, but we're at a loss as to how to make them accept it. Eliza will see through any well-meant kindness and demand to live her own life. Lord Thomas has been doing so for years already."

Sir Owen nodded in comprehension. "As I told Miss Worthingham this morning, Your Grace, I've already approached Lord Thomas with sundry ideas for his future. He won't have any of my help."

"Boy's a fool," the duke said, but he looked admiring all the same. "Demmed Taverton pride settled in the twelfth son where it don't belong. I'd give a monkey to see my heir living above a stable."

Antonia knew that Lord Thomas's eldest brother, a wastrel in his middle years, was not the sort to gladden any father's heart.

"What the duke and I have decided to do, Sir Owen," she said with a smile, "is to offer them a stud farm. Lord

Thomas loves horses. Eliza likes them, too. What we are lacking is a way for his pride to allow Lord Thomas to accept this offer.''

Sir Owen furrowed his brow for a moment. Then his eyes lit up. ''What easier? Look about for a place that has been woefully mismanaged, then come to Lord Thomas with stories of horses crying out for his attention. Neighing out, I ought to say. That sort of thing is bound to set well with my tenderhearted sister, too.''

''Blast. We had it settled to offer him my Leicestershire seat,'' the duke grumbled. ''You won't find a better place in the country.''

''Take my advice, sir, since you seem to want it, and have your agents look about for a place that needs those two. That's the only way they'll come over to our way of thinking.''

Antonia looked at Sir Owen with respect. ''You're right, sir. I know that will serve.'' Eyes shining, she turned to the duke. ''It must be a place falling down, Your Grace. Perhaps the stables could be infected with some dread disease; or the wicked overseer could have been beating the young colts. Or—''

''My dear Miss Worthingham, we mustn't descend to melodrama,'' Sir Owen said with a laugh. ''Let us settle for mere mismanagement.''

Taverton had been nodding and looking serious as the young people went over this latest idea. ''You might have something there, young man. I'll set my people on it.''

Antonia sighed in satisfaction. ''I know this will work. And Sir Owen's mama won't be able to complain to see her daughter married to a duke's son and respectably settled in the country.''

''In a place falling down around her ears,'' Sir Owen added with a wicked grin.

''We won't have to tell Lady Longfort that part.''

The Duke of Taverton stood up heavily. ''Well, you youngsters may settle the details of Lady Longfort's comfort. Now, if you will excuse me, young woman, I'm off to try my luck with that charming godmother of yours.''

"He is so very gallant when once one gets past that gruff exterior," Antonia murmured to Sir Owen, gazing with fondness on the duke's retreating back.

"You, Miss Worthingham, are the surprise of the day," Sir Owen returned. "To think of you confronting that old bear in his den. I'm all admiration. But then . . ." He hesitated and shrugged, giving her a knowing look.

But then, what more could he expect from the Lady? Antonia finished his sentence for him in a suddenly gloomy silence. Sir Owen saw her distress and expertly talked her out of it, making no further reference to her supposed smuggling career.

Antonia's unexpected status as one of the season's ornaments, not to mention her plans on Eliza Longfort's account, had made her lose all track of time. With Eliza's happiness safely in the hands of Taverton's men of business, who were looking out a suitably run-down stud farm, Antonia returned her attention to society and, to her surprise, began to enjoy herself enormously.

Merry evenings at balls and routs went by in a whirl. On every occasion, Sir Owen was there to bear her company: to dance with her, to bring her a glass of lemonade, to hold her chair for her as she sat down at some musical soiree to listen to the performers.

Antonia flirted with him to her heart's content. An edge of desperation became discernible in her manner as the days went by, which more than one *tonnish* gossip put down to Miss Worthingham's evidently futile attempts to bring Sir Owen to the point. But in reality, the slight frantic note was simply Antonia's knowledge that the season was fading fast, as was the false Lady's presence in Sir Owen's life. And when Laura left the country, as she soon must, the Lady would be gone forever. Sadness began to tinge Antonia's every emotion as the days went by.

Meanwhile it was springtime in London, and Sir Owen was mightily intrigued by the supposed Lady. Antonia smiled into his eyes on every occasion, willing herself to enjoy his company while she could, missing him already as she looked ahead to the time when he must realize that, whoever the Lady was, she was not Antonia Worthingham.

And as often as she could, she wrote letters down to Kent full of her adventures and demanding, in delicate phrasing, to know exactly what Laura's plans were.

Laura's letters were never clear anymore, being always silly accounts of this shopping trip and that batch of wild strawberry jam laid down, but hidden within the crossed pages of nonsense, Antonia was able to glean that yes, Laura did still plan to elope overseas with Fontanges, and no, they had not yet come by a safe transport.

One day Antonia realized that the next dark of the moon was approaching fast. Sir Owen Longfort would be expecting the Lady to be with her men down in Kent. Antonia smiled to herself and began to lay her plans, for dark of the moon would coincide nicely with a message she had just received from the Duke of Taverton.

"What has you looking so sly, my dear?" Lady Pomfret asked. She and Antonia were sitting in her private boudoir, free, for once, of the presence of gentlemen young or old.

Lady Pomfret had declared a day of rest, and the only signs of masculine admiration in evidence were the common offerings of flowers. As usual, Lady Pomfret had chosen those that would most suit the peach and silver decor of her sanctum, and yellow, pink, and white blooms nodded from strategically placed vases, as Lady Pomfret leafed through a fashion periodical and Antonia scrutinized the almanac.

"And whatever can you be doing with that depressing volume?" her ladyship demanded. "I always call it fatiguing to dwell upon the passing of the days. Are you perhaps thinking of a new crop for Easton Grange?"

Antonia shook her head and immediately schooled her features into innocence. "By no means, Godmama. I merely ran across this volume in your library, and I thought it would amuse me."

"And it seems to have done so. Why?"

Antonia hesitated. She could hardly say that she was busy making certain the dates she had in mind for fooling Sir Owen were correct. "I was thinking of making a short trip," she confided.

"A trip? You aren't one for staying at home, are you, Antonia? Where must you go this time, and to see what aged former retainer?"

Having been about to offer that very excuse, Antonia was naturally a little miffed when Lady Pomfret saw through her so quickly. "If you wish the truth, Godmama dear, I'm worried about Eliza," she said. This was true enough. How much would she have to confide?

"Eliza Longfort. I see." Lady Pomfret looked wise and waited.

Antonia chose her words with care. "You must know, ma'am, that Eliza and I wish to visit St. Albans in Hertfordshire, merely for a flying visit. With our maids to bear us company, it will be most proper."

"St. Albans! What can you young things wish to do in such a poky place?"

"I—I assure you it's most proper," Antonia said, hating her own evasiveness, yet not knowing how else to carry her point. She couldn't talk about her schemes with the Duke of Taverton until she was certain they would work.

"I am not your guardian, child, nor do I control your movements. Since you are underage, though, you must consult Messrs. Whatever and Failing as you did when you went down to Eton that other time."

"Oh, thank you, ma'am." And Antonia, radiant with the ease of her plot thus far, went off to compose a letter to her trustees and to her old governess.

It happened that Mademoiselle Bluet had recently written that she wished to accept Laura's invitation to spend a week at Easton Grange. Mademoiselle had wished for Antonia to accompany her. Antonia wrote to suggest the exact days for the trip, but managed to avoid saying definitely that she would be going herself.

The plot was coming together famously. It remained to hint Sir Owen into an awareness of her intention. This was not difficult. At the play that very evening, Sir Owen presented himself at Lady Pomfret's box in the interval and, having elbowed his way with care through the press of older gentlemen already collected in the box, he sat down beside Miss Worthingham and began to exert his charm.

"May I venture to say how lovely you look tonight, my dear?" he murmured in his most seductive voice. His gray eyes held a glint of humor, but his sincerity was also apparent. "You are a veritable goddess of spring."

Antonia was pleased that he had noticed her new gown of soft green sarcenet with blue velvet violets trimming the shoulders and scattered about the skirt. Her short sleeves were slashed to reveal the same blue velvet, and pearls were scattered through her unbound hair in careful disarray. She managed to laugh as though she were Laura. He must never guess that his compliments, instead of meaning nothing to her as they would to any fashionable beauty, were being treasured up in her heart forever. "I'll have to become a goddess of summer before long, sir. How quickly the time is passing." She paused significantly. "It seems only yesterday that the moon was full."

"The moon?" Sir Owen flashed her a look of instant awareness. "Why, yes. Now it's almost dark again, to be sure. How difficult for you, my dear Miss Worthingham. I would wager you must be planning a trip out of town in the near future. To Windsor, perhaps?" He grinned.

Antonia looked severe. "I have no plans to go out of town, sir, I assure you." She tried to look startled and slightly guilty; that ought to arouse his suspicions that she would be flying out of town as quickly as possible.

"Naturally not," Sir Owen said with a bow, and he began to make amusing comments on the theater crowd and the performance. His words were everything most proper and most conventional.

Antonia sat contentedly beside him, looking as proper and conventional as he was even while her mind worked busily at the details of her trip to St. Albans. Sir Owen would probably set people to watching Lady Pomfret's house. Well, he would see a carriage leave for Kent. The trip to St. Albans was simple enough. What luck that the Duke of Taverton had sent her that message! She felt herself growing more excited by the moment at the thought of the little cloak-and-dagger business of getting out of town. She had never done any such thing before. It would be great fun.

She glanced at Sir Owen, and he smiled at her, a smile eloquent of his happiness at being with her. Antonia could not help wishing, in a confused way, that all could be open and honest between them. Even though that honesty would mean the end of his admiration.

16

Sir Owen Longfort reached the crossroads near Easton Grange in Kent on a beautiful spring evening just at sunset. As he watched the red ball descend below the hills to the west, he could hear the roar of the sea behind him. Contentment welled up within him.

This very evening, he was sure, would see the end of Antonia Worthingham's smuggling career. Though sensible of a touch of regret that the Lady's time was ending, Sir Owen was happy. He had a much more vital role prepared for Miss Worthingham, and smuggling did not fit into it.

He was determined that, whatever happened, no harm should come to her. She would not be held up to public disgrace, nor would her men be hauled before the magistrate. He would simply put a stop to the game. And if she were caught by another than himself, a riding officer perhaps? He would somehow see that she went free.

Lord Hambrey, his host for the next few days, had previously received with skepticism the notion that the Lady's Gentlemen were not responsible for landing the spies. "We have the one Frenchie ready to swear to it, remember," he had written in his most severe style. But Sir Owen was certain that whatever else Antonia might be, she was no liar, and that the French spy was untruthful himself or simply mistaken. One thing Sir Owen intended to do while he was down in Kent was to interview this Frenchman himself. The prisoner was being temporarily held in custody at Lord Hambrey's estate.

Sir Owen turned aside from the road into a stand of trees just as Antonia's hired post chaise rattled by and went off down the lane to Easton Grange. The baronet headed for Ham Hall and a meeting with Lord Hambrey before the night's work commenced.

He would have been mightily surprised had he been present when the occupants of the hired coach were set down at the door of Easton Grange, for he had been certain that he was following Antonia and her old governess. Mademoiselle Bluet did indeed descend at journey's end, assisted by Charles, Lady Pomfret's youngest footman.

But though the carriage door remained open for some time, no younger lady appeared in its opening.

Hours later on that same evening, Sir Owen, decked all in black with his face professionally darkened with soot, not merely masked with a silk scarf as he had done on the last occasion, prowled the handy vantage point above the cove, which he was convinced, from his study of the area and his study of the Gentlemen's habits, that the smugglers must surely use this time. The spot was about a mile distant from the place where he had been hit on the head on that other night, the night he had first seen Antonia.

Smugglers, he had reason to know, changed the exact locale of their landing every time, and a combination of logic and elimination as well as a report from a man he had posted in the area had led him to select this spot. The night was not only moonless but cloudy; no free trader could resist such conditions.

And sure enough, the lapping of the waves eventually sounded louder to Sir Owen's ears, as though oars were being laid to water. He waited, holding his breath, and somewhat to his own surprise was rewarded: a line of dark shapes, each burdened with another, rounder shape, climbed up the track from the cove.

Sir Owen was well concealed in the hollow he had discovered earlier between two rocks. He looked out at the passing Gentlemen, wondering how soon they would be able to unburden their backs and shift their load to pack ponies. Or would they simply carry the contraband overland to its hiding place? That was not unheard of, though it was much more common for the farmers of the district to find, come morning, that their horses had been borrowed and now stood winded in the stalls, as often as not alongside a token payment of brandy or tobacco.

The baronet held his breath as a light feminine laugh floated to him on the night air. Antonia! And the next thing he knew, he saw her in the shadows, the last to emerge from the cliffside track. An uncommonly fine figure outlined by the wind's whipping of a black dress; a flash of some precious stone on the bosom; the Lady!

"That went off smoothly, Jack," a woman's soft voice said. "Too smoothly. Do you take care."

"Aye, ma'am," whispered a gruff dark figure beside the female. "Godspeed you, ma'am."

Sir Owen was puzzled by this comment. Was the Lady parting from her Gentlemen? Did Antonia really mean to give up the smuggling game? And what was amiss with her voice?

Then he saw something that interested him more than any question about the Lady's possible motives. The hulking shape called Jack lumbered off after his cronies, leaving the Lady alone at the top of the cliff.

Now was the moment Sir Owen had been waiting for. He was unwinding himself from his cramped hiding place, all set to approach Antonia and tell her she had been caught out, when something happened. A few stars came out from behind a cloud. The Lady took off a scarf and shook out her hair in the wind, laughing softly as she looked out to sea and ran her fingers over her head.

The hair was only a shadow, to be sure. But Sir Owen could tell without a doubt that this Lady had tight ringlets, not floating soft tresses.

This discovery led him to a closer scrutiny of the Lady's figure, her height, her carriage . . . and to surprising conclusions.

*   *   *

The next morning Barrows, the butler at Easton Grange, opened the door to Sir Owen Longfort. The baronet stood smiling brightly, his hat in his hand.

"Is Miss Worthingham in?" he asked. "I bring greetings for her from her London connections."

Barrows grunted and made a motion with his head that Sir Owen interpreted as "This way, sir."

In the morning room sat Laura Worthingham and a very small female whom Sir Owen recognized at once as Mademoiselle Bluet, the former governess he had met at Eton. The ladies were busy at needlework, looking innocent as two lambs.

"Why, Sir Owen," said Miss Worthingham, holding out her hand. "It *is* Sir Owen, is it not? I'm so wretched at names. What a pleasant surprise."

He greeted her in his most gallant manner, all the while cataloging her looks from the raven ringlets, arranged casually in a ribbon, to the slippered feet. She was a beauty, there was no doubt about it. Her face was entrancing, her figure spectacular, and not the least of her attractions was the sparkle in her eye, the sense that she was being barely held back from violent action of some kind. Animal spirits sang out in Miss Worthingham. Yet Sir Owen knew that fifteen minutes after leaving her, he would have forgotten the precise details of her lovely face, simply because it was not the face he loved.

"A surprise indeed, Sir Owen," a heavily accented voice remarked from the other side of the room.

Sir Owen was recalled to his social duties. He hoped that his scrutiny of Laura Worthingham would pass for simple admiration. Most men must approach her with the mooncalf stare he had hoped would excuse his careful measuring of each detail of her appearance.

"Mademoiselle Bluet, I am most happy to see you again," he said with a bow. He had seen the governess and Antonia mount up into a coach in Curzon Street and had known where they were heading, but he acted completely shocked to meet her. "You have a holiday, evidently, from your boys at school?"

"A small visit I make, merely to see how my Laure goes on," Mademoiselle Bluet said with severity. "The boys, of course they are watched over by my good friend Mrs. Black. And you are here for what?"

"Merely passing through the neighborhood, ma'am, and I had to stop to say how do you do." He looked around the room as if puzzled. "How very odd. I did expect to find Miss Antonia here. Perhaps I misunderstood something she said in London."

"Perhaps you did." Miss Worthingham gave him a penetrating look from the large violet eyes that had inspsired many a man to poetry of the very worst sort.

At this moment Barrows appeared at the door again, boomed out, "The Simpkins ladies," and lumbered away.

The two most gossip-prone spinsters in the neighborhood fluttered in and made a great show of greeting their dear Miss Worthingham, Mademoiselle Bluet, whom they remembered very well, and—why, Sir Owen! What a delightful surprise to see Sir Owen!

Sir Owen wondered at the speed of country gossip, and also at the spinster ladies' resources. Had they been crouching behind the bushes to watch him come in through the gates of Easton Grange? He spent the next moments in a positive cloud of matchmaking innuendoes. Evidently the elderly Simpkins sisters took his sudden visit to Kent as the most meaningful sort of compliment to Laura Worthingham.

While Miss Worthingham twinkled at him from across the room, apparently enjoying his awkward position, and Mademoiselle Bluet exchanged pleasantries with Miss Simpkins, Sir Owen found himself locked in deadly conversation with Miss Cecilia Simpkins, who thought his sudden appearance in the neighborhood the most romantical thing in the world.

"You are quite like a knight of old, sir," said Miss Cecilia with a sigh and a hand on her heart. "I don't mind telling you, Sir Owen, for I know that you are too much the gentleman to be insulted, that the neighborhood once expected unbelievably great things for Miss Worthingham."

"Indeed?" Sir Owen held back a yawn with difficulty. His observations of Miss Worthingham completed to his satisfaction, he was now wondering if the proper length of time for a morning call was not already past.

"Oh, yes. My sister and I wouldn't have been surprised to see her snare a royal duke during her season. But you see it is all working out for the best. Evidently dear Miss Worthingham was but waiting for the right man." A meaningful leer from behind an antiquated lorgnette completed this observation. After a pause, the lady added, "Where were you, sir, during Miss Worthingham's season? Called away to your estates, no doubt."

"I believe I was in town," Sir Owen said. "And though I can't recall the occasion, I suppose I must have met Miss Worthingham at that time."

Miss Cecilia was visibly astonished at this sort of casual attitude in an ardent lover.

Sir Owen hid a smile, wondering whether he ought to have furnished fuel for the Kentish gossip-mills by rhapsodizing over the stunning impression Miss Laura Worthingham had made on him so many years ago. And then what would have happened to delay his suit by seven years? He could spin a tale of terrible machinations of some villain who had kept him and Laura apart. That would please Miss Cecilia.

He decided not to bother. He suspected, at any rate, that there was a man on Miss Worthingham's mind, and if she were interested in some fellow, the gossips would eventually be satisfied. Laura Worthingham had barely glanced at his worthy self; yet a suspicious sparkle in her eyes, a certain faraway look accompanied by a high color, made it clear to anyone who cared to look that she was deep in somebody's spell.

Sir Owen got up to take his leave as soon as it was decent, much hampered in this project by Barrows, who carried in a tray of refreshments and thus rendered it impossible for anyone to escape the room without at least a token chunk of seedcake and diminutive glass of wine. But at last the baronet went on his way back to Lord Hambrey's.

Laura Worthingham waited until the room had been cleared of the Simpkins sisters before turning to her companion. "Well, Miss Cornflower," she said, using the name Antonia and she had been wont to call their governess in the old days, "what do you suppose that was all about? Not the Simpkinses' visit, Sir Owen's."

"He will have her," Mademoiselle Bluet pronounced, setting a stitch in the pair of boys' breeches she was working.

Laura considered these cryptic words for some moments before she spoke. "I hope you are right, indeed I do. Antonia needs someone. But tell me, mademoiselle, do you think he's still fooled? Does he still think Antonia is . . . you know?"

"We must pray that it is so, Mademoiselle Laure," the small Frenchwoman said. "You did tell me he would visit, and that he would be shocked not to see her. But I think, *ma chère*, that he wasn't as surprised as you thought he would be not to see Antonia here."

Laura's eyes were keen. "Did you get that impression? So did I. I wonder what he knows. But it's no matter. We've done all we can to confuse him, and Sir Owen may suspect all he wants." A touch of melancholy softened her features. "I've made my last run."

His host had not yet seen Sir Owen that morning and beckoned him into the library when they met in the gallery of Ham Hall.

"Well, my boy." Lord Hambrey settled behind his desk and motioned Sir Owen to a plush-covered armchair across from it. "Did you see what you meant to last night?"

"Yes and no." Sir Owen grinned.

"But you're pleased about it, to all appearances. Land another French spy, did they?"

Sir Owens shook his head. "From what I could see, nothing of the kind occurred, though naturally we can't rule it out. One of the landsmen hauling a keg could have been a French spy on his way in. Anything is possible." A smile played about his lips. "I never spoke truer words. Anything is indeed possible, my lord."

Lord Hambrey scrutinized the younger man with suspicion.

"Whatever you did see has set you up enormously. It was the Lady, I suppose. Has she taken to running in the goods unclothed?"

The men laughed together at this thought, and Sir Owen told of seeing the Lady's silhouette, of the shadows of men hauling kegs on their backs, and everything save his suspicions.

He would swear now that Antonia Worthingham was not the Lady. He was pretty certain that her sister was, and that the two Worthinghams had been running a rig on him designed to ensure Laura Worthingham's safety.

The thought didn't enrage him in the least. He remembered his brazen accusations to Antonia Worthingham, his initial refusal to believe her denials, his insolent stealing of kisses. He deserved what she had done to him, and more. And what had she done? Merely played along with the opinion he had formed all by himself, aided by one glimpse of Antonia's face when he had been the next thing to unconscious.

Suddenly he could not wait to get back to London. Interviewing the captured Frenchman was anticlimactic, though now that Sir Owen as good as knew Laura Worthingham was the Lady, all previous opinions he had formed of the Lady's patriotism were invalid. What did he know about Antonia's sister? Nothing encouraging. Laura Worthingham might be in the business of landing ten spies per week for all Sir Owen could tell to the contrary.

To the outmoded dungeons of Ham Hall, Sir Owen and Lord Hambrey went as soon as they finished a comfortable luncheon with Lady Hambrey in her morning room.

The Frenchman was housed under guard of a couple of Lord Hambrey's staff behind the picturesque gothic dungeon. The Iron Maiden and sundry other frightening implements used or at least purchased by Lord Hambrey's ancestors had long been cleaned of cobwebs and prominently placed. They now made a good scare for lady houseguests.

In a small, secret room behind this frightening display, Lord Hambrey and Sir Owen found a wiry, dark young man glaring over a book.

"I lent him my Molière, but the chap won't cheer up," Lord Hambrey muttered into Sir Owen's ear.

The Frenchman looked up in evident disgust.

"This is Sir Owen Longfort," Lord Hambrey said. "Please do tell him what you've told me about your reasons for being in England. I would introduce you, Longfort," Hambrey went on, "but this fellow won't out with his name."

The young man smiled slyly; or perhaps it was not slyness, but merely the only smile his narrow, ill-tempered face could manage. "A stupidity, would it not be, for me to disclose my name to you, good sirs?" he said in moderately accented French. He closed his book, marking the place with a dirty playing card.

"You make a good point," Sir Owen said. "Well, man, out with your story. Why are you here?"

"I land to go to London, to live as an émigré while I find out what my people wish to know and relay the information back through these channels. The *contrabandeurs* of this coast, they are most efficient. We exchange much information," said the man without hesitation. "But you see my problem, good sirs. I have done nothing, and here I am held prisoner. I walked up out of the water and was taken. And I have the so-vivid memory of the last man we landed, who was killed by your officers."

Sir Owen and Hambrey exchanged glances. They had heard nothing of such a case.

"Do you see what I mean, Longfort?" Lord Hambrey said, shaking his head. "He comes out with the story we want to hear. Then there's that other nonsense. No one around here has seen, let alone killed, another spy in recent months. Suspicious, I call it."

"Monsieur knows best," said the Frenchman with a half bow. "We know our man disappeared without a trace."

"He can give you places and dates, too, for our local smugglers. No names; no one hereabouts has names, for the secret has been too well guarded over the centuries. I'm fed to the teeth with the man," Lord Hambrey said.

"You do seem to be a convenient prisoner," Sir Owen

told the Frenchman. "What is your true mission, I wonder? Can you really have sacrificed yourself merely to incriminate the local Gentlemen?"

The prisoner shrugged, removed the playing card with a flourish, and went on with his reading.

Sir Owen could now understand Lord Hambrey's frustration. The two men walked back to the upper reaches of Ham Hall, grumbling in unison over the spy's deuced coolness of head. "He's probably looking for his fellows to spring him from this trap. Well, they'll catch cold at that," Lord Hambrey said. "The old place is tight as a drum."

"I believe he's lying," said Sir Owen. "About being landed by the local free traders, I mean."

Lord Hambrey shrugged. "Yes, the story comes tripping too easily off of his tongue. Perhaps someday we'll find that out. Meantime, if we catch a smuggler in the act, it's treason we must charge him with, thanks to this fellow's testimony." He heaved a heavy sigh. "If you can call it testimony when a Frenchie tells you what he wants you to know."

To Lady Hambrey's disappointment, Sir Owen wouldn't even stay for dinner that evening but rode off into the night in a manner she called most quixotic and dangerous. He was in London, though, by next morning, and by early afternoon, with the help of a short sleep, a bath, and a change of clothes, was feeling fresh and ready to do battle.

Miss Worthingham wasn't to be found in Curzon Street. She had gone on a short trip to St. Albans, Lady Pomfret said.

Sir Owen wondered how St. Albans fit into all of this. He had definitely seen Antonia get into the very carriage that he had followed down to Kent. At which point had she managed to descend from it and go elsewhere? And why had she gone? He realized that he had been counting upon finding her in town.

Another surprise greeted him at dinner that evening when his mother informed him that Eliza was gone on a short journey with Antonia Worthingham.

"Over to St. Albans, they said, and I gathered that it was

to see some old servant of Antonia's. I believe it is a pretty enough place for Hertfordshire, but they are missing so many delightful invitations.''

''Quite so,'' her son said in a grim voice.

''I do hope you aren't angry with Eliza for going off without your permission,'' his mother rallied him. ''She is no longer under your guardianship, after all, and she did get my leave.''

''Eliza will do as she pleases.'' And Sir Owen applied himself to his dinner, wondering if his sister and Antonia Worthingham between them would drive him into bedlam, or if perchance they already had.

A day went by without a sign of the young ladies, and then suddenly they returned. Sir Owen walked into his drawing room in Mount Street and found Eliza sitting on the sofa.

''Aren't you going to ask me how I do, Owen?'' Eliza said with a coy look.

''Or where you've been, perchance?'' Her brother flung himself into a chair across from her. ''Mama told me some faradiddle about a visit to Hertfordshire to see Miss Worthingham's old servant.''

''Oh, so you know that was false, do you?'' Eliza looked at him carefully. ''What else do you know?''

''Nothing, Sister.'' Sir Owen had no patience with any roundaboutness on this subject. ''Tell on.''

Eliza smiled. ''Antonia and I went on this journey, with our maids, of course, to see a place the Duke of Taverton has had left on his hands. It's a stud farm, Owen. The most dreadful place you can imagine.''

''I didn't know you thought that badly of stud farms,'' Sir Owen said, beginning to see the light. ''And why visit one in that case?''

''You don't understand, Brother. This place has been woefully mismanaged. The duke is at his wit's end to see the place come about, for the steward he's placed there is not having any luck at all.'' Eliza paused. ''His Grace has asked for my help, Owen. He wishes me to convince Thomas to take over this farm, and after seeing it and the poor horses, I can't do less.''

Her brother immediately saw the reason for the young ladies' trip. He admired Antonia for being able to arrange the thing, and at the same time to convince him that she was on her way to Kent. How had she done it? He mulled this question over for a moment. "Tell me," he said, a smile slowly coming to his countenance, "did Miss Worthingham meet you at Hyde Park Corner?"

"I did think that rather strange," Eliza said with a shrug. "She and her maid simply appeared in the street and got into the carriage. But Antonia had some perfectly logical excuse for her action, though I called it downright folly for her to be out in the streets where any vehicle could have run her down."

"I would imagine she always does have a logical reason," said Sir Owen. When he had followed Antonia's coach out of London, there had been one confusing moment near Hyde Park Corner when he had lost sight of it. She was a clever girl, Lady or not. "And so Miss Worthingham is back in Curzon Street," he added.

Eliza smiled. "You must wish to see her at once. Please don't bungle this, dear Owen. She would be so very good for you."

Sir Owen didn't dignify this with an answer. He was loath to admit to his female relations that he had any designs upon Miss Worthingham. He was eager to see her, though, and to hear what story she would tell.

17

Antonia, feeling very much the sophisticated woman of mystery, arrayed herself in her best morning gown for Sir Owen's call. She expected he would come to see her the very next day after she and Eliza arrived home from St. Albans.

Though she had known in her heart that he would visit, and soon, when he actually did arrive at her godmother's doorstep at the expected hour, she was a bit unsettled. It was always so odd to have one's plans work out perfectly, and many of Antonia's plans had been coming off to admiration in the last days.

There was that audacious switch from her own to Eliza's coach in the bustle of Hyde Park Corner; how marvelously that had been done thanks to the aid of Charles, her old friend the footman. He had cleared a path for Antonia and the terrified Steelman right through the worst traffic in London, then returned to the hired post chaise to escort Mademoiselle Bluet to Kent.

And the visit to the stud farm had done its work well, quite as Sir Owen had predicted it would. Eliza was now the determined champion of some large-eyed and appealingly distressed horses, and would surely convince Vale to accept the farm from his father.

Antonia had received a heartening letter from Laura that morning that did not say a great deal, as usual with Laura's recent missives, but did manage to communicate through the patina of country gossip and domestic arts that the smuggling had succeeded as usual and that Jean-Baptiste was much improved. Antonia knew, then, what part she had to play with Sir Owen: the successful smuggler, the audacious Lady who had outwitted the revenue officers yet again.

When Sir Owen was announced, Lady Pomfret, as usual during the morning hours, was sitting surrounded by her superannuated court. Two young men who had been calling upon Antonia were just leaving. Antonia thought the baronet looked askance at her two callers; and, as they were both presentable young men whom she cared not a rush about, she was gratified by the idea that Sir Owen's furrowed brow might betoken jealousy. She settled her jaconet muslin skirts with pleasant feelings of feminine power as he approached her chair.

"Are you not going to ask me about my trip to Kent?" she opened the conversation when he had shaken her hand and sat down close beside her. Her own boldness pleased her.

He was looking at her with an expression she had never seen in his eyes before and was not able to interpret. "Do you wish me to do so? By all means, then. How was your trip to Kent, Miss Worthingham? Though my sister gives me a very different idea of your recent wanderings."

Antonia laughed lightly. "Oh, Eliza is a good friend. She has agreed to stick to that story to spare me trouble."

"I see." Sir Owen favored her with a very knowing smile. "Then Eliza must have visited the stud farm without you, for there is no doubt from her vivid descriptions that she was indeed there."

Antonia was demurely silent.

"You had a successful run, I hope?" Sir Owen said in a very low voice.

Tossing her head, Antonia entered into the spirit of the pretense. "I admit nothing, but might I remind you, sir, that movers of contraband cannot be prosecuted unless they are found with the goods. I merely expected you to quiz me on my activities, and so I beat you to it."

"So that is what you think of me? A quiz and nothing more."

"By no means, sir. I consider you a very clever quiz."
Antonia found she was enjoying what she supposed must be
fashionable banter. By his delighted countenance, Sir Owen
was, too.

He leaned even closer. "Your opinion of me notwith-
standing, you must let me tell you how much I admire you.
I do, you know. Enormously."

"Do you?" Antonia stared into his eyes. If she was not
completely mistaken, such compliments went beyond the line
of drawing-room chatter.

"Most strongly. Knowing what I now do about you,
ma'am, has caused my admiration to flower amazingly."

"Has it?" Antonia said faintly. She thought she caught
a hint of satire in his words. Yet he was looking at her so
tenderly. Well, it made no matter. His words made his
position clear. He admired the Lady, not Antonia.

Suddenly Sir Owen captured her hand and kissed her
fingers quickly, so the others in the room would not see,
though, they all being such nearsighted specimens, there was
probably little such danger.

Antonia shivered in mingled dismay and excitement. More
than anything else, she wished at that moment that she truly
were the Lady.

"What fun," exclaimed Lady Pomfret next day at the
luncheon table, where she was going through the post. "Do
but look, Antonia. A masked ball! The first this season; I
mean to say, the first respectable one. How clever of Lady
Montaigne. What more original way to celebrate dear
Alicia's engagement?"

Antonia accepted the card and looked it over without much
enthusiasm. "I must say I've never heard of a masked
engagement ball."

Lady Pomfret sighed in satisfaction. "Heavens, it's been
years since I went to a party in character. It was at Ranelagh,
I do believe, several years before it closed. A masked ridotto.
I wonder if my dress was carefully put away? I should still
fit into it."

"What did you wear, ma'am?" Antonia asked obediently.

To her mind, there was nothing immediately exciting about the prospect of a masquerade. She had never attended one before, never got herself up in fancy dress at all as it happened. She secretly thought such practices a little silly.

"You need not fear your godmother appearing ridiculous, my dear," said Lady Pomfret, smiling in reminiscence. "My costume was ever so dignified, stately even. I was a Roman matron. Now what shall you dress as?"

"I hardly know, ma'am. What are the common characters? And might I not wear a domino over evening dress instead and avoid the problem?"

Lady Pomfret wagged her finger. "No charge of mine shall appear in a *common* character. No, my dear, you shall not be a shepherdess, or a French lady of the *ancien régime,* or a country lass. And I forbid you to wear a domino, for all that says, dear Antonia, is that a person possesses no originality of mind. Or worse, too much dignity to enter into the spirit of a thing."

"I assure you I have no unbecoming dignity, ma'am," Antonia said with a laugh. "The truth is, I've really no idea what to wear."

"The masquerade is some days away. We will contrive."

As the meal went on, Lady Pomfret continued to discuss her Roman matron ensemble, the proper jewels to wear with it, the most becoming headdress. Her ladyship's excitement began to rub off, a very little, on Antonia.

A thought struck her. "There was a famous smuggler on our coast in Kent," she said casually, pushing her cold lobster salad around on her plate. "In the last century. A female who is said to have stood up to the dreadful Hawkhurst gang and fought to keep honor in the free trade." The more she voiced her thoughts, the more she liked the idea. She would attend the masquerade as her own Great-Aunt Harriet, as a young woman, to be sure. For one night Antonia would truly be the Lady. Immediately she wondered what Sir Owen would think of her audacity.

Lady Pomfret was looking at Antonia narrowly. "And I suppose you have the clothes you need stored down at Easton Grange?"

Antonia stared into a pair of shrewd eyes. She had never even dreamed that her godmother knew anything of the smuggling activities going on in the Worthingham family. Quickly she lowered her own gaze to her lap. How many secrets did she think she was keeping from people who knew everything already?

"I think it's a splendid idea, my dear," Lady Pomfret said after a moment had passed. "You will make a delightful lady smuggler."

No reference was made again to what her ladyship might or might not know about the Worthingham family and the celebrated Lady of the Kentish coast, but Antonia happened to remember that Lady Pomfret and Miss Harriet Worthingham had been bosom-bows in their youth and drew her own conclusions.

Lady Pomfret sent her dresser and Steelman to the attics directly after luncheon to look over her Roman matron attire, and also to see if a certain mourning evening gown from her own young days was still in passable repair.

Antonia found Steelman in her chamber later on, brushing out a beautiful gown of black silk brocade, made tight to the waist with panniers and a draped overskirt trimmed in costly black lace. Brilliants were scattered over the lace. The neckline looked to be scandalously low.

"The very thing for a lady smuggler," said Lady Pomfret, who had accompanied her goddaughter. "How lucky that the gown should be trimmed in lace."

Antonia appreciated the joke, lace being one of the prime articles to be sneaked into the country. "But it's so very tiny," she said in regret, examining the waistline.

"Never fear, ma'am, it ain't that small, and there's a sight of material in the seams we can let out," Steelman contributed.

"Yes. I was a bit smaller than you in my younger days. I'm afraid you must lace yourself rather tightly even when the gown is let out." Lady Pomfret frowned. "I know you modern misses are nearly naked under your gowns, as am I these days, I must confess, except for the merest whisper of stays, but it was not so in my youth. I do hate to think of you spending the evening so rigidly boned.''

"The sacrifice is nothing if the gown can truly be made to fit," Antonia said. "It's so beautiful."

Lady Pomfret laughed and held the creation up to her still-willowy figure. She surveyed her reflection in the glass. "I must say, I wore this gown less for mourning than for the way it became me. It will be so for you, too, Antonia dear. And your hair unbound—this is one occasion when you simply must go with your hair unbound."

"But everyone will know me instantly," Antonia objected, for the style had become her signature over the season.

"Fiddle! Do you suppose that those who count will really be fooled, whatever the disguise? Sir Owen would know you, my girl, if you wore a sack over your head." Lady Pomfret laughed sunnily as Antonia blushed and looked at the carpet. "You will not find it necessary to black your face, I hope, child, though I do seem to remember that such a custom is current among the Gentlemen."

Antonia caught herself on the point of saying that Laura, custom or no custom, had always refused to black her face because of the detrimental effects of soot to the complexion. "I think not, since I'm merely trying to give an idea of the Lady, not ply her trade. I'll simply wear a mask."

Thinking happy thoughts of the masquerade, which was beginning to sound like great fun, and Sir Owen's surprise at her costume, Antonia went off, accompanied by Steelman, to order a gaudy emerald brooch made of paste.

Antonia's mood varied between elation and melancholy. She went about her daily activities with a heavy heart, for she knew that the masquerade, which Lady Pomfret was anticipating with such joy, and which she herself was looking forward to since she had hit upon the Lady as a character, must effectively mark the end of her season.

Many of the *ton* were dispersing already to the country or ordering their bathing dresses and seaside bonnets for Brighton. Antonia's letters to Laura grew increasingly frantic. Sir Owen thought Antonia was the Lady. All would be well if, when she went back to the country, the real Lady's operations had ceased. Laura must leave soon if she really meant to do so.

Laura's missives became more frequent than usual, but told of nothing but neighborhood gossip. Then one day they ceased to arrive. Antonia didn't know what to think, for she had expected to receive some message, some hint that Laura and Fontanges were leaving the country at last.

This new silence could be merely Laura's carelessness as a correspondent. Or it might mean that Antonia would never see her sister again, unless, as Laura had suggested, she married a man who would take her on a voyage to the Americas. Antonia grew positively depressed as she considered this possibility.

She was in this mood of uncertainy, mourning Laura as well as the end of her season—which she viewed, not as a social whirl, but as time spent with Sir Owen Longfort— when she and Steelman walked out one day to purchase various furbelows in black for the masquerade.

"Why the long face, my dear Miss Worthingham?" a jolly voice cried as she and Steelman headed down the pavement of one of the shopping streets. Antonia spied, at the bottom of the stairway to Gray's, the jeweler's, the comfortably overdressed figure of Mr. Daingerfield.

"How do you do, sir?" She summoned up a smile to go with her respectful curtsy.

"I do very well indeed, my dear. And the answer to my question?"

Antonia shrugged. "I suppose I'm a little disheartened, sir, at the thought that my visit with Lady Pomfret is drawing to a close."

"But why must it be so, my dear young woman? She certainly enjoys your company. You do her a world of good."

"No more good than she does me. But I have family responsibilities, sir, calling me back to Kent."

A couple of young men descended the steps of the jeweler's just then, and Antonia realized that she and Daingerfield were very much in the way. The gentleman offered her his arm, and followed by Steelman, they strolled down Sackville Street.

"Are you not going to ask me, Miss Worthingham, what business I had at the jeweler's shop?" Mr. Daingerfield asked in his genial way as they negotiated a corner where a performing monkey was plying his trade to the great confusion of the foot traffic and the delight of some school-room misses.

"It would never have occurred to me, sir, but if you wish to tell me, by all means do so."

Mr. Daingerfield winked at her, and, stopping in the relative shelter of a shop's awning, he took a small box from his pocket and snapped it open.

Antonia gasped. Mr. Daingerfield was so unassuming and approachable a man that she often forgot how obscenely rich he was reputed to be. On a bed of velvet lay a ruby brooch of truly alarming size, surrounded by diamonds.

"Do you like it?" Mr. Daingerfield surveyed the stones dispassionately.

"I—it's quite something," Antonia stated. "I've never seen anything like it."

"Yes. It's for Lady Pomfret," the gentleman confided. "Do you think she'll take it?"

Antonia's eyes opened wide. "Do you mean to say—is this to be a declaration, sir?"

Mr. Daingerfield shrugged. "I have no idea. Her ladyship and I have a most unusual understanding, but there are times in a man's life, Miss Worthingham, when fate must be seized by the throat, as it were. I intend to accompany this offering —which will set off, to a nicety, her newest evening gown of ivory lustring—with a lecture on our advancing years and the simple practical difficulties of visiting in the winter. For a man of my years, one slip on an icy pavement could be disastrous."

Antonia let a giggle escape her at such a reason for matrimony. "I do wish you luck, sir, though I cannot imagine Lady Pomfret married."

"She might enjoy it," Mr. Daingerfield said. "She could

go back to her old style and be Lady Louisa, as she was when I first met her.''

"But you've said you've asked her before.''

"A number of times, my dear, and never to good effect, as you may perceive by my state of single-blessedness.'' With a chuckle, Mr. Daingerfield returned the amazing brooch to the pocket of his dandified coat. "She's looking forward to this masquerade the Montaignes are giving. I intend to ask her there, where she'll be in a good mood.''

"Is that wise, sir? The ruby wouldn't at all match the Roman matron ensemble my godmother is wearing.''

Mr. Daingerfield appeared to puzzle over this for some moments before stating that he would take his chances.

Antonia found herself looking forward to the masquerade even more. Would the night really see the end of Lady Pomfret's independence? Antonia didn't know whether she hoped it would or not. She liked Mr. Daingerfield very well, but she had told him the truth. She couldn't imagine Lady Pomfret married.

18

Lord and Lady Montaigne's great house at Richmond blazed with light and laughter on the night of their daughter's betrothal ball. Alicia, in the character of Diana the Huntress, stood at the head of a sweeping marble staircase beside her fiancé Lord Bentish, he attired as a Greek philosopher. The couple was flanked by the young lady's parents, who had chosen the common route, so disdained by Lady Pomfret, of finding their characters in the *ancien régime* of France.

Lady Pomfret was looking marvelously well in her Roman matron dress, the stola of purple satin a fitting contrast to the gossamer white of the gown. Her white hair was bound up in a classical style with purple ribbon and surmounted by a veil. Mr. Daingerfield, whose dignity, he had confided to Antonia, would not allow him to dress in character, looked mysteriously right standing beside her ladyship in his ordinary vivid evening clothes, a black domino thrown over them.

Antonia was very aware of being dressed in a ridiculous manner, most unlike her true self. On stepping down from the carriage in the Montaignes' front sweep, she had experienced a moment of trepidation until she had time to look about her and see that many of her fellow guests were sporting truly outrageous apparel.

Surely her black gown, décolleté though it was, would cause no stir when Lady Montaigne herself was nearly popping out of her own antique bodice, and a woman across the ballroom, got up as a shepherdess, had actually done so, or so the scandalized whispers went. As for the gentlemen, they ran the gamut from the sobersides in dominoes to a less than modest young man whose bare knobby knees emerged from a classical tunic to less than happy effect.

When they had entered the ballroom, Antonia stood for a moment close beside her elderly companions and looked around. How difficult it was even to begin to find one's friends in this sea of varicolored costumes! There was no use in searching for Eliza's favorite ball gown or even for Sir Owen's blond head. He would surely wear some disguise for this great occasion.

"Antonia, my dear," Lady Pomfret called over the chattering of many voices, "do stay by us. We are going to the card room, but I shall see to it I get a seat near the door so that I may watch you out on the floor. That black does stand out, my dear, at least among the ladies. How right you were to wear it."

Antonia smiled and followed the elderly couple. Despite a display of bosom she would not have tolerated in one of her everyday gowns, and the tight stays that seemed likely to cut her in two if she breathed too deeply, she was pleased with her appearance. The looking glass this evening had shown her an exotic figure clothed all in sumptuous black, eyes glowing with unusual intensity through the slits of a black mask bordered with paste diamonds. The paste emerald brooch glittered on her bosom, looking every bit as real as did Laura's. Antonia was confident that no other lady at the ball possessed such a dramatic and worldly costume as did she.

Her secret feelings of conceit were justified when, before she and her guardians had gotten halfway across the floor, a tall young man garbed as Charles II claimed her hand for the first set of country-dances.

Antonia complied with pleasure, fluttering her black feather fan and doing her best not to flirt. But somehow flirting came quite easily from behind a mask.

* * *

Sir Owen, like Mr. Daingerfield, had elected not to come to the ball in character and wore his usual impeccable evening clothes, covered by a wine-red domino. Now he leaned against a silk-hung wall and shook his head in admiration. Antonia as the Lady! What a spectacle. His glance rested more than once on the splendor of her figure, more exposed than he'd ever seen it in the close-fitting black gown. He did not only admire her audacity.

One of the most appealing aspects of Antonia's gown was its secrecy. Who among the ball goers would remember that old story of a daring Lady smuggler? Sir Owen felt that Antonia had dressed for him alone.

Tonight, when she was dressed as the Lady, would be a most appropriate time to tell her that her game was over, that he knew everything about her and her sister.

"Do you see her, Owen?" asked the porcelain-pretty shepherdess by his side, tugging at his sleeve. "She looks so very original. I wish I had a mind for these things."

Eliza's originality, so vivid in other areas of her life, had certainly failed her on this occasion, Sir Owen had to admit, surveying his sister's commonplace costume. "Perhaps flights of fancy don't run in our family. Look at your brother," he answered, touching his own ordinary domino. "I presume the lady you were referring to is Miss Worthingham? The black-gowned lady?"

"She told me she represents a smuggler from her very own neighborhood down in the country," Eliza informed him, tracing a pattern on the floor with her ribboned crook. "I hope you can get the next dance with dear Antonia. You were so very dilatory about the first one."

"Don't worry, my anxious sister, I plan to monopolize Miss Worthingham this evening. But for now I can only watch her."

"You do have your romantic side, Owen. See you keep it up. And do remember to cast a brotherly eye on me as you promised Mama you would." Lady Longfort had the headache and had not been able to bring herself to attend something so fatiguing as a masquerade.

With an airy laugh, Eliza walked off on the arm of the
Shakespearean who had engaged her for the dance.

It was no unpleasant task to be obliged to keep an eye on
Antonia from afar, Sir Owen considered, watching her go
down the dance with grace and a quiet dignity. How very
lovely she was—how lovable! He must indeed take care to
be beside her when the music stopped. He would bespeak
two dances, he planned, and supper. Then, after he managed
to get her alone, expose her in her lies and ask her the
question he could feel ready to burst from him, it would be
quite proper for them to spend the remainder of the evening
together.

He kept looking at her, wondering if the answer to that
question he was longing to ask would indeed be the yes he
longed to hear. She had surprised him more than once. Was
he only imagining that she felt something for him?

When the set was over, he immediately started toward
Antonia. But due to an ill-placed waiter with a tray of iced
champagne, a fainting female, and a pair of squabbling
newlyweds, Sir Owen found his path to the lady of his choice
disastrously blocked. By the time he approached her, she
was going back to the floor on the arm of a burly Highlander
with hairy legs, and the music was starting up again.

Worse, he saw Lady Cyril Bromley bearing down on him
with a determined tread. Her Cleopatra wig and transparent
gown of pleated linen made her easy to spot in the crowd.
Deftly, Sir Owen turned aside and lost himself in the press
of people. Lady Cyril, he saw when he had reached a safe
vantage point, found a willing partner in an overly painted
Louis XIV.

Sir Owen propped up the wall for the duration of this
dance, too, knowing that at the nearby door to the card room,
that strict Roman matron Lady Pomfret was surveying him
with amused eyes.

Antonia had cast many a glance about the ballroom, but
she had not yet seen Sir Owen. She had glimpsed Eliza, in
a pink and white shepherdess dress, a large leghorn bonnet

topping her golden curls. Eliza had had the first set with a young man Antonia had recognized as Lord Cavenham, but now she was going down the dance with someone garbed as a stable hand. Antonia took a closer look and started. The man's features were masked, but it was Vale, all right. No wonder Eliza looked so smugly satisfied, an expression that even her pink satin mask could not disguise.

The tune of the second country-dance came to an end, and Antonia curtsied to her kilt-clad partner, whom she did not recognize and who seemed to leer down her décolletage in a disconcerting manner. Before he could offer to escort her back to her chair, a tall figure in a dark red domino approached.

"I've found you at last," said the unmistakable voice of Sir Owen Longfort. "You will excuse us, sir? I'll take care of this lady. We have had an engagement to dance this age."

The Highlander went off, looking a bit disgruntled. He was soon seen bowing over the hand of a scantily-clad classical goddess.

"That gentleman finds much to amuse him at an affair of this sort," Sir Owen remarked, smiling at Antonia.

She was grateful that he was looking into her eyes and not at her unusually exposed bosom, as the Scot had spent the dance in doing. "Indeed," she said, determined to find humor in the situation. "I'd wager he won't approach a single domino this evening. Dominoes are such modest garb."

"I collect you refer to my own tasteful attire," Sir Owen said. "Thank you very much. And may I say—my Lady— that you have chosen the cleverest costume in the room? If only the world knew what I know. Yes, it's a famous joke."

"I meant only to be a bit daring," Antonia said, modestly casting down her eyes.

"And so you are. Shall we dance? I can hear the fiddlers striking up."

They moved off onto the floor and were soon lost in the intricacies of a waltz country-dance. Antonia felt herself dreaming as she touched hands, curtsied, and crossed the floor with Sir Owen. If only life could be a dance.

When the tune was over, the first words Sir Owen uttered were to bespeak another set. "And may I take you in to supper?" he asked with a tender look.

"Yes," Antonia said in a dazed way. Was it only the costume of the Lady that entranced him tonight, or did he really wish to be with her as much as she longed to be with him? She could not have planned this situation better even in her dreams.

Another dance flew by, and Antonia felt a peculiar languor invade her limbs whenever she looked at Sir Owen. Her mind was drifting, even as she drifted in the dance, into strange country, and though the terrain confused her mightily, she didn't dislike it at all.

Supper was a merry meal. Antonia and Sir Owen joined Lady Pomfret and Mr. Daingerfield for the procession into the rooms, where a sumptuous repast was laid out on groaning tables. They sat down at a small table for four, and the gentlemen went off in search of forage. Only then did Lady Pomfret begin to question her goddaughter.

"Well, child," she said without preamble, "has he spoken?"

Antonia pretended to misunderstand. "Of course he has, a number of times. I shouldn't at all like a silent dancing partner."

Lady Pomfret sighed. "You know what I mean, my dear, and that you're being evasive gives me to think that perhaps he did. Speak, that is. Never mind, I won't press you for your little secrets."

"But he didn't, ma'am, and I don't believe he will," Antonia stated, not without a touch of sadness.

"Hmmph." Lady Pomfret eyed the young lady with severity. "You haven't done your job, then, my dear."

"Done my job?" Antonia bristled up immediately. She was about to expostulate, to say that naturally she wouldn't be so bold as to force a declaration from an innocent male, when all thoughts of Sir Owen receded. Her eyes focused on the large ruby glittering on Lady Pomfret's Roman stola. "My heavens," Antonia gasped, "you've accepted him."

Lady Pomfret saw where the girl was looking. "Him? Oh,

you've noticed the ruby. Mr. Daingerfield must have confided to you, dear.''

"He did. I confess I was surprised to hear he was contemplating matrimony.''

"Absurd, didn't you think? Well, I soon talked that silly man around,'' Lady Pomfret said comfortably. Her slender fingers caressed the brooch.

"But you're wearing it.''

Lady Pomfret winked. "I've accepted the brooch, child, not the hand that was to have gone with it. My heavens! Can you imagine me married?''

"No, I can't.'' Antonia knew that the rules of society prohibited a lady from accepting an expensive piece of jewelry from a man not her relative or promised bridegroom, but in the case of such an elderly couple, naturally an exception might be made. "He didn't look too disappointed,'' she ventured.

"He wasn't,'' Lady Pomfret said in a satisfied voice. She glanced around the crowded supper room, then leaned forward a trifle to whisper the next words. "I doubt if Mr. Daingerfield, any more than I, would wish to be bound hand and foot by the strictures of matrimony. At our age it would be too shocking.''

"Yet he gave you the ruby.''

"He gave me the ruby, child, as thanks for my practical handling of the situation,'' Lady Pomfret stated, leaning back in her chair and speaking in a normal voice. It was apparent that no one was listening to their conversation; in the buzz of talk that surrounded them, they had all the privacy her drawing room might have afforded them. "Do you know, he was ready to offer simply because of the streets in winter? The jittery man has even known sedan-chair bearers to slip on ice and injure their passengers. I solved that problem neatly. Come winter, Mr. Daingerfield will simply take up residence with me.''

"Without a chaperon?'' Antonia gasped.

"I have every hope of enticing some other young lady to bear me company. Perhaps even you, dear, though in your case I wouldn't suggest such a long engagement that you

would be free to visit me in the winter. The two of you seem
to want each other very badly.''

Antonia turned crimson. "I beg you, Lady Pomfret, Sir
Owen hasn't—I haven't—"

"I shall say no more on that score," Lady Pomfret said.
"But trust me. I shall contrive. Mr. Daingerfield sometimes
grows a little possessive, my dear, but that is only because
of our odd situation. I assure you he was delighted to hear
of my scheme for the winter months.''

"You've spoken before of your odd situation," Antonia
said. "What is it, exactly? Not that you must tell me, but—"

"But you're curious. It is simply this. Lord Pomfret left
me without a feather to fly with, and I have many expenses,
what with my gaming. As you know, Mr. Daingerfield is
the richest man in town. He's been franking me, my dear,
for more years than I care to count.''

"What a generous man he is! And you've accepted his—"
Antonia cut herself off just in time. She had nearly uttered
the dread word "charity.''

Lady Pomfret winked. "You must not think he has lacked
for what vulgar minds might call compensation of a sort,
my child.''

Antonia could hardly form her next awed question. "Do
you mean to say, ma'am, that you're his—"

Lady Pomfret held up a white-gloved hand in protest. "My
very dear girl. Never let it be said that I shocked a young
lady under my care with any disclosures of a private nature.''

Antonia nodded, looking at Lady Pomfret with new eyes.
That was nothing to compare to the scrutiny to which she
subjected Mr. Daingerfield, once that gentleman returned
to the table, looking as respectable as he ever had and as
little like a rake. Antonia was forced to concede, as she
observed the older couple's fond manners, that there were
many ways to live one's life.

Sir Owen returned, bearing ices for all the party that he
had braved the crush to obtain. A footman followed him,
carrying the plates he had filled with other eatables for
himself and Antonia. "Lady Montaigne, though I love her
dearly, is notoriously mean in her estimation of how many

ices it takes to serve such a gathering," Lady Pomfret said, looking at Sir Owen in admiration. "And nothing sets me up quite so well as an ice these late evenings. Thank you, young man."

Nodding soberly, Sir Owen said, "You've guessed it, ma'am. This isn't my first time at the Montaignes'."

After a general laugh, the four ate the fruit ices in companionable silence broken only by the clinking of spoons on china. They then proceeded with the rest of the meal, chatting amiably about the latest theatrical productions.

They were not yet finished with their wine when Eliza, accompanied by a masked figure only too familiar to Antonia, stopped beside the table.

"Good God," Lady Pomfret said, looking through her eyeglass at Thomas Vale. "At least you didn't wear my livery."

The young man bowed. "I knew, of course, that all my family was invited here, and I had no reason to think I would be barred entry."

"Isn't he too good?" Eliza gazed up at him. "I told Thomas that though I of course detest the fripperies of society as much as he does, it was very sad that we'd never danced together. And so he came this evening. We've danced every dance but the first. I do wish to thank you, Owen, for granting me such freedom tonight. If Mama had been here, I would never have been able to make such a spectacle of myself."

Sir Owen coughed. He had not so much as glanced Eliza's way all the evening, so intent had he been on the pursuit of Antonia and the avoidance of Lady Cyril Bromley.

"We are here to announce our engagement, Sir Owen," Thomas Vale proclaimed. His face under his mask looked a little ruddier than usual. "We thought you should be the first to know, as Eliza's brother. Now we're off to my father."

Antonia clasped her hands. "You're actually going to speak to His Grace?' How wonderful, Lord Thomas."

"The very least I can do, for we'll be business associates in the future," the young man replied. "Eliza has told me of his problems with the Hertfordshire stud farm. I call it infamous that such a manager has been left in place so long. The sooner I get to work on it, the better."

"And that's why we shall be able to marry. We now have the means," Eliza added. She had a slight, private look for Antonia that bespoke thanks as well as conspiracy.

"I did see the duke earlier," Lady Pomfret said. "He's dressed as Henry the Eighth. Oh, there he is, children. At the head table, with the Montaignes."

Eliza and Vale looked a little fearful with the moment upon them.

"Go to it," Sir Owen urged them. "The duke is a formidable man, especially in his current dress, but he won't eat you."

The others at the table also urged the couple on with good-luck wishes.

"My mother will have a spasm," Sir Owen added.

"Perhaps she'll be reconciled. Horse breeding is a respectable occupation," Antonia returned. She looked up at the couple. "Do go on. His Grace will be so happy."

Eliza suddenly clasped Antonia's hand. "My dear, you must go with us."

"I?" Antonia was shocked. "I can't. At such a moment you will want privacy . . ."

"If we wished privacy, we wouldn't be choosing a crowded supper room for the meeting, would we?" Vale put in. "Miss Antonia—dear Miss Worthingham—we should be glad of your company."

"But . . ." Antonia hesitated, and the voices of her tablemates joined in chorus to urge her on.

"Antonia, you know you've been in on this from the beginning," Eliza whispered into her friend's ear. Her shepherdess's hat brushed Antonia's hair.

Casting a glance back at Sir Owen, Antonia accepted Thomas Vale's arm. The three mounted the dais to the head table.

The duke, in fur-trimmed robes and a jeweled hat, was talking to his host. He turned in his chair as if feeling eyes upon him. His gaze fell first on Antonia. He nodded to her.

Then he looked beyond her to Eliza and finally saw his son.

Taverton rose, leaning heavily on his stick. A moment passed.

"Thank you, Miss Worthingham," the duke said.

"I had nothing to do with this, sir," Antonia protested. But nobody paid further attention to her. Thomas Vale extended a hand in his father's direction. Another moment, and a gnarled hand remarkably like in shape and size to the younger man's reached out.

Antonia dashed tears from her eyes. She could swear that the two men were nearly in her state, and Eliza was audibly sniffling as the duke and his son broke from their handclasp and met in a hearty embrace.

The duke turned from this to kiss first Eliza, then Antonia on the forehead. "Now shall we adjourn, children, to a more private place?"

Antonia noticed that most of the guests in the room were staring at the party in evident fascination. She excused herself with smiles and murmurs, and returned to Sir Owen's table.

To the tune of a sudden burst of lively gossip, Taverton and the young couple left the room. Presumably there would be family revelations and expressions of affection in some side chamber.

"Oh, Sir Owen," Antonia said, feeling a tear at the corner of her eye, "don't you feel that everything is working out for the best?"

"Indeed I do, ma'am." Sir Owen surveyed her with a very fond expression. At least, so it looked from behind his black mask.

Lady Pomfret chose this moment to nod forcefully at the baronet. Antonia saw this signal and didn't know which way to look. She very much feared that her ladyship would next poke Sir Owen with her fan, and tell him to get on with his pursuit of Antonia.

"Her ladyship must have been reminding me to ask you for the next dance," Sir Owen said with a smile.

"But that would be too many," Antonia replied. Her voice came out in a sort of squeak, and she silently cursed her lack of self-possesion. But what could be expected when three pairs of amused eyes were gauging her reaction to Sir Owen's bold request?

"Antonia," Lady Pomfret said, "as your adviser and chaperon, I mean to accept for you. Thank you, Sir Owen, my goddaughter would be delighted to dance with you. I trust you have some special reason for exposing her in such a manner? I need not tell you that the patronesses of Almack's, who are all here, would have something to say about such a liberty as three dances taken in their rooms."

"But in a private house, my lady, with your kind permission to guard us, there can be nothing to censure," Sir Owen said. "As to my reason, in my opinion Miss Worthingham and all the young ladies here tonight have more freedom than usual. Who can tell who is really behind any of these masks? Miss Worthingham might be anyone tonight. She isn't tied down to the stultifying pose of the young lady in her first season. And since a third dance is such a harmless thing . . ."

Lady Pomfret let him declaim a little more on the subject before she cut him short, and told the young people to be quick. The musicians could be heard even now, tuning up after the supper break.

Antonia put her black-gloved hand into Sir Owen's with a smile meant to show him her sophistication, her lack of shock at being singled out in such a manner. He thought she would think nothing of a third dance, much as he had once thought she would not be offended by a kiss from a near-stranger.

Well, she would show him that he was perfectly right. The Lady would dare much more than a simple third dance.

19

The third dance turned out to be less than a romantic thrill from Antonia's point of view. The music was delightful, her partner all attention. But as the tune ended, Sir Owen led Antonia immediately to a vacant gilt chair. "Do you know, I think you're a little short of breath," he said in concern. "Will you sit down while I fetch you a cool drink?"

"Thank you." Antonia sank gratefully into the seat, then looked up at him. "I'm afraid the tight lacing this ancient dress requires will be the death of me, sir," she admitted before she realized the intimacy of her words. Mortified, she put a hand over her mouth.

He laughed. "Oh, the mention of stays doesn't embarrass me in the least. I hope you don't wear them as an ordinary thing."

Antonia looked shocked and refused to answer. He laughed at her and went away, promising to return in a nonce.

She soon caught her breath. The stays were not that pinching; that is, they certainly hadn't been before supper. She could bear it very well. Since she didn't commonly wear much boning, the change was simply a little disconcerting. Antonia put her hand on her middle, thinking up more excuses to convince herself that she was really quite comfortable, and wondering how the females of Lady Pomfret's youth could ever have stood it, going about like this every day.

Her chair was in a quiet corner near a set of doors that opened into the Montaignes' formal garden. She breathed in the sweet scents of the night. Perhaps when Sir Owen came back, she could suggest retreating to the garden. No, that would be unbelievably bold.

Suddenly she felt a tight grip on her arm. "Don't scream if you care for your sister's safety," a voice hissed into her ear. "This way."

Antonia found herself being propelled by a large figure in a black domino, out the door and into the garden. She tried to twitch her arm away, but the stranger held it fast. Past privet hedges and rose-covered arches, the man led her, past all the couples who had come out to dally in the pleasure grounds of the suburban estate. Antonia began, not unreasonably, to panic, especially when she realized that she and her captor had left the last of the flirting couples behind them.

The black-clad man stopped finally before a stone bench flanked by two high cedars. He thrust Antonia down. She glared at him.

"You have done well, mademoiselle," he said in that odd soft voice. "Not a peep."

Antonia was struck by a familiar something; this man was not a stranger to her. However, she could not place him. "What have you to do with my sister?"

A low, female laugh sounded somewhere close by, and another figure stepped out of the shadows to stand beside Antonia's captor.

Antonia found that she was able to see quite clearly. The moon was full, and there was a faint glow from those torches placed closer to the house. The second figure threw back the hood of a satin domino.

"Laura," Antonia said without much surprise.

Her sister bent down to hug her. "Wasn't it clever of us to find a way to bid you good-bye?"

The man beside Laura threw back his hood, too, and removed his mask. Antonia recognized Jean-Baptiste de Fontanges. "My word," she said, "you seem to have recovered all your strength, sir." She reached to undo the strings of her black mask, since the time for pretending seemed to be past.

"And the use of my leg," he said with a flashing grin. "Do you not admire, mademoiselle, how I have totally lost the accent when I speak English?"

Antonia nodded politely. She had only seen him in bed before, and speaking with a heavier accent, she told herself. She couldn't be blamed for not recognizing him immediately. Still, she felt foolish.

"Then you're really going, Laura." Rising to her feet, she returned her sister's embrace. "Somehow I thought you'd change your mind."

"Never, my dear. Jean-Baptiste simply cannot be found in England, and, truth to tell, though being the Lady was a good enough adventure for a while, I need something more to test my talents."

Antonia looked into Laura's shining eyes and could tell that her newest adventure had already begun. A furtive ride to London from Kent was already behind her and Jean-Baptiste, no doubt, and the fleeing pair would not feel safe until they touched American soil. Antonia couldn't help wondering if, when they did, Laura would need something else to capture her imagination. Perhaps, Antonia considered with a smile, there were gangs of smugglers in America crying out for a firm hand.

"What do you mean to do now?" she asked.

"We've been here for an hour or more," Laura said, "and it was quite amusing to dance in society again after all these years."

"And for myself," Jean-Baptiste added, "my first time in an English ballroom. My last, too."

"I can hardly believe it!" Antonia said in awe.

"Oh, Antonia, who would notice two dominoes in this crowd? It isn't as though we haven't proper manners. We did decide not to go in to supper, though, for several of the guests were unmasking." Laura laughed. "And as to your question, love, we plan to go now to the docks, where my friend's ship is waiting, and board this very night under cover of darkness. Odd, isn't it, that we should end up on a ship setting out from London? I thought it a very lucky thing that we had this chance to bid you farewell.''

"Yes." Antonia was dazzled by her sister's flow of talk. "But, oh, Laura, it's so sad to see you go at last."

Behind them, a man cleared his throat. "I hate to interrupt this touching scene," said an all too familiar voice. "But I believe I have business with all of you."

"Sir Owen!" Antonia whirled about and confronted the man in the dark red domino. He had removed his mask and his hood, and the expression in his eyes was confusing. He looked excited, yet sad and somehow resigned.

Though she felt he must know more than he should, Antonia did her best to save the situation. "These are friends of mine. They were just about to return to the party. Should we all go together?" Laura and Jean-Baptiste, she was certain, would be able to slip away if the four began a sedate promenade back to the ballroom.

Sir Owen looked at her, then at her two companions, and slowly shook his head. "I wouldn't advise a sudden flight, good people."

Laura laughed. She had pulled the hood of her domino up the instant Sir Owen made himself known, but now she threw it back, exposing her prettily coiffed head of black curls, her enchanting face, her feverishly sparkling eyes.

"Well met, Sir Owen. It seems but yesterday that I saw you down in Kent. Dark of the moon, was it not?"

Antonia caught her breath. If Laura would but hold her tongue until she and Jean-Baptiste could get away, all might yet be well. Desperately, Antonia gave Laura a nudge.

Sir Owen was smiling. "Dark of the moon it was indeed, ma'am." He looked up into the sky. "What an odd thing, to be sure, to capture a smuggler at full moon. I do presume correctly, madam? I do address the Lady?"

Laura put her chin up, but said nothing.

"And since the law would demand that a smuggler be caught with the goods so to speak, it would seem I have you at last, Miss Worthingham," Sir Owen continued.

"The goods?" Antonia burst out. "My sister has done nothing—has nothing with her—"

"This gentleman here." Sir Owen nodded toward Jean-Baptiste. The Frenchman had also tossed back his hood, and his dark eyes were burning angrily. But he made no move to run as he might have done, and Antonia thought the better of him for not abandoning Laura. "When the message was brought to me only moments ago," Sir Owen went on, "that the man I've had watched for weeks had turned up at this very ball, and with the elder Miss Worthingham at his side, I hesitated to believe the evidence. Yet here you are." He turned from the pair to Antonia. "I'm sorry you had to find out this way, my dear. Your sister isn't only the Lady. She's been using her gang to ferry in spies from the Continent."

Antonia was with difficulty getting used to the fact that Sir Owen knew that *she* was not the Lady in question. Had he always known? "Sir, that is completely false," she said stoutly. "My sister would no more bring in spies than you would."

"Then who is this gentleman, who I'd dare swear speaks with a charming Gallic accent? And why has she spirited him to London, even got him into society this evening?" Sir Owen was imperturbable.

Laura's laugh rang out again. A shrill edge to the sound made Antonia flinch. "My dear sir, how clever you make me sound. But I assure you, I do not bring in spies. None of our people do."

"Laura," whispered Antonia angrily. This was as good as a confession.

"My fiancée speaks the truth," Jean-Baptiste put in at this juncture, his tones deep and rumbling. His accent was as thick as it had been in Kent, probably the effect of the excitement.

"Fiancée?" Sir Owen looked puzzled.

"This is all quite simple, you depressing man, if you would but lose your prejudices for the merest moment and see things as they are," Antonia snapped. Once out, the words astonished her. She put her fingers to her mouth and stared, stricken, into Sir Owen's eyes. The laughter lurking there reassured her.

"Please do explain, one of you," he said. "Never let it

be said of Sir Owen Longfort that he wouldn't take the time to listen.''

"Allow me," Laura spoke up. "This man is French, true enough, but he hasn't done any spying."

"And what is he doing here, fresh from France, if not spying?" Sir Owen demanded.

Antonia took a deep breath, stepped from Laura's side to that of Sir Owen, and spoke carefully. "To begin with, sir, you accuse my sister falsely. She is not the Lady. I am."

Three incredulous gazes rested on her. "Antonia!" Laura cried.

Antonia was looking proudly at Sir Owen, her back straight, her chin lifted. "Don't be shocked, Sister," she said. "I never wanted you to know, but I can't let you stand falsely accused."

"Can't you, by God?" Sir Owen said with a laugh. "You're magnificent, my dear."

In that moment, Antonia felt as she believed Laura must have felt during her time as the Lady: regal, unashamed, with generations of tradition backing her . . . a legend in the flesh. "I am ready to take my punishment," she said softly, and realized, in a sort of amazement, that she was.

"This is ridiculous," Laura broke in. "I am the Lady, sir. My sister is trying to protect me for whatever henwitted notion."

Sir Owen looked from one Worthingham to the other. "This is something new in my experience. For months I've had my eye on one elusive Lady. Now a veritable feast is set before me. Am I to choose which one I prefer?"

"No need for that," Antonia said with a warning glance at her sister. "I am the Lady. You've known for months; you've done nothing but quiz me about my true identity. Why, even tonight—"

Sir Owen's raised palm brought an effective halt to Antonia's words. "My dear, I asked a question of the Lady. Either Lady may answer it. Who is this man? I noticed he is loyal enough to stay by you when he might have fled long since while we've been arguing." He turned to the

Frenchman. "Perhaps, sir, it is best if I simply ask you."

Jean-Baptiste laughed in what Antonia thought was a nervous manner. "At your service, Sir Owen. So you have had me watched, have you? The cottage in the woods, it is known to you?"

Sir Owen nodded.

"Then you will know that no spying has taken place; that I have received only the visits of Miss Laura Worthingham, who is my love." He gave Laura a besotted glance that neatly confirmed the last assertion.

"Is she not another spy, conveying messages for you to your superiors?" Sir Owen snapped.

"Sir!" Laura looked daggers at the baronet.

Jean-Baptiste put his arm around her and murmured, *"Ma chère,* let me go on."

Laura nodded, but she continued to look stormy.

"I was landed to spy, yes," Jean-Baptiste said. "But I have not done so. I was injured grievously in the landing—you would know that, if you have been watching. My comrades gave me up for dead; they didn't even try to save me. As it happens, I was rescued by a party of your Gentlemen and one lady. They carried me to safety, she watched over me like the angel she is, and she and I fell in love."

"Most touching," interjected Sir Owen, "but you've no proof this is so."

"Proof must I have? I can tell you this: the landings of the French on your coast of Kent have been carefully plotted to ensure that the smugglers are blamed. To draw the attention of the officials to them while French landings go on undisturbed. Have you not captured a French spy only lately?"

Sir Owen nodded, thinking of the insolent and nameless prisoner in Lord Hambrey's dungeon room.

"And let me guess. Has he not told you he was landed by the free traders?"

"It is so."

Jean-Baptiste laughed. "This I know, for that man was to have been me. When I was forgotten so easily by my fellows during the landing, then I decided not to trust them further with my life. The plan, you see, is for the man to be liberated by our connections on land.''

Antonia drew in her breath sharply.

"Jean-Baptiste," cried out Laura, who had been ominously silent, "you never told me any of this. You said you were to pretend to be an émigré, to spy on London society." She pointed a shaking finger at her betrothed. "You know I swore revenge on the one who maligned me and my men. You—you—"

He shrugged. "What, should I tell you our blackest plans against your comrades and risk losing you? You have every right to your revenge, but so do I have a right to my love. Now," and he seized the hand that was pointing at him and kissed it, "I flatter myself it is too late to lose you. Besides," and there was another Gallic lift of the shoulders, "I decided not to do what I had been told. Why stir up trouble for no reason?"

Laura hesitated for an ominous moment. Antonia wouldn't have been surprised to see her pull out a pistol. Instead Laura made a small furious sound and pulled Jean-Baptiste's head down to hers. Sir Owen and Antonia feigned sudden interest in the dark shapes of the garden foliage.

"My dear sir, can this possibly be true?" Sir Owen finally said when the couple showed signs of returning to reason.

"I swear it on my mother's grave," said the Frenchman.

Antonia plucked at Sir Owen's sleeve. "What are you going to do?" she demanded with a scared look at her sister's glowing face, the eyes burning with excitement. A vision of Laura moldering away in prison, perhaps even executed for treason, rose up to taunt her. "You mustn't . . . you can't. I am the Lady, I tell you."

"My dear Antonia, calm yourself," Sir Owen said. He reached out to touch her hair. "You have so much courage, my dear. But you don't need to spend it all at once."

Antonia looked away, unable to bear the gleam in his eyes and still less able to interpret it.

"What *do* you mean to do, sir?" Laura asked in her clear voice. "You must understand, my betrothed and I were on our way out of the country when you chose to disturb our farewells to my sister. May we continue? We have a ship to catch."

"Do you?" Sir Owen appeared to be thinking hard. He looked at Laura as though he did not see her. "A ship here on the Thames?"

Laura nodded. She and Jean-Baptiste clasped hands, and Sir Owen looked at the entwined fingers in that same abstracted way.

"Where were you going?" he asked finally. "Back to France? To the Indies?"

"We are to change in Portuguese waters to a ship that will take us to Bermuda. From there, we have plans to go elsewhere," Laura said, not quite confiding, Antonia remarked, the exact nature of the ship they were to board. Probably an agreement of secrecy she had with the vessel's captain.

"And where is this ship now?" Sir Owen asked.

"At the West India dock," came the calm reply.

"Well, Miss Worthingham." Sir Owen addressed Laura after another moment of silent deliberation. "What do you say to a compromise of sorts? My duty is clear. I have here a famous smuggler and a French spy. Every finer feeling demands that I turn you both over to the authorities. Yet I know that what you say is true. I've watched you carefully, and I admit, Miss Worthingham, that I've had your letters intercepted. If you had been sending messages on this man's behalf, I would have known about it."

"I sensed I was being watched," Laura said. She exchanged a glance with Antonia.

Sir Owen nodded. "I will escort you and your friend to this ship, see you board, and—forgive me—leave a watch on it so that you will stay there till it weighs anchor. In return, you will swear to me that neither of you have been guilty of any activities traitorous to the British crown."

"I'm ready to swear," Laura said eagerly. "On anything you like. And it will be the truth," she added with a feminine bluntness.

Sir Owen seemed to flinch at the idea that a sworn statement needed to be described as the truth. But he nodded seriously and held out his hand. Laura took it solemnly, then stood aside so Sir Owen could next grasp the hand of Jean-Baptiste, who went even further and kissed Sir Owen on both cheeks to cap his own vow upon the tombs of all his relations.

"And now, my friends, it remains only to escort you to your ship," Sir Owen said, recovering from this assault with a startled look. "As it happens, those who brought me word of your presence here have a coach waiting for me outside the back gate of these grounds. What do you say?"

Laura and Jean-Baptiste conferred in murmurs for an instant. Then, "That will be quite acceptable, sir," Laura said. "Our bags are waiting in a certain spot, also outside the gates. We don't have much." She grinned at Antonia. "A lot of bride clothes my sister gave me, nothing more."

"We'll stop to pick them up," Sir Owen promised. "And now, shall we? You'll wish to make your farewells, ladies."

"Now? Certainly not. I'm coming along," Antonia said, furious that he would actually have thought of leaving her behind.

"But—of course you may." Whatever objection Sir Owen had been about to make was quickly stifled.

Laura took Antonia's arm. "The more time we have together, the better," she said. "This is really an unexpected treat, Antonia. I thought we would have only brief words in the garden, and now we may spend the entire drive to the Isle of Dogs in catching up on news."

True to her word, Laura chattered away during the long drive from Richmond to the East End of London. Antonia could summon up no such cheer. She grew a little weepy as she realized that there could be nothing more final than this: her sister was leaving, and at once.

"Oh, Laura," she said with a sigh, "I'll miss you so much."

"My dear sister, I'll miss you, too." Laura patted Antonia's knee from her seat opposite and quickly began another subject.

The streets they drove through were dark and for the most part silent. Then they came to the docks, where some men toiled all night loading and unloading goods. There was a certain hush about the district even so; workers who would shout and swear in the daylight were quiet now, too tired, perhaps, for argument and exclamation.

The coach pulled up, and Sir Owen descended first and let down the steps. Then the others emerged into the starry summer night.

Antonia looked about her. She could hear the Thames lapping at the pilings of the nearby docks, see the hulking shadows of warehouses and ships, yet her presence here, about to say farewell forever to her closest family member, seemed somehow unreal.

"There she is." Laura pointed to a large vessel out in the harbor. "They will be expecting us."

Sir Owen had turned aside and was conferring with the coachman who had driven them. Antonia assumed that this man was the one who would watch all night to see that Laura and Jean-Baptiste did not decide against leaving the country.

Someone signaled the ship, and a small boat was soon being rowed over to the dock.

"This really is good-bye, my dear," Laura said excitedly, pressing Antonia's hand. "My love to Monty. Remember, tell him the truth as soon as he's old enough." One embrace, and she was gone. Jean-Baptiste kissed Antonia's hand and followed Laura's lead.

Antonia went to the edge of the dock and gave a helpless little wave as the small boat containing Laura and the French-man was rowed out to the ship by a burly seaman.

"What is that in your hand?" Sir Owen said into Antonia's ear.

She jumped. She had forgotten all about him. And she had no idea what was in her hand, she realized, noticing for the first time that a package had been put into it. A parting gift from Laura.

"I don't know." She wondered if she should wait to open it when she was alone. It could possibly be something of a delicate nature, something to do with the smuggling, and Sir Owen might as soon not see it. She looked up at him; the sympathetic affection in his eyes was something new in her experience. He felt sorry for her then, because he must realize how much her family meant to her.

She also realized that she could trust him with more than one little package from Laura. She undid the strings.

sympathetic affection in his eyes was something new in her
experience. He felt sorry for her then, because he most
realize how much her family meant to her.

20

Antonia gasped as the wrappings fell aside to reveal a large,
perfect emerald set in a brooch, a close cousin in looks to
the paste jewel she wore on her bosom.

"Tell me, my dear," Sir Owen said with a crooked smile,
"is she passing the torch?"

"Heavens, no." Antonia could imagine how Laura would
laugh at the very idea. "I'm the sensible one in the family.
Laura doubtless wishes me to keep this to pass on to the next
Lady. Monty will marry someday; perhaps his wife will have
a talent for the family legend." She paused and sighed. "Or
perhaps the legend will simply be buried at last."

"Not an hour ago you were ready to swear to me that you
were the Lady, only to save your sister. Do you call that
being the sensible one?"

"I said what I had to say. I'm sorry it was a lie. I feel
quite silly, you know. You've been aware of my masquerade
for heaven knows how long and here I've been mincing about
pretending to be the notorious smuggler. How you must have
laughed."

"Only with delight, my dear, I assure you. And with
admiration for your true courage. You followed through with
the whole masquerade in order to keep your sister safe."

"It was nothing." Antonia wished he would leave the
subject of her many virtues. She was embarrassed enough
as it was to be exposed as a prosaic and quiet female, not

an exotic smuggler after all. "Besides, you make me sound
unselfish, and that's not the case. I enjoyed playing the Lady.
I enjoyed baiting you and misleading you." But most of all,
she added silently, she had enjoyed becoming someone she
was not, someone who could enchant a man like Sir Owen
Longfort.

"I deserved it," he said. "You might have played me for
a fool, my dear, but I acted the fool to begin with. Imagine
setting you up in my mind as the Lady merely from a brief
look at your face."

"Your foolishness was helpful to Laura and me for as long
as it lasted," Antonia said. "The situation was so very
unbelievable, wasn't it? Fancy anyone thinking I had an
adventurous spirit."

"Did you think so, my dear? What a shame."

Those words out, he was quiet. Antonia had leisure to think
as she and Sir Owen stood side by side watching the dinghy
go out to the waiting ship. Laura and Fontanges, two distant
shapes, climbed aboard. The few lights on deck went out
one by one.

"I hope the captain of the ship will marry them soon,"
Antonia said. "Perhaps I should have reminded Laura."

"You think she'll forget a thing like that?" Sir Owen
grinned down at her.

"In all the excitement, she may. I must hope that Fontanges
is made of more practical stuff than my sister. He mentioned
once that he wanted many children; much better if their
mother were a married lady."

"How sophisticated you sound, my dear. Have you
become cynical during your sojourn in town?"

Antonia thought of the people she had been learning from;
Laura, Lady Pomfret, Mr. Daingerfield, Eliza . . . there were
so many roads to happiness, most of them strewn with stones.
Yet happiness could be found. "Not cynical, no," she
answered.

Sir Owen's arm went around her; somehow it felt so
natural there that Antonia didn't have the heart to shrug away.
She certainly had no desire to do so. She did realize, all of
a sudden, that she was alone, deep in the worst section of

London, with a man. Her reputation would be ruined if this got out, but she was confident that it wouldn't. She could trust Sir Owen with more than a mere reputation.

They said nothing as they looked out at the water. "How long have you known about me?" Antonia asked finally.

"I've suspected for a long time. I knew for certain when I went down to Kent at last dark."

"You were there? In Kent? But you never said so."

"I don't think I'm the only one who likes to maintain a little mystery," he said, giving her shoulders a squeeze.

She shivered at the touch.

"I went out in the night and saw the smuggling, as I'd tried to do once before, on the occasion of our meeting." Sir Owen continued the story. "This time no one knocked me over the head. I saw the Lady. I thought she was you at first, but then it became quite clear that a different person altogether was in question."

Antonia nodded. "It's true. No one with an eye could mistake me for Laura."

"How odd. You sound sorry. But you don't really regret that, do you? You have such charming qualities of your own. Your sister is lovely, true, but there is nothing special about her."

Antonia was certain he was roasting her. How could anyone say that there was nothing special about Laura? Family loyalty swelled Antonia's bosom. "How dare you, sir?" she snapped, wrenching her way out of his embrace. "First you almost arrest my sister, then you insult her."

"But I let her go," he said, sounding bemused. "And I said she was lovely." He stepped forward and grasped Antonia by the shoulders. "Can't you forget about others for now and concentrate on yourself? If you must think of someone else, think of me."

Antonia looked up into his face. "I do think of you, all the time," she said. Equivocation was useless; he must have read her true feelings in her eyes a thousand times.

"And I think of you," Sir Owen said. He moved closer, took her into his embrace, and kissed her.

What had started as a gentle, perhaps even a comradely

salute soon blossomed into something much more interesting. Antonia found herself clinging to him like a wanton.
She forgot that she had been playing the Lady when he had
kissed her in the past; she even forgot she was Antonia as
she reveled in the sensation of being a human being reaching
out to the one she loved.

"Oh, my dear," Sir Owen murmured into her hair,
ages—or was it only minutes—later. "You fascinate me."

These words brought Antonia down to earth with a crash.
She pulled away. She could feel her cheeks flaming and was
glad he could not see them in the dark. "I forget," she said
sadly. "You forget. I'm not the Lady after all, Sir Owen."

"What?" His expression was puzzled.

"The Lady fascinates you. She always has."

"Oh, my dear." Sir Owen repeated his words of a moment
before, but this time he chuckled.

"I don't think my broken heart is a fit subject for your
levity," Antonia said, turning away.

His next words were whispered into her ear. "Your broken
heart? Are you saying that your heart is involved?"

She nodded, unable to utter a syllable.

Once again she found herself turned to face him, and the
expression of joy upon his face, discernible in the moonlight,
made her catch her breath.

"My dearest," he said, "I'm so in love with you. I do
have a chance, then? You weren't simply playing with me
to draw attention away from your sister's true identity?"

"Do you think that of me?" Antonia asked, incredulous.
"How could anyone not love—that is, I mean to say, I
wouldn't do such a thing to you. I know it sounds odd coming
from me, Sir Owen, but I'm an honest person, truly I
am."

"I know. And so you possibly think you could call me
Owen without the Sir?"

"I could try . . . Owen." Antonia smiled. "You said you
loved me. Do you really mean that you love *me*? I've watched
you, you see. I know how the Lady has intrigued you. I'm
not a swashbuckling female, though, I'm only myself. I kept
the accounts at home and visited the cottagers. Laura was

the clever one, the adventurous one. Are you sure I'm the person you want?''

"How sad that you should even have to ask that question," Sir Owen said. "If you want the truth, my dearest, I always did have a soft spot in my romantic heart for the Lady even before I saw her, or thought I did. But when it came to the point I was so glad to find that you weren't the Lady, I didn't know what to do. I had my plans all laid, you see. I was going to have to bring you to justice, yet see that no harm came to you. It would have been a ticklish piece of diplomacy; devilishly difficult to explain to my superiors that I wished to marry the notorious criminal I'd been stalking.''

"You wanted to marry the Lady?" Antonia was amazed.

"I want to marry you, foolish girl. Why do you think I've been mauling you about like this?"

"Well," Antonia hesitated, wondering whether to voice her one question about his character. It would expose her as less than honorable, but do it she must. "I thought perhaps you mauled ladies about quite often. I know you're on most intimate terms with at least one woman. It shames me to have to confess such a terrible thing, but . . . I read your letter the night you were hit on the head and brought to our house.''

"You read what letter?"

"It was from a woman," Antonia said in the direction of the dock planks.

"Oh." Sir Owen laughed heartily. "I know what letter you mean. Not fit reading for a gently reared young lady. And then I had the audacity to kiss you on our first formal meeting. What you must have thought! A libertine of the first order, no doubt.''

"Something of the sort," Antonia said. "I'm dreadfully sorry I read that. Are you—will you—I can't marry you if I'm not the only one.''

"Are you asking me to give up the lady of the letter?"

"Yes," Antonia said, setting her jaw. She must have all of him; she somehow knew that no relationship of hers could function otherwise. Many husbands juggled mistresses and wives, and many wives juggled lovers and husbands, but she would not get herself into such a situation.

"I can't give her up," Sir Owen said.

Antonia nodded and wished her chin would stop trembling. She might have expected such an answer. The female of the embarrassing letter would doubtless make up for any loss of adventure he might experience by not marrying the real Lady.

"Look at me, Antonia."

She raised her eyes. He was smiling broadly and touched her face with a gentle, almost a reverent hand. "I can't give up that lady because she happens to be a middle-aged man with a paunch, a high-ranking gentleman who smokes too many cigars. The letters from passionate women are my signal, darling, that I have to meet with those who give me my instructions."

Relief flooded through Antonia. "Then you are an agent of some sort?"

"I would hardly have proposed to haul your sister and her lover off to justice had I been an ordinary citizen."

"Oh. No, I suppose you wouldn't have. Then all the time you thought I was the Lady, you also thought that my sister was helping a Bonapartist to spy?"

"What else could I think? Even when I was certain you were the Lady, I believed you implicitly when you said that you had nothing to do with spies. I knew in the bottom of my soul that you were telling the truth. And since I had had watch kept on the cottage in the woods ever since the Frenchman's arrival and knew that your sister saw him often, I jumped to the conclusion that she must be helping him. The question of a love affair never entered my mind."

"How did you find him in the first place? The smugglers were very careful when they brought him to Hannah's, I believe. Heavens, they must have been. They have never been caught."

"Ah, but they were not aware that old Hannah was reporting back to my people as well as to your sister's."

"Oh." Antonia shrugged. "Hannah was evidently loyal enough to my sister not to betray Laura's private feelings to your people. That is something."

"That is a great deal. Had Hannah not been so confoundedly closemouthed, I would have guessed earlier that there was no harm in Laura's visits to the Frenchman. Now may we return to the subject at hand?'' Sir Owen kissed Antonia's hand. "I believe we were discussing marriage before we meandered into talk of your sister's affairs.''

Antonia looked at him with a hesitant expression. "I simply can't believe that you could love me. Not when you've been so entranced by the Lady.''

"But, my dear, you were the Lady,'' Sir Owen reminded her. "Ah, Mademoiselle Bluet warned me this might happen.''

"Mademoiselle Bluet?'' Antonia repeated with a blank look.

"When we visited her at Eton, she saw at once how it was with me. She warned me that you wouldn't believe I loved you. Said you spent too much time doing for others to think that someone would care for you . . . that sort of thing. I don't remember exactly what she said because I knew it was nonsense. I knew I could make you believe I loved you within a quarter hour at the very most.''

"Did you?'' Antonia said, smiling now in her most welcoming manner. "Would you like to try?''

He said nothing, but his eyes shone with a strange light as he bent his head to hers once more.

"I believe you,'' Antonia said a little later.

"I'm not certain you do. I think it will take many exercises of this kind to be sure.''

"Well, I shall simply have to suffer through it,'' Antonia said. "The Lady can do anything, isn't that what the legend says?''

"*You* can do anything. I don't know about the Lady. What is this, my dear, that's bruising my rib cage?''

Antonia laughed. "It's the Lady's emerald.'' She had pinned it to her midsection to keep it safe, since her gown lacked pockets and her reticule must have been left on a chair in the Montaignes' ballroom. "Will you keep it for me? Perhaps I should have you put it away. I know how you are about lady smugglers. You might wish our daughter to follow in the Worthinghams' footsteps.''

He put the brooch into his pocket and kissed her cheek. "My dearest love, I can't be sure you won't need it yourself one of these days. You see, my Antonia, I know you better than you know yourself."

"But does any one person ever know another, dear Owen?"

"We can but try, my own love," he answered with a contented sigh, pulling her close. "We can but try."